THE HIGHWAYMAN

By the same author

Queen of the Witches

THE
HIGHWAYMAN

JESSICA BERENS

ARROW

Published in the United Kingdom in 2000 by
Arrow Books

1 3 5 7 9 10 8 6 4 2

First published in the United Kingdom in 1998 by Hutchinson

Arrow Books
The Random House Group Limited
20 Vauxhall Bridge Road, London, SW1V 2SA

Random House Australia (Pty) Limited
20 Alfred Street, Milsons Point, Sydney, New South Wales 2061, Australia

Random House New Zealand Limited
18 Poland Road, Glenfield, Auckland 10, New Zealand

Random House (Pty) Limited
Endulini, 5a Jubilee Road, Parktown 2193, South Africa

The Random House Group Limited Reg. No. 954009

www.randomhouse.co.uk

A CIP catalogue record for this book is available from the British Library

Papers used by Random House
are natural, recyclable products made from wood grown in
sustainable forests. The manufacturing processes conform to
the environmental regulations of the country of origin

Printed and bound in Norway by
AIT Trondheim AS, Trondheim

ISBN 0 09 952061 3

To: David Jenkins

Chapter 1

Fairview Castle had once been a hotel noted for the excellence of its international cuisine. In the past there had been turnip rémoulade, filo parcels, and squid rings. Chef Alexandre had experimented with snails while Michel 'Le Chou' du Pont had invented a range of multi-tiered pastries whose delicacy and flavour had won five awards, including the prestigious *'Dessert de l'Honneur'*, presented annually by *Sweet Trolley* magazine.

Now there was only dinge.

A tangled crisis of brambles led to rusting iron gates. One, cloaked in dripping creepers, hung off its hinges. The other presented a rotting 'For Sale' sign. They opened into a courtyard where grass sprang rudely through cracked flagstones. Here, a decrepit wooden barrel full of stagnant water offered itself to those insects designed to dip and skim and float.

Gangling cow parsley straggled around a mildewed front door whose crumbling lintel displayed the Ruthven family coat of arms. The colours had washed away but a hideous Hydra was apparent, as were the words of the family motto – *Nemini Fidens* (Trusting No-One).

A washing line, limp with sodden cerements, was the only sign that any human being still inhabited this neglected corner. A huge pair of underpants drooped alongside preternaturally elongated tights and an antique bra.

The atmosphere of necropolitan gloom concealed an inescapable truth. Fairview Castle was, in fact, built in 1962.

Roger Ruthven, canny entrepreneur that he was, married commerce with history when he designed a hotel to cater for the boom brought to Minehead by the arrival of Butlin's. Constructed along the lines of the nearby Dunster Castle, his modern edifice offered the tourist all the delights of medieval life without the inconvenience. His guests had enjoyed eating their breakfasts on heavy reproduction Tudor tables. They had been impressed by the the suits of armour (bought in an auction at Christie's) and amused by the paintings of mythical Ruthven ancestors. The hotel was a success.

Now inches of dust lay softly on oak tables and tough cobwebs interweaved rotten beams. Broken windows allowed bats to inhabit rafters while ancient, untreated drainage encouraged damp. The corridors were populated by shifting penumbra while draughts blew behind tapestries causing them to lift and flap.

The kitchen had once resonated with the sound of slicing, slivering, stretching and hammering as culinary arts were practised. Today it was silent, but it was not empty because the lifeless body of a middle-aged woman was lying face down on the floor.

Margaret Ruthven came to with a jolt, sat upright, and stared wildly around. In front of her a fire had died in the grate, beside her a copy of *Coping with Old Age* lay splayed in a pool of beer. Myopically she groped around for her Polaroid sunglasses which, though they reduced her world to monochrome, were filled with prescription lenses without which she could not see.

She was disappointed to discover that the ridges of the stone tiles had formed a red criss-cross pattern on her forehead but relieved that the painful challenge of dressing did not present itself.

She was wearing a yellow T-shirt bearing the name 'Simon' and a pair of Bermuda shorts printed with a loud jungle pattern. These items had been left behind by an adolescent guest and would doubtless have suited a lean teenager named Simon. He might even have received flattering attention in a discotheque. On the fifty-five-year-old body of Margaret Ruthven they presented a disturbing portrait. The clothes were short and tight. Propelled by some arcane law of physics her matter sprang hither and thither. Snakes of flesh protruded above the waistline (such as it was) and below the sleeves.

Stiffly, Margaret Ruthven heaved herself up and slid two flat feet into a pair of Dr Scholl sandals. Bending her body from the lower back to prevent the pain rising and clawing at her neck, she shuffled forward. The oblivion of the night had left traces of narcosis but she knew that this was temporary, that soon, fear, harrowing and exquisite, would kick in. There was an estimable limit of time before her flesh started to crawl in a cold sweat and her eyes would see shades that existed for no one but herself. Knowing these things and wishing to avoid them, she cast herself off.

Staring at the floor and still bent forward she arrived at an industrial-sized fridge filled with six hundred cans of Special Brew. The dark glasses feasted upon this array. Her eyes filled with tears of gratitude and her stomach lurched with the heat of love in an ecstasy so intense she wondered, briefly, if she was having a religious experience.

She emptied the amber contents of a can into a pint glass and swallowed it with a movement of the wrist so quick and so graceful that it was almost invisible. Then she poured another and attempted to see the day.

A fern had shrivelled in its urn. Blotches seeped on peeling walls. Pus oozed through a plug-hole. Putrescence hung in the air. Margaret Ruthven relished ordure. She saw honesty in dereliction because it accurately represented her life. Rotting objects reflected her hostility and dregs exuded the stench of her disappointment.

Listlessly she sat at the kitchen table. She had long ago consumed the contents of the Fairview wine cellar. Now she took psychopharmaceuticals and, in front of her, the labels of dozens of brown bottles described days spent careening between anti-manics, tri-cyclics and narcotic analgesics.

She arranged the pills into groups. Benzodiazepine hypnotics to one side; Monomine Oxidase Inhibitors to another. The phenothiazenes were the most interesting. She rattled the Vertigan bottle. Empty. There were three capsules left in the Melleril packet. She took one. A nice thioridazine to start the day.

She was still sitting at the table when a thin man appeared. It was sometimes difficult to discern the exact character of things through the dark glasses, but as she leaned forward, the shadowy form took on some identifiable and familiar features. She realized, judging by its youth and the timidity of its mien, that it must be her son Rupert.

'What's that on your head?'

'A bandana.'

Rupert's custom was to steer as wide a berth from his mother as possible. As animals have a sixth sense that tells them when there is danger in the jungle so he had developed an instinctive acuity that served to protect him. Today, however, there had been a miscalculation and he found himself in occupied territory. His mother, Kent cigarette in stained digits, beer glass in front of her, was staring, with a distant and tearful eye, at a locket that lay open in front of her. In it there was a photograph of the late Ian. Rupert remembered, with a tremor of apprehension, that today, March 12, was the third anniversary of the Jack Russell's death, but he did not have time to consider the implications of this festival as the locket was not the only object lying on the kitchen table. Amidst the debris of ash-trays, pill bottles and glasses, in the centre, where some people place vases of tulips, lay a Heckler & Koch MP5 sub-machine-gun.

As casually as limited courage allowed he indicated the unlicenced firearm.

'Where ja get that?'

'Car boot sale.'

He was overcome by a compulsion to hold the steel in his palm, test the weight, tinker with the safety catch, but he refrained because he knew that the situation was already fraught with risk. His mother was never friendly in the face of investigation. He had once asked her the time and incurred a kick to the shin that had caused his leg to go numb for two days. She was a dangerous woman at the best of times. Now she was armed and dangerous. He managed to ease himself out of the room without taking his back from the wall. He was too young to die.

'Where are you going?'

'To work.'

Rupert worked in an amusement arcade where simulated warfare was a part of everyday life and, over the months, he had learned a little about guns. The HKMP5 was a semi-automatic weapon, carried by the SAS and the FBI, but also favoured by terrorist organizations all over the world including, most notoriously, the Baader Meinhof gang.

He found it hard to believe that his mother had fallen in with a cabal of guerilla revolutionaries. Where would she have met them? She had stopped going out since the off-licence had agreed to deliver. Furthermore she had no qualifications for membership. She was possessed of no firm ideology. Her beliefs oscillated madly from left to right, dancing to a set of stimuli that were unaffected by the leader columns and out-patient disasters that usually mould an individual's political convictions.

These fluctuations were underpinned by an inclination towards anarchic principle. She believed, for instance, that the police force should be abolished, but would this libertarian distrust of authority be enough to attract those engaged in professional sedition? He could see that she was psychically attuned to the sociopathy required by insurrection, but she was ageing, asthmatic and overweight. Her body could never be employed to slither underneath a car and plant Semtex. Any militant nihilist with eyes in their head could see that her metabolism retained water. In the event that she did manage to lower herself underneath a vehicle, she would undoubtedly become stuck.

Rupert rode his motor bike to Lucky Bob's Amusement Arcade. The Big Boss was waiting. He was wearing a T-shirt that said 'Life's a Bitch, Then You Marry One' and one fat finger was stabbing against the face of his watch.

'It's ten past,' he said.

Walking towards his rotund employer, Rupert became a gore-master of the Shaolin tournament. Here, at Lucky Bob's, his identity twisted and he was Dan the Man, legendary high-kicker, master of the shadow upper-cut and Kombat Tomb Fatality. Leaping, kicking, indomitable. *Down. Down. Forward. Forward. Low punch. Forward. Forward. Kick.* A terror to all earth warriors, Dan the Man moved with lightning stealth. Everyone knew that when it came to combat the Big Boss was all flash and no impale facility. *Forward. Punch. Kick.* Only his shoulder charge was effective. *Kick. Punch. Thrust.* The Big Boss had better watch it. Dan the Man was working on a move so lethal that it would make the Ripped Torso Fatality look like a kiss in the back row of the Regal.

Forward. Forward. Low punch. Even Lau Gar would be afraid, Lau Gar himself with his Slicing Hat and Army of Rotters. Ha. Lau Gar would be splattered.

'Sorry,' said Rupert.

'Yeah. Well get on with it. We'll be busy today with the rain 'n' all.'

Dan the Man eased himself through the neon-spattered killing field. Wurlitzer music and pop tunes mingled with the sound of hundreds of homeboys meeting their violent ends amongst the trash cans of Bronx slums.

At last, unwounded, he reached the kiosk marked

'Change' and climbed on to the stool behind the window. Victorious in the Shaolin Temple, Dan the Man knew he sat as the symbol of triumph over the forces of evil.

'Five pounds' worth please.'

A hand pushed forward a grimy note. The head was invisible because the body was too small to meet the level of the window.

Dan the Man pressed his mouth to the circle cut into the arch of glass.

'How old are you?' he asked the tiny fist.

'Ten,' came the disembodied reply. 'So wot? I'm allowed.'

Dan the Man pushed the pile of fifty-pence coins forward. The fingers groped blindly until they located the metal column, then snatched it away.

He watched the little figure dart past Big Bertha and Virtua Racing Cars before stopping at Splat-A-Crab. A simple game, the player, armed with a mallet, hammered rows of surprised looking shell-fish as an electronic device propelled them out of rock formations.

The Big Boss had been right. They were busy.

Old men, hypnotized by the banks of Joker Poker fruit machines, sat in docile rows stoically feeding their pensions into thankless grooves. A Rastafarian family situated themselves at 'Zeke's Shack' where air-guns allowed them to take pot-shots at animatronic effigies of hill-billies. The life of Zeke (an elderly man in dungarees) was tormented by bottles of poison that dropped on to his head, by corpses of cats that flew at him, and by 'cacti' that jumped out of their pots, yelped, and twisted in to the air.

Youths in baseball hats inserted themselves into replica cockpits. The Formula One Devil Drive, complete with stick shift option and 3D graphics, was equipped with a device that gave the driver's body a realistic jolt when his vehicle (minimum speed 200 mph) smashed into trees.

Teenage girls clustered around pinball machines. Giggling, they patted painted mouths with Silk Cut and taught each other to inhale. One appeared at Rupert's window.

'Yes?' he said.

Her hair had been organized into an arrangement of plastic daisies and she was wearing a badge saying 'Hello Boys'. Hands twiddled daisies, mouth opened and then shut again.

'Yes?' he said again.

Another girl appeared and pushed the first in the back so that her forehead nearly smashed against the glass.

'Fuck off Nathalie.'

'Go on then, tell 'im.'

Rupert did not savour these moments. He tried not to speak to women. He did not know how their minds worked, what they would do, or, much worse, what they expected. His life was divided between murdering Loopy de Luxe, devising ways to avoid his mother and mending his motorbike. He had little time left to work out how to cater for the class of person that the Big Boss described as 'local totty'.

'MY FRIEND'S GORRA CRUSH ON YOU!' the face suddenly shouted. Then her cheeks turned a frightening scarlet and she ran away screaming.

The Big Boss, strolling by, noticed this frisson and knew that Rupert's motor bike and leather jacket imbued him with a sexual kudos of which their owner seemed sadly unaware.

'Ask one of them tarts out, you stupid git,' he said.

'What if she says no?' said Rupert. 'What then?'

'Just ask another one. They're all roughly the same, take it from me mate, they are all roughly the same.'

Rupert did not agree. They all seemed very different.

'You berregeramovon,' the Big Boss continued. 'I was engaged at your age. Mind you, that was Jean's mum – gave me a look that could have opened an oyster at two hundred yards.'

'What did you and Jean do on your first date then?' asked Rupert.

The Big Boss rolled his eyes and leered in a way designed to relay the message that there had been unusual sexual acrobatics but he, as a gentleman, could not divulge them.

Rupert spent the rest of the morning pushing cardboard tubes of coins at the crowd who came to play pool and fish for necklaces and twiddle cranes that dipped into glass cases full of skeleton heads. His post on the stool provided an observation point from where he could see most of the activity in Lucky Bob's clinking terrain. The Big Boss liked him to 'keep yer eye open'.Rupert tried to do so, his heed motivated by fear that if there was trouble he would receive the blame.

The Big Boss could not have known that his employee's assiduity was often undermined by a constricted focus. Rupert spent most of his time mentally guarding the *Combat Rotters* game. He had come to think of the machine as his own and watched it with the protective vigilance of one who has just smoothed their new Porsche into a rough neighbourhood.

His worry was wasted. Customers took little interest in *Combat Rotters*. It was not a popular game. Everyone preferred *Venom* and *Exterminatorsaurus*. This had not affected Rupert's loyalty and he took pride in the singularity of his taste, but he did sometimes wonder why so few were captivated by Loopy de Luxe when no other arcade game offered a villainess as beautiful or as depraved. A bitch-goddess with the body of an Olympic athlete and the head of a wolf, she was a mutant in a mini-dress – one half superwoman, one half dripping gums and blood-spattered teeth. She stalked on all fours, and her weapons were her claws, black, lethal, sharp as razors. She was cunning and terrifying and Rupert loved her.

The Big Boss, always to the point, said that no one liked *Combat Rotters* because 'it ain't bin on the telly'. He sometimes threatened to replace it with the new *Turbo Street-Fighter III* but he only said this to taunt. He knew that Rupert's performances on *Combat Rotters* were an attraction. Crowds would gather when he took his position in front of the joysticks and they were never disappointed. Taking on the character of Dan the Man, Martial Artiste *Extraordinaire*, Rupert could kick and punch his way from level to level with coordination, determination and dexterity.

Some unworthies sneered at Dan the Man with his film-star looks, muscular physique, and unlikely hairdo. The man was pathetic, they would say, he did not have the Kombat Tomb Fatality of Baraka or the Deep Freeze Shatter Fatality of Sub-Zero, master assassin of Shang Tsung. There was always a queue of aspirants keen to knock Rupert's initials from the top of the digitalized scoreboard. Arrogantly they would face the Man in battle, only to find themselves pulverized by the lightning speed of his wrists. *Splat. Kick. Punch.* No one took on Dan the Man and lived.

The object of *Combat Rotters* was to save Fortune Cookie, the daughter of Mr Chow, King of Chinatown. She had been kidnapped by Lau Gar, Commander of the Tribe of Rotters. Lau Gar, once a god, had been demoted for nefarious activity. Now committed to iniquity, his most dangerous attribute was the ability to take on the appearance of his enemies, a skill that had confused Dan the Man for many weeks until he had mastered the complicated Ashi Garnami leg-entanglement technique.

Lau Gar was supported by a legion of malevolent freaks, all of whom had to be maimed if Fortune Cookie was to be liberated from the Cell of Despair. Butterball, for instance, was vicious, yellow, and possessed of Ninja invisibility. He leapt out from behind a Firewheel Tree, flailing a katana. Dan the Man knew that defence was pointless. The most effective strategy was to cut off the warrior's arms with a lightning series of slicing karate chops. This meant that a shadow kick could be delivered to the knee-caps which, if accurate, caused his legs to fly off. Some novices thought that this marked the end of Butterball. They were wrong. He was equipped with a Dismembered Torso Fatality that could only be arrested by jumping up and down on his stomach.

The final destination was the Citadel itself, a labyrinthine pagoda festering with Lau Gar's macabre henchmen. Dracon (a bloodsucker), Cinch (a uniped) and Oligarch (a Russian) were invigorated by magical powers of resistance, but they were all cast aside by Dan the Man's frenzied assault. Dauntless, he would march forward as the blood of Lau Gar's champions surged down the corridors of Budoka. *Kick. Kick. Thrust. Advance.* To the Cell of Despair guarded by Loopy herself. Bold, mighty, vicious and semi-naked,

Loopy had disqualified herself from the human race, but Dan the Man did not care.

She was skilled in all the oriental arts. It was as if Korea, Japan and China had united to present her with the knowledge of the Ultimate Truth. Rocket Kicks, Spinning Fists, Hundred Hand Slaps – she was savage, peculiar and impenetrable. Dan the Man had, in the past, subjected her to neck locks, judo chokes, groin kicks, and eye gouging, until, finally, he had discovered the secret of her infirmity. Loopy's face was her misfortune. Punching her was a waste of time, only a battery of impact-kicks to her snout effected prostration.

Rupert was often sorry that he had to kill her. He did not like to think of how he would feel if the Big Boss should keep his word and send *Combat Rotters* to the scrapyard. In the massacres of the Swamp and Citadel there was life. His enemies had become his friends. The loss of Loopy would be a blow from which he knew he would never recover.

''Ere.'

The Big Boss was lobbing chips into the recess that lay in the middle of his beard.

'Do you wanna go for yer dinner? Jean'll take over.'

The Big Boss's wife eased her round bottom onto the stool.

''Allo Darlin' 'As tricks? Married yet?'

Rupert, to his irritation, blushed. Jean was so overpowering with her tight denim and mists of Charlie. Today she was more frosted and highlighted than ever. Silvery streams trickled through the blonde fall of permanent curls, an opaque veneer of pearly hue encased her nails and a crescent of some glittering substance rose over thick navy-blue eyelashes that mocked and flirted.

'Course not.'

Rupert felt like shouting at her but he managed to combine a brazen sneer and a certain *froideur* while manoeuvering his eyeballs into a location that was as far as possible from the cleavage that opened, like a dangerous ravine, in the large area exposed by a tight scoop-neck T-shirt.

The Big Boss's Jean wondered if there was something wrong with Rupert's eyes, but she failed to perceive the undercurrents and knew nothing about chagrin. She plunged in for the kill.

'Yah! Virgin are ya?'

'Don't talk daft, Jean.'

Her husband interrupted not because he wanted to stall his wife's emasculatory parry but because gainsay was the mode of their communication.

Rupert felt sweat drip like blood down his back. His forehead vibrated.

'Course not,' he said again.

He crammed his motor bike helmet down on to his head and jangled his keys.

'Don't be long!' the Big Boss shouted after him.

'I bet he is,' said Jean.

'What?'

'A virgin.'

'Don't talk daft ya silly bat and watch the cash – them kids'll 'ave it from under ya nose.'

'I got eyes in me head ain't I?'

'You might have eyes but you certainly ain't got brains.'

'Have.'

'Haven't.'

'Have and no returns for ever. Anyway he can't be moron sixteen.'

'E's seventeen.'

'Ow ja no?'

'Told me.'

'Bet he lied to get the job.'

'Saw his motor bike licence dint I?'

It was a happy marriage and one that had lasted for twenty years.

Chapter 2

March had cast a pall over Minehead and Rupert rode through a town whose esplanades and promenades were shrouded with grey cumuli.

A freezing wind whistled between Furzecot and Littlecot. A hunched form, anorak stained dark with water, moved, with zombie gait, towards the public bar. A septuagenarian staggered on a stick, one withered hand pressing a transparent rain-hat on to the perm supplied by Nicole's Tonsorial Salon. The only other human motion was in a rented room at the Town Hall where the lips of the Hard-of-Hearing club moved noiselessly up and down.

The sea, flecked with brown froth, had become a swamp of disturbed mud and sewer. Slimy rocks exposed themselves through sweating seaweed and the faint stench of decaying fish emanated as seagulls circled.

Fishermens' cottages cowered under dripping thatch while frenzied weather-vanes spun round and round. Front doors were half-hidden by walls of sodden sandbags which offered no protection against the wash so empty Domestos bottles battered against carefully restored leaded windows.

In the desolate high street white faces pressed against water-flecked window-panes as shopkeepers' eyes haunted country restaurants and gift shoppes for signs of life. They longed to see a child shoplifting, or a father wishing to buy a bird-house cunningly crafted from a coconut. Summer, with its demand for Ensuite Facilities and Delightfully Different Butter Biscuits, seemed a lifetime away.

Butlin's, at the end of town, was a wasteland. The ferris wheel, static, towered over silence. The Polyp, the Chair O Planes and the Dragon Coaster glistened with the mist of drizzle.

Rupert paused, as he often did, in front of the Ghost Train. The words 'Abandon Hope All Ye Who Enter Here' had been painted in dripping blood over the gates. The sign had been there since he was seven and his father had taken him on the ride. Afterwards both Rupert and his father had re-emerged into the daylight panting and pale. His father had said that the Ghost Train was worse than being shot at in Korea. This had been a comfort to Rupert who had thought that he was alone in his horror.

A glancing memory of brown trousers and Viyella shirt meshed with the nightmare scenes of agony they had seen that afternoon. An early amputation. A corpse, face bathed in green light. St George stretched in sodden rags on a crucifix. Rats and whisperings and the sound of diseased limbs being dragged across the floor. Rupert could still see the waxen features of the hellish tableaux but he had to concentrate, these days, if he wanted to recall his father's face.

His father had liked games – Monopoly, football,

pretending to be the the King of Siam, anything, but the fleeting images of these old scenes were fading. The feelings were easier to remember. Waves of disbelief or shock. These were easy to sum up. People had said 'he has gone to Heaven', but they never said that he would not come back. No one explained the meanings of the words they used. He had not known if 'dead' was a colour or a feeling or a country. He had been left with night-time nightmare shows when, gazing into the gloom, he imagined Heaven and wondered where it was and who his father made friends with once he was there and whether he could see him, Rupert, in his bed, surrounded by hateful shadows. This so-called Heaven. No one bothered to tell him anything about it. It was years before he realized that his father would not return.

He had been given some cuff-links and books on fly fishing, a few tweed jackets that he could not look at, let alone wear. This was all that remained, apart from the old dull ache and a collection of questions that he never asked himself because he knew better than to awaken old misery.

Rupert rode into a side street and parked his motor bike. Cold rain battered plastic furniture and a searching wind knocked over signs advertising sundaes and tubs. Once inside Antonio's Kebab House, however, the customer was treated to a climate similar to the hothouse at Kew. Equatorial humidity might have encouraged exotic lilies to burst into blossom but it also steamed up Rupert's vizor and rendered him temporarily blind. This made it difficult to read Antonio's bill of fare but Rupert was not inconvenienced as he knew the contents off by heart.

He always went to Antonio's Kebab House for his lunch. He did not like kebabs especially, but kebabs were not the only dish on the menu. There were also burgers (Hawaiian), burgers (chilli) and burgers (Neopolitan).

The atmosphere was coloured by Antonio, a compact man whose sense of humour was influenced by his brother Dimitri who ran a joke shop next door. Antonio was not beyond serving his clientele whilst wearing a plastic axe through his head. Today, for his own amusement, he had placed a battery-operated hand on the counter. Its prosthetic fingers wiggled, twitching in the nervous throes that are supposed to be the body's reaction to sudden amputation.

'Very funny 'Tonio,' said Rupert, removing his helmet and gloves.

'Good innit.'

Antonio's brown face split into a delighted edentate grin and his eyes lit up with glee.

''E's got lossin if you want one. Five pounds. Cheap at twice the price if you ask me.'

In the summer it was possible to sit outside Antonio's, which was preferable. Spinning bow-ties did not always manage to counteract the lacklustre character of Antonio's interior decor. Today rain prevented escape. Rupert sat at a tiny white table, opened his *Games Monster* magazine and ate a cheeseburger while Antonio wiped formica surfaces and bobbed about behind glass cabinets containing battered fish.

The environment was familiar and Rupert felt at ease. The plastic landmarks were immutable. Rupert liked the way that the salt-cellars stuck to the tables. He would have been unnerved if Antonio had taken down the posters of Greek statues or introduced new items to his menu. Here, amongst ketchup and cans of Lilt, there was no pressure. The present was safe and the future did not matter. The Big

Boss was always trying to talk to Rupert about his future. 'You're a bright lad,' he would say. 'You're wasting yourself. You should get a proper job with proper dosh.' Rupert took no notice. He liked working in the amusement arcade and he did not wish to do anything else. Furthermore the Big Boss was at least thirty-five years old and he spoke the gobbledygook of embarrassing senility that one could only address with polite detachment and then hope to forget as soon as possible lest retention should lead to disabilities.

The peace was suddenly and brutally shattered by the raucous shriek of motor bikes.

The noise subsumed the sanctum and introduced danger.

They slammed the door open and thundered in, boots and spurs hammering on the faded lino.

There were three of them.

Three, in Antonio's opinion, was three too many. He knew varmints when he saw them and his senses had not been so assaulted by chip fat that they were unable to detect the smell of beer.

Three, in Rupert's opinion, was a gang. His head rose reluctantly from the magazine but he brought it down again and studied the outlaws through the open fingers that cradled his forehead as he pretended to read.

They walked in single file, a strange queue whose serration was varied by their disparate sizes. The tallest led. A pale, thin creature, his dyed-black hair had receded leaving an islet of fuzz to float in the middle of his cranium. An over-sized black tuxedo contrasted with the anaemic wash of his skin and a pair of immaculately clean jeans cracked with creases that had been starched into white lines as straight as road markings. The evidence of fanatic ironing might have negated the glowering malevolence of his aura, for it spoke of a domestic stability that is no friend to the reputation of the disenfranchised, but it was offset by a broken nose, sullen inflated lips and the impassive eyes of a snake.

Behind him a youth in leather was as dark and sinuous as liquorice. Black leather jacket, black leather trousers, black cowboy boots, lank black hair that flopped into slanted eyes and over a thin, wet, cruel mouth.

The person bringing up the rear raised the possibility that the trio had not only purposely arranged themselves in order of size, but also in order of beauty. He was small, so small that it was a disability. He looked like an aged child. There was no tangible evidence of damage suffered to the spine at birth, certainly something had been damaged but it was difficult, from perfunctory observation, to pinpoint the exact nature of the medical misfortune. The process of his creation had left him with tiny hands, tiny feet, and a very large head. A harvest of sandy straw had matted itself into a thatch on top of this disproportionate goitre. Small confident eyes pitted a complexion whose ruptures communicated that a diet had escaped all trends in low-fat eating.

'Whatcha gonna have Nil?'

Neil, the pale superior, gazed at the menu behind Antonio's back as the other two waited reverentially for the decision that would influence them.

'Dunno. Kebab probbly. Watchoo genav?'

'Dunno. Kebab probbly.'

'They got wet chips?'

The shrill whine was the voice of the sandy-haired minute.

'Fuck off Shorty. This ain't an Indian.'

'Dint say it woz.'

'Yor' a wet chip if you ask me.'

'Fuck off Neville.'

'Fuck off yerself.'

Neville violently pushed Shorty who fell over and, like a a child's toy, bounced straight back up again.

'Fuck off.'

Neil leaned on the counter, slammed his crash-helmet down, and pushed his long lumpen nose forward so that it moved into (but did not gentrify) the neighbourhood around Antonio's face.

Antonio's eyes darted to the etiolated palms that had joined his joke hand on the counter. Tattooed lettering spelled out the word SATAN on Neil's fingers.

'Three shish.'

'Oy,' whined Shorty. 'I don't want shish.'

Neil swung around and glared down with a basilisk stare that, in the animal kingdom, pre-empts a fight to the death, but his menace was neutralized by their difference in size. His gaze fell on top of Shorty's head where, unnoticed, it failed to spark obedience.

Neville, though, squirmed in a peristalsis of awe.

'Tough,' snorted Neil. 'I got the money ain't I?'

They sat down at a table opposite Rupert, who was constricting every muscle in a strenuous attempt to make himself smaller. This fatiguing grip on tendon and ligament did not, as he had hoped, cause him to seep unnoticed into the background, but merely precipitated painful cramps as unnaturally twisted joints cried out for oxygen. He persevered, silently praying that some isometric miracle would cause his body to contract into a ball and roll to safety.

He read and re-read *Games Monster*'s review of *Violent*

Bastards. 'Fast, fluid animation on a 704×480 high-resolution display runs at fifty frames per second,' it said, 'The Bastards and their enemies, the Pathetic Plebs, have been given extra moves including up to ten-hit combos and bone-snapping grapples. At the end of each bout you can tap in a secret code and tear the arms off the loser . . .'

Then, for one fatal second, primal wariness relaxed and Rupert glanced up.

This senseless abandon might have gone unnoticed but untenable dynamics were against him and he found himself irreversibly connected with Neil's unblinking gaze. The message of his stare was difficult to discern, but to avert would have unleashed tidings of cowardice that, in circumstances such as these, were no less dangerous than courage. Rupert met him with a mixture of dignity and humility.

Neil indicated the crash-helmet on the table.

'Wot bike you got then?'

'Honda a hundred.'

A cacophony of whooping and cheering greeted this news. The delighted trio banged the table and punched each other.

'Chryce,' spluttered Neil. 'Ya mus need the wind behind ya.'

Shorty, overcome by mirth, had his head in his arms. His tiny form shuddered, as if in a seizure, and his feet, which did not meet the floor, swung back and forth in a regular clockwork motion that caused the heels to bang against the chair legs.

Rupert's Honda 100, which he had bought on HP when the Big Boss had given him the job in the amusement arcade, represented all he had in the world. More importantly, it offered freedom of escape. Small though the machine was, and unencumbered by the chromatic appurtenance that earned prestige in Superbike circles, it nevertheless travelled at 60 mph and sixty miles was a long way from his mother.

Your Bike magazine had given the model three stars for 'power and guts', a review that Rupert wore with some pride. Power and guts were crucial components and they were particularly crucial in this microscopic dot of time that seemed to be stretching to eternity.

Condemnation of the H100 invaded the same recess as the slurs discharged by the Big Boss's Jean. The valiance of the motor bike was linked to secrets that must be guarded and protected with steely fortitude. To dishonour them was to generate a chaos whose first sacrifice was self-respect.

Jape could not effect this because jape was the symbol of social interaction, an instrument in that occult process known as the making of friends. Jape was close to, but very different from, jeer. Jeer did not wish to insinuate itself, it wished to exclude and condemn. Rupert hoped that jape was not destined to be extinguished by jeer for, in this event, he would be forced to fight.

Employing a combination of courteous neutrality and *sotto voce* ingratiation, he said, 'It's all right. It gets me about.'

Rupert's voice described his middle-class origins rather than his life. To be 'posh' was to be pulped and, in an effort to survive the comprehensive, he had once tried to cultivate a Somerset accent tinged with the street vowels he heard on the estates. But he did not have an ear – the dialect arrived with an exaggerated sneer which mocked the very people it was supposed to befriend and caused him more trouble than the voice he had inherited from his parents. Eventually he had dropped the attempts and learned to live with disapproval.

'Ya. Provided your mother's pushin',' gasped Neville. 'Ya posh git!'

As his eyes tightened into hairlines of derision his vermiform body rippled, rose and looped as if charmed by an unseen pipe.

It was unlikely that Margaret Ruthven would push the motor bike unless she found it parked in front of a keg of beer. Rupert grimaced and the gang mistook his expression for good-hearted acceptance of their ridicule. Unseen threads bound them together and, in the enervating presence of a stooge, the bond tightened. Here, star-crossed, was a play-thing. A butt for the bike joke. They all flexed themselves ready to fire ammunition from a bottom-less arsenal, but it was Neil who opened his mouth first. The glistening protuberances of his lips quivered with the excitement of emitting irony.

Joy was cruelly snatched from him, because Rupert spoke first.

'Oh well.' He shrugged. 'Gotta go.'

Neil rarely experienced interpolation. He was accustomed to a hushed and respectful silence. In his view it was the world's duty to shut its gob. Humility and attention were his dues and he expected them with feudal arrogance.

As an understanding of insult established itself, the saveloy lips slowly closed and a gleam sparked into his eyes – the dangerous glint of the thwarted narcissist. He glanced surreptitiously at the others but the moment had been too subtle to affect the torpor of their understanding. If they had observed his displeasure he would have sensed their dread. But dread, to Neil's surprise, did not hang in the air.

Rupert waved and exited.

Dan the Man had defied death.

He was invincible.

Street-fighting men ride street-fighting bikes and, conscious of this, Dan the Man expected to see the pavement outside Antonio's filled with low-slung hybrids of highway terror all stripped, power-jumped and tricked out with suicide clutches. There would be swastikas and flames and signs that the gypsy jokers had made runs to one-horse towns. He himself was not a commuter on a small road bike but an anarchist who risked death daily. One day he would buy aluminium armour, a superbike – liquid-cooled, electronically-triggered, digitally controlled, and squirm-resistant. He saw himself riding around Minehead with a tinted speed screen, fibre-glass farings and tyres designed to travel at 140 mph. Minimum. Mini-*mum*! There was glory in desperation and honour in retaliation. His Honda made him a man who would have taken a curve at 70 mph, if his bike had gone that fast.

And so Rupert paused to admire the possessions of those who knew how to deal in extremes and who had nothing to lose. These devils of road history would own a Thunderbird pre-unit chop, perhaps, or a Triumph Trophy with bolt-on plunger, stainless steel oil tank and Sudco Mikuni carb.

No panhead or shovelhead met his eye. No fat-bob fender or silver drag pipe. What he saw was a Kawasaki 250 (old) and a Yamaha 125 (trail).

These little machines were not designed to burn enemies up at intersections or bust tarmac in lonely outposts.

Rupert jumped on his pedal and opened the accelerator. He was no longer inferior. The gang, like him, rode small

Japanese bikes. They were related. He wheelied forward in a smoky wail. Power and guts.

The afternoon passed as usual at Lucky Bob's. An old woman won £25 on the Mocky Horror fruit machine and the Big Boss concealed his dissatisfaction by moving his stomach through the crowd shouting, 'Huge prizes to be won! Everyone's a winner at Lucky Bob's!'

'Give us ten.'

Rupert recoiled. Three shish.

The voice needed no expression. It was calm in its knowledge of obedience. A quicksilver flicker of inexplicable excitement darted down Rupert's spine. It brought an urge to be wanted by this stranger and to be a part of his domain, foreign but friendly with the common language of biking lore. Here was a nomad with the charisma of one who knows he has been miscast and who does not care.

Rupert looked through his glass circle. It was replete with Neil's mouth.

He leaned forward so that the tip of his nose pressed against the glass.

'Hullo again,' he said.

The eyes registered recognition.

'Oh. S'you. Honda a hundred. You work here then.'

'Yes.'

'Praps we'll 'ave a game some time.'

'OK.'

The warmth of this exchange dissolved into apprehension when Rupert saw the gang make their way to the *Combat Rotters* game. They gathered around the machine and it was as if their spurs were digging into his entrails.

Neil and Neville inserted coins and took up the wide-legged stance believed to maximize coordination between eye, brain and wrist.

Duty confined Rupert to his kiosk and prohibited close inspection but, by straining his neck, he could see that things were not going well for the Prince. Judging by the crowd that began to gather around the machine, Loopy de Luxe herself was about to be challenged.

'What's happening?' he called out to a passer-by.

''E's got Cinch. I've never seen anything like it.'

The only way to find Cinch, who appeared as a shadow, was to win fifty rounds in a row.

This was bad.

Very bad.

Rupert sat down and stared sadly through his glass. There were no customers now for a crowd pulls a crowd and all were dragged ineluctably towards the game. His mood was further depressed by the sound of regular cheering.

'Dracon is down!' someone yelled.

The crowd was now so large that some people were jumping up and down to see the picture on the screen. There was pushing, jostling and 'gerroff'. Suddenly, and for no particular reason, the agitation took on a different rhythm, a rhythm that spoke of physical fray. Grunt and threat ascended to a crescendo of crack and scream, superseded, finally, by the splinter of glass. Some bodies split away and ran for the exit. ''E's got a knife!' yelped one. A youth in a blood-spattered Madonna T-shirt sprang up in front of the glass and then collapsed out of sight.

Rupert was immobilized by panic. Stiff with indecision he saw that the misshapen mêlée was becoming more frenzied. If he stayed in the kiosk he might be condemned as a coward but if he left his post, and launched into the tumult, a looter might steal the cash.

Then, from nowhere, the Big Boss arrived. He surged into the rabble, hurling bodies left and right until he came to the core.

The next thing Rupert saw was a procession move past his window. The Big Boss was in the middle with Neil and Neville on each side. Both were in the inflexible grip of his hands. Shorty bobbed behind, unnoticed.

'Weren't nothin' to do with us,' Neville whined. '*They* started it.'

'We stuffed twenty quid in that machine!' Shorty shrieked.

Neil was silent but, as he moved past, Rupert saw his face. It was pinched with malice.

'Out,' said the Big Boss.

Chapter 3

Loud laughing and sobbing often echoed down labyrinthine corridors and through empty chambers. These noises sounded as if they were discarnate, but they were not. They emanated from Margaret Ruthven, a woman seized by diverse internal dramas. Sometimes she rolled around the castle screaming for no other reason than she felt like it. She did not care if anyone heard her or not. Gripped by convulsions she knew nothing, only the howls that reverberated between dripping brickwork and mouldy cornerstone.

Sometimes, when the terrible screeching abated and a semblance of logic returned, she slid ungratefully back into her body and wondered how far her cry had travelled. Had it been heard in the high street, out there in the tea-shoppes and burger bars? Had it broken a cucumber frame? Had They heard it?

These musings never lasted long because she knew the answers. She knew that her larynx could bleed, her lips could dry up and turn into dust. No one would hear her just as no one had heard Roger Ruthven's final shriek as he lay writhing and dying. She had come across him twenty minutes after the last breath had left his corpse. His eyes had protruded, staring at her. His hands lay stiff where they had clawed at his bruised throat. His fishing-line had, apparently, twisted itself around his neck while he was practising casting in the courtyard. A freak gust of wind then accidental death.

Roger Ruthven's fate had been seen as a fascinating mystery and his legend became entwined with local folklore. His name joined Mother Shipton, the witch of Watchet, Eleanor Lovell, buried alive at Bawdrip and Sarah Biffin the armless artist from East Quantoxhead. The tragedy inspired rumours of a castle curse which acted as an advertisement and energized business.

Hordes of tourists gathered to gaze upon the patch where the body of the hotelier had been found. Margaret Ruthven made no effort to encourage them, quite the opposite in fact. 'Poor Roger,' she would say. 'But he was very dull you know. I think he might have bored himself to death.' The crowds soon decreased as the novelty faded away, the food became more repulsive and the personal manner of the hostess led most visitors to agree with the popular theory that she had killed her husband.

The end finally came when, in the throes of *delerium tremens*, there had been a fight with a family from Huish Champflower and somebody had been punched on the nose.

Margaret Ruthven had not minded. She cared not a jot for Les Routiers or Tourist Board accolade. The guests demanded a relentless joviality that was alien to her nature. Sometimes, when her senses were unnaturally heightened, after a course of Amitriptline for instance, mixed (danger-ously) with amphetamine, images became larger and detailed to a grotesque degree. Faces with malformed simian features would float in front of her, swelling until they took on a hyper-real magnitude and definition. Harrowing stimuli bought women who looked like men and men who were women. Tufts sprang from the wrong gender. Hectic flora undulated on summer dresses and brown crouton teeth clamped down on the remains of pig.

Margaret Ruthven consumed pods, beans and capsules, but they could not protect her against acrid deodorants, fat fingers, soup like placenta, loud opinions, golf-bags, two-tone cycle helmets with ventilation ports, waterproof polyester, or babies.

The teenagers posed the most threat. Victims of seba-ceous disorders, their pores would splay into black holes that, if studied by the new quantum scientists, would undoubtedly prove that those who fell into them would be destroyed by forces of unimaginable fortitude. The open pores were terrifying. They could consume her, force her to bash against event horizons, then travel eternally in imaginary time faced with the fruitless task of finding a unifying theory.

For Margaret Ruthven there was no unifying theory, only chemically induced flushes of love and hate. Love came as gushing hysteria; hate was bitter, dark and pervasive. Love was the beginning of a drink. Hate was the end of one. Both had driven everyone away. Valerie had once arrived with a plastic box full of hair-brushes and rollers. A gardener had once cut back roses. Now she was alone. The bailiffs had taken what they could. The health and safety officers had no reason to call after the hotel closed.

She had been relieved when the business collapsed but, over the years, she too had come to believe in the curse of which so many spoke. She lived with doom as if it was a parasite which the body could not eject.

On some days an invisible phalanx stalked her. It went through her drawers, leafed through her books, waited on the doorstep, flicked the letter-box, knocked on the various doors that led into the castle and then disappeared when she went to answer them. As mocking voices filled her head, countless eyeballs seemed to watch her. Every window-pane framed a face staring at her, every creak hailed a footstep. They were always around, listening, following, creeping. She would look up to the sky and see a hundred satellite cameras trained to record her thoughts with sophisticated equipment developed in secret by The Government.

On other days the combination of substances that she ingested exerted a different effect – perception remained distorted but it was not paranoid. Filled with self-love, she assumed infallibility. She knew that she could do anything, be anything, say anything. This determined arrogance was, in a way, more terrible than her other moods. She would affirm it with several cans of Special Brew then spend the afternoon engaged in singing, for which she accompanied herself on the piano. Dissonant barrel-house blues reverberated around the room that had once been designed as a lounge for hotel guests.

Her falsetto tones, marked with a nasty vibrato, were harsh and off-key. Her playing was heavy – it did not emote the ragtime *joie de vivre* of junk-house jovials so much as the nephritis that tended to carry them away. If anyone had been unfortunate enough to hear her they would have told themselves that honky-tonk should have remained in the

Piney Wood sawmill camps from whence it came. Ethno-musicologists interested in debate might offer that Margaret Ruthven's lifestyle gave her much in common with Burnt Face and Peg Leg and all the others who sang of the sadness of lives that were full of squalor, drinking and debt. Certainly she spoke the truth when she sang those words written by Blind Willie McTell: '*I drank so much whisky, I stagger when I sleep. My brains are dark and cloudy, and my mind's gone to my feet.*'

It will come as no surprise to learn that, as a child, Margaret Ruthven devised a dizzying array of means to attract attention to herself. She had been born in Wimborne to Derek and Sue. He was a solicitor, she was a housewife with a collection of china dogs, and neither understood how they had managed to create such an extreme person. At the age of three she pushed a chest of drawers against her bedroom window and climbed out on to the roof. As a teenager she devoted her energies to creating a number of psychosomatic illnesses. This was partly from boredom and partly because she liked the lifestyle. The assembly line of symptoms allowed her to stay in bed, eat meals off trays, and listen to pop music on the radio. She enjoyed writing (and rewriting) her will, and she enjoyed mystifying the general practitioners who imparted prognoses that served to terrify Derek and Sue.

By the time she was fifteen she had given herself insomnia, hot flushes, swellings, a nervous tic, a stammer, water on the knee, allergic rashes, anaemia, an underactive thyroid and boils. At the age of sixteen she made page four of *The Lancet* when, after limping for seven weeks, she convinced various specialists that she was suffering from a freak lipid-storage disorder.

Eventually a new, younger doctor joined the Wimborne practice, a doctor whose own daughters wore dental braces that they had made out of paperclips and thick black glasses in which there were no lenses. He knew that there were no limits to teenage eccentricity and, having read Margaret Ruthven's notes (by now a weighty volume of some five-hundred pages) he decided that the majority of her symptoms could be put down to an over-active imagination. He took Derek and Sue aside and suggested that they send their daughter to drama school. She needs to express herself, he told them. Such a thing was outside Derek and Sue's ken. Their cultural experience was confined to garden centres and *The Pirates of Penzance*. Doctors, however, were always right, and Margaret was sent to the Camberwell School of Dramatic Art.

It was here that she met the first of her four husbands. Kevin St Kevin had been mesmerized by her red hair (which in those days was natural), her green eyes and her voice which, distinct, deep and resonant, could always be heard at the back of the auditorium. Kevin St Kevin, to his credit, but also to his downfall, believed in love at first sight. The marriage lasted six months.

Margaret Ruthven married his best friend because she couldn't think of anything else to do. The best friend, whose name she could never remember, had wondrous black hair combed into a quiff but, having been a very promising Polonius, he submitted to social conscience, and stood as a Labour candidate. Disparate aspirations separated them. He attended meetings with the TUC; she went to play Dame Pliant in Birmingham.

Over the years Margaret Ruthven's career took her from tragicomedies set in Welsh valleys to social realism set in bedsits in SE19. There were violent orgies enacted in west London pubs and Gothic interpretations of Salome at the Edinburgh Festival. She was the Duchess of Malfi with a Lancashire accent and Lady Fidget with a cigar. Her Lady Macbeth was (according to one review) 'a tedious moll', but her Medea was a 'convincing mixture of raw sexuality, jaded cynicism and faded femininity'.

On New Year's Day in 1972 she saw someone being sick in the checkout line in Woolworth's and this led her to reassess her life. She had learned to make a dramatic entrance and she had learned to project but her future seemed to hold an expanse of wet provinces, dirty dressing-rooms, local reviews, paltry pay, uncomfortable corsets, and fat casting directors who endlessly rejected her for endless television adaptations. She was tired of telling strangers that her talent lay in character; that she could do comedy; that she danced . . .

She served herself some exhilarating cocktails and rang her agent to announce her retirement. He told her that he had lined her up to play Lady Wishfort in *The Way of the World*. She argued that Lady Wishfort was thirty-two years older than her, furthermore she did not understand the plot and neither, to her certain knowledge, did anyone else. Congreve had probably mystified himself when he was writing it. Her agent would not listen and she was dispatched to The Pit where she met Simon Tree.

Simon Tree was a legend but he was a legend who was growing old with an all-year tan and alimony. Exalted as a genius when he was at Oxford University, he had directed an innovative production of *Hedda Gabler* (in which he had played Hedda) and, offstage, he had worn pink suits and turbans. Plays and pink suits have long granted success in a milieu with a tradition of homoerotic mythomania. Simon Tree, promoted by loving dons, acclaimed by besotted neophytes, found himself touched by fame.

He left Christchurch with a third but a string of West End hits quickly made him a millionaire. Then cynicism set in with gin and cravats. His face was often flushed, his jowls had swollen, he was known to have a hysterical temper, but he was still the man whose personal magnetism had led (it was said) seventeen women to become officially engaged to him. Grey hair was combed smoothly back from a high forehead, ice-blue eyes flashed with dangerous intelligence, and, at six foot three, his stature dominated the room.

Simon Tree had glared at Margaret Ruthven through a nimbus of du Maurier smoke. He saw the wrinkles clinging to her neck, he saw hair that needed height, he saw a body that would grow big and a mind that would explode like a lettuce left to go to seed. Margaret Ruthven fell in love with him.

He cast her as Richard III (in which she appeared in a wheelchair) and then as Queen Marguerite in Dumas' *The Tower*. She was brave in a leather corset but her perform-ance was compared to a 'brisk swim in an acid bath' and the play closed after two weeks.

They lived in Pimlico for three years. They met Ian Fleming, the Bee Gees and Harold Acton. They were written up. Then Simon Tree announced that he was leaving her.

'Is there someone else?' she had asked.

'No there isn't. I'm bored, that's all.'

'Bored?'

'Yes. Bored. We don't fight like we used to.'

'I thought you didn't like fighting.'

'I do like fighting but I always win and it's boring.'

This was true. Simon Tree was blessed with cruelty, wit, and the ability to think on his feet. This meant that his verbal parrying skills were insurmountable. He always had the last word and, thanks to a mixture of percipience and sadism, it devastated the person who dared to oppose him. The rare occasions that Margaret Ruthven managed to provide a pertinent philosophical point to which he did not have an immediate counter-statement, he resorted to physical superiority and threatened to cut off her legs with a knife.

'I could have a baby,' she had suggested.

'I'd rather have a brain tumour.'

Simon Tree packed his monogrammed slippers and went to Kent.

Roger Ruthven had appeared at a convenient moment. She had no money and she needed somewhere to live. Simon Tree's departure had marked the end of sentience. Now life offered only the practicalities of survival. Roger adored her, which was irritating, but he was stable and chaos had drained her. She chose a marriage of convenience and a year later (by mistake) gave birth to Rupert.

She had never particularly wanted a child and she did not understand the small man that she had created. He ran around asking for things. The guests played with him, his father took him fishing and various teachers claimed that he was clever. He made drawings and disappeared then came back again. He talked a lot and wore a Batman outfit and spent hours doing boring things with a football.

The everyday clatter of feeding and washing did not bring her peace of mind or fulfilment. She went through phases of exertion because exhaustion provided an anaesthetic and prevented her from thinking. But disconnection appeared at regular intervals and brought the all-consuming darkness that she was beginning to accept as her destiny. There was no self, only a mannequin to clothe with gestures and a body to be supported by multi-coloured axiolytics. These sedated her but they also introduced side-effects such as shuddering limbs and swollen breasts. A physiological side-show diverted her from the fear that she would never be cured of despair but cast no light on its causes.

'I am desperate,' she said to Roger Ruthven in September 1982.

'Oh dear. What's brought this on?' He was reading *Catering Monthly*.

'I'm very depressed.'

'What about?'

'About nothing. I'm depressed.'

'Have you seen Dr Carr?'

'I've been seeing Christopher since 1978.'

'What does he say?'

'He says I'm depressed.'

'Perhaps you need a holiday.'

Sometimes she wanted to tear his skin off with her fingernails. At least when she told Simon Tree that she was depressed he always said, 'You can't be as depressed as I am because no one is.'

'I hear voices,' she told Roger Ruthven.

'So do I,' he replied. 'I think it's the Shadwells. They want their bill.'

Then he had folded up *Catering Monthly*, placed it on the pile with all the other *Catering Monthly*s and said, 'Cheer up. It might never happen.'

If she had loved him she could at least have hated him, but even this luxury was denied her. So she took an imaginative compilation of Ativan, Tranxene and Dalmane, laced it with a Palfium suppository, and woke up in a clinic where a man qualified by a Biro and a clipboard announced that she had schizophrenia. At least this was something, a definition. The unholy glamour of schizophrenia.

'Is it curable?'

'Uh. Not really. Manageable I would say, but curable? No.'

He put her on chlorpromazine so she sat in a chair for a year or so. No one seemed to mind. The cleaning lady hoovered round her.

Now the days unfurled slowly. Sometimes the drugs would cause her tongue to swell to twice its usual size. Sometimes her eyes refused to blink and she thought they would pop out of her head and roll under the sofa. She concentrated on protecting herself against Them. She did not know who They were, she was not even sure of the nature of Their mission, but she was aware of Their eternal presence and she lived in the knowledge of Their malice.

Her Circadian rhythms, massacred by drugs, had fallen into a disarray which segregated her from normality. This morning, brooding on Ian's death, she added a Nitrazepam to the thiordiazine. Then, after checking the room for electronic bugs, she slouched over a three-year-old copy of the *Daily Mirror*. Mice scratched in the cupboards. They made her think of Aunt Mabel. As a child her first sight of Aunt Mabel had been the vision of the woman standing on a table where she had leapt after seeing a mouse run across the kitchen floor. Margaret, who had not seen the mouse, assumed that this was an adult code of manners, like shaking hands, so, thereafter, she leapt on a table every time she saw Aunt Mabel.

She smiled to herself. The sedative was beginning to kick in.

Vacuity might have toned this day if the fridge had not turned into an instrument of terror.

The appliance suddenly emitted a tattoo of staccato clicks. Then it jumped forward, growling.

Margaret Ruthven's bosoms heaved as anxiety possessed them. It was obvious that a person was hiding in the fridge and, if not a person, then a host of evil forces that had collected into a poltergeist. The noises became louder. The fridge shook. A spray of blue sparks spurted out of the electric socket. The metal casing was old; person or presence could not be contained for long. The imponderable was about to escape.

Margaret Ruthven picked up the machine-gun and, without standing up, fired a round at the fridge door.

Everything went quiet.

She crept towards the door, now shredded by black bullet-holes, opened it an inch and pushed the barrel of the gun through it. Encouraged by the continuing silence she opened it wider and was relieved to find that the Special Brew cans had not been pierced. The drink was safe and the haunting entity seemed to have disappeared.

She snatched a can of beer, pressed it to her lips, emptied it and took another without noticing the spume that flowed down her chest. Then she went to visit Ian's grave.

The Jack Russell had been buried in a walled garden that Roger Ruthven had intended to turn into a crazy golf course. The project was never finished but the gardener had subsequently persuaded Margaret to buy a job lot of stone statuary at a reduced rate and a family of shepherdesses, cupids and lions had had their heads blasted off when Margaret Ruthven was teaching herself how to shoot the machine-gun. Most of them now stood in disconsolate groups, as if they were waiting to be served sherry after a wake. A crumbling wall, hampered by ivy, was surrounded by a tussle of overgrown dogwood, corkscrew hazel and hydrangea, all of which had meshed into each other as they fought for the light.

Ian's grave was marked with a circle of flint and a small tombstone that stated his name and the year of his death. Overladen with nostalgia Margaret knelt down and saw, to her horror, that the tomb had been interfered with. The earth had been stirred up, foliage had been flattened and a vase of flowers lay on its side. Dead daffodils lay strewn on the ground. To the right, underneath an unkempt privet, she saw the clear outline of a man's shoe.

This was the day then. This was the final day. They had arrived.

Grabbing the MP5 she heaved herself out of the walled garden and, without thinking, ran out of a back gate and into a lane that wound up the hill behind Fairview Castle. She could hear the splash of Their footsteps following her. Strengthened by terror her legs rotated automatically and she staggered over fields, only stopping to listen for the crunch of Their feet.

She had not left the grounds of the hotel for many years. Dazed with drink, confused by panic, semi-sedated by hypnotics, the world became a blur of hedgerow and fence.

There was no direction. She simply ran.

Chapter 4

Clive Swinburne did not believe in God but he did believe in Madame Blanche's prescriptive skin-care products, a range of *savons douceurs* and *crèmes biologiqués* with miraculous powers of rejuvenation. Her *lait fleur*, with its extract of rose petals, had been particularly beneficial, as had the *crème collagen* for wrinkle-prone complexions that needed special protection against sun, wind and pollution. This, with its neroli and lavender, had eliminated the tiny lines that were the bane of Clive's eye-sockets. Thus encouraged he had embarked on a ten-day intensive treatment utilizing Madame's Ampoule Number 2 which, for $100, came with elastin, micropolysaccharides and DNA.

He studied himself in the rear-view mirror as he drove his hired Toyota Carina (Executive) through Exmoor's ecologically sensitive areas. His complexion had never looked so good but there was no one around to appreciate the purifying effects of waste removal.

Now the Biosomes Night Repair Cream (with liposomes,

AHA and Vitamin A) was running out. He had faxed his assistant, Brent, in Hollywood to Fed-Ex a new supply, but Brent had become unpredictable since the release of *Dances with Wolves*. A new pride in his Native American heritage had caused him to change his name to Twilight Moon Rhythm and he had embarked on a complicated vision quest. Once reliable, he now spent his time at shamanic seminars or learning to play the love flute and was often so exhausted by his efforts to empower himself that he overslept and was late for work.

Brent's personal search had turned into a full time job, Clive thought resentfully as he nosed the car past sodden fields full of heart-breaking lambs, a full time job for which he was paying while his skin, without the liposomes, ran the risk of drying up and cracking like some godforsaken plateau in the desert. Brent was probably doing it on purpose, witholding the life-saving supply in some heinous Indian spell of revenge whose effect would be to cause epidermal crinkle. Brent's own face, of course, was blessed with the natural oils of the olive-skinned. He did not have to worry about moisturising.

Clive wished that Brent's 'path' would infuse some sympathy for the plight of others – others like him, for instance, who were getting on, who had spent too much time in the Tanning Salon and not enough drinking Evian water and needed a disciplined daily skin care regime using the products formulated by Madame Blanche with the expert help of a team of Parisian scientists.

His problems were increasing now that he was as far away from civilisation as it was possible to be without special breathing apparatus. There would be no fax machines in Porlock, no E Mail or fibre-optic support of any kind. The only form of communication would be the shouting to which the locals seemed so prone. Clive felt like shouting at Brent. He would have shouted at Brent more often if he had not been aware that volume turned his voice into a trembling tremolo.

He had been touring this designated area of natural beauty for three days now and he was nervously exhausted. He had taken Polaroids of Rose Cottages and slept in old coaching inns that, despite declarations of superior accommodation, offered no sight of a spa or gym. He had seen the remains of a woolly mammoth, he had seen terrier shows, he had visited Oare Church where Lorna Doone had been shot and he had felt at home in Lynmouth when his credit cards had been stolen.

He tried to feel grateful that he had been dispatched to England to find locations; he had, after all, long wanted to see the country from which (according to his mother) his forebears came. At least England spoke something akin to English. In the past Clive had found himself in places where scorpions ran about in rest-rooms and menus had offered seal brains.

Clive, as Karl's employee, was the victim of Karl's whims and Karl had felt (with every fibre of his artistic being) that Lorna Doone country was the only setting in which to photograph Hatch Hamstone's new advertising campaign. What Karl wanted Karl tended to get because he was the highest paid photographer in the world.

Karl's caprices were often complicated by impulses of grandiosity. One season he had ordained that Hatch Hamstone's tailored combat fatigues and flak jackets must be photographed in Guatemala. Clive had spent weeks arguing against travelling to a country torn by civil war. He spoke darkly of genocide and the fact that they would not get insurance. 'Why can't we go to Belize,' he had suggested. 'It's right next door and they don't have a scorched-earth policy there.' But Karl had availed himself of connections with the IMF and UN and he had managed to persuade them that the shoot would be of benefit to the tourist industry. Visas had been issued, 'carnies' of clothes had been sent to San Marcos and teams of makeup artists had been lowered from helicopter gun-ships into the jungle village of Ixtahuacan.

They had spent many miserable days living in tents, washing in buckets, eating beige-coloured beans and jumping as every rustle in the undergrowth hailed the arrival of a death squad. Then the inevitable had finally happened and a supermodel went up in a mortar attack on the Pan American Highway.

The cost incurred by this tragedy had been easily consumed by the millions of dollars worth of publicity garnered by Hatch Hamstone when the world press noted that he had grotesquely exploited the people's struggle.

Now Karl could do no wrong. Hamstone's people had sprung a hair-raising budget, a portion of which was awarded to 'production design'. So here was Clive, in valleys and glens, trying to find a suitable place to photograph Hamstone's new peasant collection – a repugnant selection of dirndl skirts, pie-crust frills, broderie anglaise blouses and mob-caps.

Clive was not a rural person. He had been born in San Diego and he lived in Los Angeles. He was a creature of the boardwalk. Hussocky grass meant ticks that carried Lyme Disease (rash, aching joints, paralysis of the face); dry heathland housed poisonous adders.

'Do the snakes bite?' he had asked a man in a tweed cap.

'Course they do. You gotta dog?'

'No.'

'Well keep it quiet. The bluebells aren't out.'

He had become accustomed to absurdist drama. On his first night, before his senses had acclimatized, he had stayed in a converted wood mill. Outside, on a 'beer garden patio', old people painted Dunkery Beacon. Inside he had been cornered by an ageing androgyne in pebble spectacles who told him that today was National Bog Day.

'You don't have to be an ecologist to be a bog enthusiast,' he had been informed from the recess of a nylon hood with Eskimo trim. 'You should come to my Blooming Bogs lecture, then you'd know the difference between your yellow sedge and your marsh pennywort. You gotta dog?'

'No.'

'Well keep it quiet. The bluebells aren't out.'

Now he was heading towards Porlock. He was praying that this would be his last port of call. He had had quite enough.

The guidebook suggested that Porlock was where John Ridd had purchased gunpowder. An ancient fishing village, it was described as 'an exhilarating land of hills, combes, sparkling streams and deep woodlands'. Here, if one chose to look, 'the mighty buzzard soars above wild ponies and red deer'.

Clive did not trust the guidebook. The only deer he had seen were staring glassy-eyed from wooden shields in low-beamed taverns. Hats had been hanging from their antlers with a uniform conspicuity that led him to conclude that hats hung from their antlers in the wild. The guidebook's falsity was further corroborated by descriptions of a 'mild equable climate'. A mild equable climate, to a Californian, meant enough heat to cause a riot, not a sheet of rain that insinuated itself into every crevice of an alpaca-lined wool-mix greatcoat designed by Giorgio Armani.

Certainly there was none of the 'breathtaking visibility across the Channel to the Welsh mountains and inland to the Mendips'. Visibility, thanks to mist and drizzle, stretched to three inches in front of his face.

Gloomily Clive buttoned up the Armani and conscientiously took Polaroids of the high street. It sure was old. And low. He had never seen such small houses. The main drag, through which he could have roller-bladed in three minutes, was so narrow that, should he have driven his Ford Explorer down it, the sides would have been scraped. He had wanted to bring his sports truck to England. It was, after all, his second home (and a great deal larger than many people's first homes) but the Hamstone budget would not accommodate this expense and he had had to resign himself to living life without the comfort of his 4×4 which had a console for a spill-free soda-drinking experience, and an Igloo Thermoelectric Cooler which connected to the cigarette lighter.

Clive loved his car more than he loved his boyfriend, Fenton, and Fenton had been aware of this. He had claimed that that was why he left Clive ('I can NAT compete with power mirrors!') but Clive suspected that the real reason was that he would not allow Fenton to wear his Pilsbury Dough Boy Talking Watch to charity fashion galas.

He nosed disconsolately into a saddlery where there was an invigorating smell of leather and took photographs of the ancient church of St Dubricious, an edifice of red stone whose round, crude design exuded the tranquility some-times brought by age. He sighed. He preferred Frank Lloyd Wright.

'I'm turning into Madam Jade,' he said aloud as he drove the car past a multi-gabled guest-house and away from the woods in which lepers had once lived.

Porlock Weir lay against a backdrop of mauve moun-tains, grey shingle and choppy sea. There were bobbing fishing smacks and a car park with what passed as a valet, the first Clive had seen since he left L.A. He handed over his keys, assuming that the car was to be parked for him, but the man threw them back. A tussle of egos only ended when Clive pointedly parked his car at the opposite end of the turf to that indicated by the attendant.

He took Polaroids of the tiny white boats, the ancient cots, the traditional blacksmith, the cute signposts, and was about to return to his car when, peering through a leaded window, he saw an exhilarating selection of high-quality gift items.

He swung into the shop, coat and scarf flapping with an enthusiasm that was equalled, if not surpassed, by the proprietor, a woman who had not seen a customer for six months. Their instant love throbbed with the passion that is the bond between supply and demand. She was wearing a sleeveless Husky waistcoat, a black cashmere polo-neck and a necklace of chunky amber beads, but even this did not matter. It was a look. Who was he to judge? She owned a shop. That was all that counted.

She was sorry, but she did not supply cosmetics. She herself had to drive all the way to Taunton to buy the Clarins range. They compared *extraits de cellules fraîches* with *Hydra Systemes* for half an hour that sped by in three minutes, then they moved on to Luis Vuitton, stocked in the shop but long discarded by Clive as 'it always gets muddled up with other people's on the carousel'. He had replaced his collection with a black series from T. Anthony in New York, seven bags in all, numbered and cross-referenced with a directory. This was was supposed to be managed by Brent but, since he had taken to following the steps of the Ancient Ones, he could not be trusted with tasks that required concentration. Clive had removed the responsibility after a trip to Puerto Vallarta when a hairdryer (number one) was packed in number seven (knitwear) and had been left at home. This error had condemned Clive to a series of flat hair days for which he had still not forgiven Brent.

The chunky amber vibrated with affection while Clive skipped and shimmied through tapestried cushions, Arran jumpers, William Morris sponge bags, and Hermés silk. He was flitting his fingers through a shower of silk ties when she informed him that the Beast of Exmoor had ripped her cardigan from the washing line.

'Oh dear,' he said from amongst the textured silks.

'Yes. It was torn to shreds.'

'The Beast of Exmoor, you say?'

'Yes. Ghastly thing. It never appears in the day but people have seen its shadow in the moonlight and they say it is not a species known to man. Half-tiger, half-dragon, with revolting reptilian tail and claws as long as fingers.'

She held up a gnarled nicotine-stained forefinger to demonstrate.

'It attacks livestock in the middle of the night, biting away the chicken wire with its teeth.'

'Sounds terrible.'

'Yes. It is. Terrible. They can't catch it you see and no one knows where it will strike next. It's a myth now. Like the Loch Ness monster.'

'Good for the tourist trade then.'

'I suppose so,' she said sadly. 'But it won't bring back my cardie will it?'

Clive bought a tie and darted out.

He cruised the high street to find the most expensive hotel. One with Royale in its name. Or Palace. One which offered a Milky Way of asterixes. He wanted room service, he wanted fountains and faux palms and mini-bars clinking with bottlettes of Grand Marnier. He wanted kitten-soft towelling bathrobes whose prices were automatically included in the leviathan bill that would be covered with indiscriminate generosity by Hatch Hamstone.

Where was the chateau that screamed hydro-massage and lymph drainage? He wanted neural therapy, ozone therapy, vitamin therapy and a collagen injection into the face. He wanted an individually designed diet menu and a series of cures which would balance mineral ratios and encourage efficient cell function. He wanted a seaweed bath and *cuisine minceur* and white-coated *curistes*. He wanted to be told more about the Feldenkrais technique of body alignment. He wanted to see Joan Collins lying on the sun deck.

He was forced to settle for the Blackmore Hotel whose façade was an attractive sun-faded yellow but which, more importantly, flagged its status with signs saying that every room had colour TV, satellite channels and direct dial, computer-controlled telephones.

He hustled suitcases one to three into the crepuscular area that doubled as a lobby and bar and, blinking in the low-beamed semi-darkness, looked around for a bellboy. A light-footed vision in a pleasing pill-box hat would have been a dream come true – what emerged from the shadow, however, was a nightmare.

The patent leather shoes were tricked out with silver buckles. The navy bloomers were tied with flowing silver ribbons. The brocade waistcoat (with unrestrained lilac chinoiserie) was topped by a crisp muslin cravat moulded into an elaborate quatrefoil. The Brandenburg overcoat, bombazine, was sky blue, and embroidered with pink sea creatures. The head was magnified by a waterfall of chestnut ringlets, a shower of curl and love-lock that flowed to the shoulder with exhausting abandon. If this was not enough (and it most certainly was), the wig supported a wide-brimmed hat that shivered with a frenzy of ostrich feathers.

Clive wondered if he was having a trauma-syndrome flashback.

He had travelled all over the world to fulfil Karl's desires. He had surveyed the mosques on the Bosphorus. He had lazed in the Kowloon ferry and eaten in the caviar bar at the Mandarin Oriental. He had been to Necker and St Lucia and Venice. Furthermore he had attended fashion shows in London, Milan, Paris and New York, men's *and* women's, prêt *and* couture. He had witnessed the unsinkable and the unthinkable, the lumpy and frumpy, the hair-raising and self-raising. He had seen costumes that defied both death and gravity. He thought he had seen it all. The nameless dread that stood in front of him could not boast art as a mitigating circumstance.

'For Christ's Sake!' Clive blurted out, 'What the hell are you wearing?'

54

The parade of plumes fluttered and quivered for a minute. Then, with no word of warning, no debate about style and substance, hat and hair were snatched off the head and placed on the top of the bar. The residual features, much diminished by this gesture, belonged to a balding middle-aged man with small, dark, darting eyes.

Accustomed to inspecting travellers and judging much from their appearance, Miles Falconbridge saw an impeccable American with three expensive leather suitcases each bearing Concorde tags. The streaked blonde hair, gelled and slicked, was scraped back in rows from the forehead, the shirt was crisp and white, the eyes clear and blue, the nails manicured and polished. A criss-cross of white fissures gleamed underneath a radiant tan, but it was still difficult to guess the visitor's age. He could have been thirty. He could have been fifty.

'Oh don't worry,' the hotelier said, patting the wig with friendly affection. 'I don't always wear this stuff. It's just our enactment.'

A breeze of gentleman's cologne blew around the room. It was accompanied by an expression that reminded Miles of a marinated artichoke heart.

'Enactment? Enactment? What *are* you talking about?'

'The dress rehearsal for the Civil War.'

'Civil War? I thought that was in Ireland.'

'No no no. We have a Civil War Weekend in June. Celebrates the Royalist Skirmish. I organize it. We've just finished a rehearsal. I am Mine Host, or yours rather. Miles Falconbridge. Were you looking for a room?'

'Yes,' said Clive. 'Big. With a bathroom. And a telephone.'

'Perhaps you would like our suite? It has a four-poster.'

'Is it the most expensive?'

'Yes.'

'I'll take it.'

Miles Falconbridge brought his fist (framed by a lace sleeve) down on a bell and banged it with unnecessary violence.

'I'll get my daughter to show you. Grace! Grace!'

Footsteps clattered down a corridor and a teenage girl appeared.

'Ah, Grace. Please show Mr er . . .'

'Swinburne.'

'Please show Mr Swinburne the Duke of Monmouth.'

At first Clive thought that Grace's beauty was an optical illusion caused by the dim lighting and intensified by the ugliness of her father.

But as she floated across the courtyard, and he studied her more closely, he knew that travel fatigue had not strained his eyes. His instincts were intact. She was extraordinary.

The symmetry of her features – high cheek-bones, strong chin, grey eyes – added definition but they did not explain the whole. The lines were finely cut, leaning to delicacy, but they were unimportant specifics. The countenance was not in the length of the neck, the simplicity of the haircut, or the youth of the skin; it was in the carriage of the girl herself.

She seemed to have wafted from an unknown stratum. Surveying her surroundings with the inpenetrable composure of an alien emigré, her outward serenity, old and young, was enhanced by innocence. She had probably not been anywhere, or seen much, but her presence was not that of an arriviste.

It was possible that her unaffected purity, underpinned by lack of curiosity, was the consequence of stupidity. Something seemed to have left her eyes a long time ago.

He glanced (with the reflex of one who has weathered many casting sessions) at her legs.

They were not long enough to carry their owner down a Paris runway. Legs, however, had become less important of late. Indeed, thanks to the uniform length of those worn in California, commonality had suffered them a decline in fashion emphasis. They were useful for wrapping around film director's necks, but they were no longer required for a successful entré into modelling. They were not even needed to transport the girl from appointment to appointment as this service was provided by a limousine.

In the future, if Darwin was right, legs would become obsolete. The model-girl would evolve into face, neck and breasts, all of mesmerizing beauty, and these fabulous torsos would be lifted into photographers' studios by a specially designed system of pulleys. In the event of advertisements for trousers, old legs would have to be plucked from photographs in archives and pasted on by the art department.

Grace's legs caused Clive no worry. She was blessed with everything that Karl sought in his models. She was possessed of no defensive affectation, she was very young, she was British, and, most importantly, she was unknown. Karl had long refused to photograph professionals. He plucked his subjects from surf, souk and street. His 'discoveries' were the material of which his reputation had been made.

Clive was confident that he had found the star of the Hatch Hamstone advertising campaign and he knew that no one (including himself) would turn down $100,000 to wear a cambric smock and mixed-wool shawl.

The girl's British *froideur* might have intimidated some people but Clive knew that vanity always welcomed the cool clichés of the talent scout.

'Have you ever modelled?'

She blinked.

'At school. For life-class. I'm going to art college.'

She did not simper or tell him to stop being silly. She was being polite to an unimportant stranger because he was a client in her father's hotel.

'No, I mean for a photographer. I work for a photographer in Los Angeles. Karl Künterbunt. He's very famous. Do you read *Vogue*?'

'Not really.'

'Oh. What do you read?'

'Books sometimes.'

'Oh.'

The only books that Clive had ever read were *Traveller's Health* and *The Bargain-Hunter's Guide to Shopping in Hong Kong*.

'Well he does a lot of work for *Vogue* and I am his Production Manager. We are shooting an advertising campaign for Hatch Hamstone. He's a designer. Have you ever heard of him?'

'No.'

Jesus Christ. Hatch Hamstone's face was on billboards from Monte Carlo to Miami. Her ignorance was beginning to give him an identity crisis. It was as if he had been swept up in some Somerset earth-mystery and had crossed a portal to another reality. Perhaps he was not Clive

Swinburne, influential right-hand man to the most celebrated photographer in the fashion industry. Perhaps he was a figment of his own imagination. He looked down and checked his shoes. To earth himself.

'Would you mind if I took a Polaroid to show him?'

Grace had stopped minding about anything since her mother died.

'No,' she said.

Clive stood her against the white wall. She was wearing a tight knitted cardigan and a pair of jeans – a simple statement and one that did not offend the eye. As the Polaroid threw up the image Clive knew that he had been right. The camera served her well – it elevated her mien and exaggerated her presence. He had long ago given up trying to define the aura that made a woman unique, but experience had provided him with the percipience to recognize it. In Grace he saw an attitude and a face that could make their owner, or those who owned their owner, millions of dollars.

'I'll ring you.'

'OK.'

Later, lying on his four-poster bed, the last of the *crème biologique* spread moistly on his worried forehead, Clive rang Brent in Los Angeles.

'Where are my fucking liposomes?'

Brent's hurt tone came through as clearly as if he had been speaking in the next room which, thank God, he was not. He was, in fact, sitting with his tasselled mocassins on Clive's desk. He had just finished eating a bowl of Golden Temple Cinnamon Puff cereal sweetened with honey collected by Mayan Indians of the Yucatan Peninsula. Now he was surfing a web site entitled 'Sacred Initiation'. The California sun was shining through a window on to his new braids.

'I Fed-Exed them yesterday,' Brent said.

'The Biosomes Repair Cream?'

'For mature skins, yes.'

'There's no need to rub it in, Brent. What about the *Eau Pour Les Yeux*?'

'Yes. I sent that. And something called a *Crème Buste*.'

'Don't be absurd, Brent. That's to firm women's tits.'

'Oh. I'm sorry. The package was so cute. Anyway, I sent them to Claridges.'

'Claridges? Claridges? You freak! I left Claridges four days ago.'

'Perhaps they'll cab it to you.'

In the small silence that represented assimilation of the expense of this idea, Brent read, 'The degree of your humanity can be measured by your ability to know another person's pain and joy but you can care without taking everything personally.'

Pain rather than joy seemed to be the order of the day.

'How's it goin'?' he asked soothingly.

'I ache all over, my skin is ruined, I've put on six pounds, and this country does not believe in the manufacture of inter-proximal tooth aids but, other than that, OK I suppose.'

'Hidierama?'

'Yeah.'

'Have you found a location? Karl's having kittens. His assistant keeps ringing from the Cayman Islands.'

'Saying what?'

'It was kinda hard to hear. They were photographing Andie McDowell sitting on an elephant and there was a lot of noise in the background, y'know? Crashin' and thumpin'.'

'Andie or the elephant?'

'The elephant, I assume.'

'Well, let's hope they can tell the difference. Anyway, you can tell Karl that it's perfect here. And I've found a girl for him.'

'That's good. There's nothin' here. She isn't tan, is she? Karl's right off tan at the moment.'

'No she's not. She's amazing.'

Clive was already feeling protective about his 'discovery'. His feelings about her appeared to be humanitarian but they were borne of the survival instinct. He knew that Grace's beauty was now inextricably linked with his reputation. If she was a success it would support Karl's lucrative relationship with Hatch Hamstone and, as a result, Clive's status within Karl's tiny but violent empire. His importance as a person of taste and prescience would be reaffirmed and he would be seen as a creator of cultural diktat, as he had been when he had found the Frundsberg Twins in a park in Amsterdam and persuaded Karl to use them for the now notorious Itsy-Bitsy Intimate Apparel campaign. The Frundsberg sisters were the first Siamese twins to appear naked on double-page spreads in glossy magazines all over the world and they had helped to put Karl Künterbunt on the map. Clive, meanwhile, had been made an honorary member of the Siamese Twin Liberation Front and was still invited to their annual hoe-downs in Palm Springs.

If the unpredictable caprices that created beauty were against him and Grace was condemned, aspersion and possibly ruin would be his punishment.

'What's she like?' asked Brent.

'Cute. Cute. Cute.'

'Hair?'

'Mouse.'

There was a silence at the end of the phone and then a shocked voice.

'Mouse huh? Well that sure is a first.'

'Don't try to patronize me, Brent. I taught you everything you know. Leave the smart remarks to the experts. When you do it it's like Quasimodo trying to become a cheer-leader.'

Today Brent was learning to care without taking anything personally. Luckily for Brent.

'I think you're bein' a little paranoid. I was tryin' to be supportive. But mouse? Will Karl go for it?'

'It's not mouse in the sense that we usually think of it. It's more of an interesting silver grey.'

'Grey? Jesus, how old's the woman?'

''Bout seventeen, eighteen . . .'

Clive heard a soft whistle which he knew was not a fault on the line but the wind blowing through Brent's pursed lips.

'Bit old,' he said. 'Cut?'

'Bob. No fringe. Beautiful forehead.'

'Body?'

Clive felt suddenly very tired.

'Yes, Brent. She has a body.'

'Sexy?'

'How should I know? I've got Polaroids. All I can tell you is that this girl's going to blow Karl's mind. She's exquisite. She has attitude, and she'll look 'darling' in those mob-caps.'

'When are you comin' back? Hatch Hamstone wants a meeting.'

'Two days. Thank God.'

'Oh well. If you need anythin' you know where I am.'

'Well make sure you're there. I don't want any more fuck-ups.'

'I've got braids,' Brent said, to change the subject. 'Two. With beads. Mario did them for me. He's got gold teeth now . . .'

'Has he. Good. Don't go out without your pager.'

'I hear you.'

Clive put the telephone down and spent some minutes entertaining the hope that a fatal accident would put Brent in the ancient burial site of his heritage. Perhaps the Santa Ana wind would blow his beaded braids into his eyes and blind him as he was driving his (leased) Jeep Wrangler down the Hollywood freeway. There was always hope. Brent was not a good driver. Clive had once seen him attempting to change lanes on the 101 at the same time as reading *People* magazine.

He placed a mint 'Travellers' Mask' over his eyes and tried to sleep sitting up to avoid puffiness.

Downstairs Grace poured herself a Britvic orange juice.

'So who's the American?' her father asked.

'Dunno.' She shrugged. 'Works for a photographer.'

'Rich then?'

''Spect so.'

'Well you'll have to look after him tonight, I've got the Bed and Brekkers.'

Miles Falconbridge's position as President of the Porlock branch of the Bed and Breakfast Corporation (BBC) gave him access to the minutiae of local politics. As tourism had swelled in Somerset, so too had the members of the BBC. Its numbers ranged from those who ran season holiday lets in Bossington to those of a more exalted status, such as Falconbridge himself, whose four-star hotel had won Country Restaurant of the Year every year for as long as anyone could remember.

The BBC represented the majority of West Somerset's hoteliers. This was a mighty force in itself, but the organization's power was augmented by the occupations and interests of its members. These stretched well beyond the catering industry. Ettie Cust, for instance, administrated a Victorian guest-house in Watchet, while her husband Ted worked with the Rangers and her son Brian sat on the county council. The BBC's authority was founded on its access to 'intelligence'. Members gossiped at 'do's, dinners and PTA events. Information spread and the BBC utilized it. Thus it had grown from a collective designed to protect mutual interests to an institution that, as a campaigning body, posed a serious threat to anyone who dared to oppose it. Over the years it had had its way on paths (permissive, way-marked and bridle), ponies, afforestation policies, foot-bridges, peregrine falcons and disabled toilet facilities. Its influence extended to all aspects of local concern. No Woodland Craft Week or Howling Headland Tour was possible, in effect, without support from the BBC.

Miles Falconbridge had enjoyed his term of leadership –

now in its third year – but he was not popular with everybody. There were some (deranged, no doubt, by professional jealousy) who whispered that R.D. Blackmore had lived next door to Noel Coward's parents in Teddington. He had had no documented affiliation with the Blackmore Hotel. But even Falconbridge's detractors had to admit that he had the interests of the local businessman at heart and worked harder than anybody to ensure that the annual sum of £144 million spent by tourists continued to flow into the pockets of those he represented.

Grace said good-night to her father and, as she walked to her bedroom, stopped and peered into a mirror. The attentions of the American were mystifying. She could not imagine what motivated them.

A pale, suspicious face gazed back at her. She rarely looked at her own reflection. The image was not her. It did not describe her thoughts, her actions, the effect of her experience. It said nothing about her. She was glad of this; she did not wish to be read like a large print novel. This face, neither monstrous nor inspiring, ordinary if anything, served to retain all her secrets. The dead daughter of a dead mother, grieving, skulking, watching, waiting for some kind of medicine that would help. Those who saw her face would never know that they looked at a wild crone who saw beauty in perversity, who was drawn only to the brutish and the discarded.

She had never wanted to be like any girl in any magazine. She had never wanted to wear their clothes or own their hair. The rules of commercial contour were of no interest to her. They were the consequence of some unseen vote, a vote that she had never been given. Girls who were blonde and thus beautiful, cottages that were thatched and thus pretty. It did not work because it was not true.

At school she had chosen to be a nobody – a nobody with no personality. Blank-eyed, invisible, floating at the back of the crowd of girls who strode home at 3.30 pm, looking at themselves in the windows of newsagents and pushing each other with felt-penned fingers.

She had a centre parting, excellent disguise, and a school uniform worn with none of the embellishments developed by the pretty and loud, and then copied in displays of affection by those who hoped that by wearing them a spell would occur and they too would become pretty and loud and chosen for teams.

Grace was not noticed or referred to. She was not even insulted by the more developed bitches when they sat on the wall swinging their brown legs and smoking cigarettes. She was not insulted because there was nothing to insult. She had made herself as blank as that.

She had enjoyed the power. She saw everything – the minute power-struggles, the mind control, the torture inflicted by girl on girl. She knew who was breaking down and who was menstruating and who had been to Rhyl to see their aunt. As a persona nobody was a great success. It was easy, too. She slipped into it every day – not thinking, not flinching, not speaking.

And so, while some had tried to learn the reproductive cycle of the frog, conjugations, and maps illustrating the battle of Ypres, and others tried to understand the lessons given by a progressive English master (later fired) who introduced the works of William Burroughs, Grace learned about the power of silence. This severed her from her contemporaries who knew nothing of its subtleties. They thought that those who were the tallest and shrieked the loudest were the winners and leaders. But even the beauties were weak because they had no secrets. Everything was displayed like medals on their chests – their flaws and ambitions, shining for all to see and read.

Grace could have chosen to undermine them. She knew how, because she knew how to make them shrink and worry. But this was not the purpose of nobodiness. The purpose of nobodiness was to see and remember and never be forced to interact. Invisibility was designed to protect.

Possibilities stretched out, tempting, in front of her, hundreds of identities, millions of characteristics and characters, all perfectly formed and ready for her to steal. 'All structures are made to be smashed,' the progressive English master had told them. 'Understand *dimensionality*! There is no such thing as definition.' Grace had believed him. Sometimes she was at the centre of a chaos of ideas, pulled this way and that.

Anonymity, easily worn in the classroom, had been more difficult to sustain in the art department, where a natural flair set her apart from those who struggled with the still lifes and charcoal. Artiness, however, did not make one a star in this constellation. The pretties and sporties created the competition and visual gifts were not revered.

The art master forced Grace to speak. She who spoke to no one and for whom the adult world was inhabited by automatons. At first she only spoke back because she felt sorry for him. She did not think that he would have anything to impart. She assumed that his motivations would be sinister and that he would have to be watched lest he tried to destroy the work. There was no telling. The work was friable and fragile and could easily be destroyed.

Words, certainly, could destroy it. Then it would vanish for ever. The art master could kill it and by so doing he would kill her. He did not know this and she did not know how to defend herself.

They met in the late afternoon when everybody else had gone home.

His eyebrows sprang out of his face, huge and white and possessed of a life of their own. Grace saw them wriggling about on his forehead and, although she liked them, they said too much. He wanted to be fierce but they made him funny and they told his age, told everyone that soon he would have to retire and face himself. Then he would see all the things that he had not done and had not been able to do. His comedy tufts said that their owner would soon have to look at all the paintings he had not painted. Grace decided that she wanted her own face to be a blank. She would shave off her eyebrows so that she could be ageless and unreadable.

He was always rude to her, which she enjoyed.

'I suppose you want the bloody acrylics,' he would say. 'Do you know how much they cost?'

'Fuck off.'

'I've lost the key to the cupboard.'

'No you haven't. It's hanging around your stupid neck as usual.'

'I suppose you'll make a mess that I'll have to clear up again. I've got better things to do, you know.'

'No you haven't.'

And because he always made out that she was in his way, she knew that she wasn't. The dance was complicated.

Once he asked her if she had a boyfriend and she said she didn't like boys much.

'Don't like anything much, do you?' he had said.

'I like birds. I like it when they eat the crops and because of them everyone might starve to death. I like that. I like crows and vultures and turkeys and I loathe cranes. And I like penguins because they murder each other.'

She told him that penguins would push each other into the sea to test to see if there was a seal hiding in it. The sacrificed penguin would then be eaten.

She did not tell him that boys, by and large, repelled her; boys, that is, of her own age. She was driven by the work and contained by it, while others, not so lucky, were driven by the struggle to fight off searching fingers.

Once he had asked why no one came to the end of term shows and she had changed the subject. And once, letting his guard down for a second, he forgot himself, forgot that he was sixty, that insult was their intimacy, and told her that she had beautiful hands. Had she inherited them from her mother? Grace had allowed the question to dissolve into the silence.

Her paintings grew larger and larger, ghastly big. The final triptych covered the entire wall of one end of the room – a huge painting of St Christina The Astonishing – wild woman of Liège, damned for madness, hailed for wisdom, as forbidding as it was possible to be. Suppurating with disease, she perched in trees, staring down with an expression of bitter hatred, appalled by the rank smell of sinful human flesh.

Grace was fixated. St Christina's weeping pustules were lovingly detailed. She was a vast ghoul, naked, ragged, dirty, but bathed in a strange incandescence. The art master surveyed the work unfolding in front of him. He told her that he saw unnerving nihilism and admitted that he could not help being jealous. He wanted to buy St Christina from her. Grace said OK. She didn't really care about her now that she was finished. She was glad she was hideous and she was glad the art master wanted her but she would have been happy to leave her behind when she left the school.

They made a portfolio and they both knew it was good. Grace wanted to include her 'conceptual' pieces made with nails, but the art master said no. The adjudicators hated Marcel Duchamp. He was right. She was given a scholarship to Taunton School of Art which should have marked the end of her nobodiness. St Elmo's School for Girls was not known for the achievements of its graduates; indeed, in its history, no pupil had ever passed on to any form of higher education. Girls from St Elmo's became secretaries and then married vets and farmers. A scholarship should have caused a stir, particularly as there had been no excitement since Tracey Tarlton got pregnant. But Grace was overshadowed by Cecilia St John, who had been accepted by RADA. This achievement placed Cecilia and her breasts on the front of the local newspaper where they were accompanied by the caption 'proud day for St Elmo's'.

Grace had spent her last day in the art room composing hurtful caricatures of the art master, while he washed brushes and lectured her about her life. He had seen them come and go, he said, he had been in the business for forty years and he could tell her that the art market was a casino. He had looked at her work and he knew that the naive zeal spoke of a wild, easily damaged soul, a soul that might drag her to places that no one should have to go. She faced hardships but she would be in more danger if she remained an obsessive outsider. Life as a stranger could be a terrible life, he warned. The isolated always felt flayed by the unseen forces of the world that they could not enter, and then they started to hate and hate destroyed a woman quicker than it destroyed a man. Men were more equipped to loathe. Women buckled under hate's pressure.

Grace had listened, incredulous. She was drawing him, but he was portraying her with an intensity that left her breathless. How had he seen so much, shuffling about in those boots with the rusting keys around his wrinkled neck, Ready-Specs pinching his nose? And now, on her last day, she was being taken seriously. This had never happened before. She felt disarmed and pleased. He had given her hope but he had drawn her away from nobodiness. He had stimulated a new desire. Now she wanted to be seen and she wanted to be extraordinary. These were new needs. The art master had ignited them, but she did not know how to fulfil them.

She had handed him the cartoon in which he was illustrated with a bright orange face. He pretended to be hurt and huffy and they quickly returned to insults and normality for the difficult minutes that were saying good-bye. Neither had been able to speak of meeting again – both knew that now they were no longer teacher and pupil, they were human beings moving in different realms with no means to transmute the relationship. He was a big old man. She did not know what she was but she knew that she would never see him again.

The next morning Clive told Miles Falconbridge that if his daughter kept out of the sun she could make $100,000. Miles Falconbridge was impressed by this figure and asked what his daughter would have to do to earn it. He found it difficult to believe Clive's answer ('look cute and wear mob-caps') but the American had a platinum American Express card and a multi-coloured business card on which there were ten telephone numbers, including those for his office, his car, his personal assistant and his bathroom. Further-more he had provisionally booked the hotel for fourteen people at the end of May.

Miles relayed this inspiring information to his daughter who told him that if he thought that the American sincerely planned to return with $100,000 then he was thick. Did he not remember Nathalie Ryswick? A man who worked in Smidgens Super-Mart had promised to give her £7.50 if she touched his leg. She had touched it and he had refused to hand over the money. Her father retorted that this was not the same thing at all. Mr Swinburne was not a pervert from the supermarket. He was a tycoon from Hollywood with a telephone in his bathroom. Artists, he reminded her, did not make money, and, as far as he was concerned $100,000 – which, by the way, he had calculated on his automatic calculator and it came to £66,666.666 – was enough money to buy as many nails, or turps, or whatever she wanted, for as long as she wanted. If she turned her back on this once in a lifetime opportunity then it was she, not he, who was stupid.

Grace would have told him that she did not want to be in any magazine but she knew it would encourage her father to recount long anecdotes about the hardships that he had suffered when he was her age and she would have to hear how he had spent two years sitting in the dark because he could not afford to pay the electricity bills.

Miles had never thought of his daughter as a 'beauty'. She tended to look pale and odd and she had not inherited the fine dark features of her mother's side of the family. These things, in his view, were to her detriment. The local lads avoided her and this did not surprise him. They did not like those who sneered and yawned. Amos Beckinsale (a perfectly inoffensive young man) had once rung her up and asked her out. Miles had overheard Grace on the telephone refusing the invitation and telling him that she would rather pluck out her own eyes and donate them to a worthy cause.

Chapter Five

Clive had to admit that Dunster Castle was quite chic. And big. Not as big as San Simeon, but big. Comforted, as always, by unashamed display of wealth, his discerning eye studied the taste of yore. He wandered through massive stone archways and looked at baronial chimney pieces, eighteenth-century sideboards, and a portrait of Sir John represented as a Triton. He gazed dutifully at overweight cherubs and at an oak staircase with newels carved into bowls of polished fruit. The library, more Hearst than Hearst, was a profusion of colour and texture. Here, an unknown hand had coordinated Turkish carpets, chintz chair covers, gold tassels and lapis lazuli wallpaper.

He walked outside to take some photographs of the exterior. The castle was on a hill and Somerset spread with enigmatic tranquillity, to the sea.

As the sun set and darkness closed in, Clive strolled towards the gazebo thinking how elegant his Church's brogues looked. Then, realizing he was alone, he practised his runway step. Prancing down an imaginary catwalk, legs high-stepping, hands in pockets, he whirled the overcoat so that an unseen audience could appreciate the beauty of its lining. He was at final twirl for the photographers fighting at the front when both his illusion and the stillness were split by a distinct, ear-splitting crack.

An unworldy ingénue might have dismissed this detonation as the exhaust from a car in the village below. Clive, however, had lived in Los Angeles for fifteen years. He recognized the sound of gun-fire when he heard it. Logic shoved aside a drive-by shooting and replaced it with the more credible explanation that here, in the arboreal hush of Fuchsia Path and Vine Walk, a nameless wacko had destabilized.

Clive leapt away from the gravel path, where he was a clear target, and dived behind a shrub. Palpitating with horror he saw that the window of the gazebo was open and the barrel of a machine-gun was poking through it. The face of the sniper was hidden by shadow.

He had been led to believe that offensive weapons did not exist in England. 'They never had cowboys, you see,' Brent had told him. 'It's not in the culture. Even the cops don't carry.' If this was the case then there was the possibility that the folly housed an aggressor whose hostility was specific. An adversary with a secret resentment had followed him to Somerset in order to murder him.

Clive had many enemies. The marksman could be any one of a huge crowd. Hundreds of rows, squabbles, sulks and feuds flickered through his mind but fear confused his thoughts and it was hard to compile a short-list.

He remembered Jacques, the maître d' at Harry's Bar in Florence. Clive had thrown a Gucci loafer at his head when, arriving five minutes late for his booking, he discovered that his table had been given to Princess Grace. She, mouth full of salted almonds, had refused to be moved. All three, Clive, head-waiter and monarch, insisted in loud voices that the table belonged to them and the storm only passed when the princess whispered to Jacques that she was not being royal but she had gained a little weight and motion was impossible because her Marc Bohan dress (apricot) had suddenly split up the back. Later, in the kitchen, Clive and Jacques had laughed for hours about this. He had dabbed the waiter's forehead with iodine. He thought that Jacques had forgiven him.

There were other possibilities. Clive had once sued an old Mexican 'clinician' following the failure of an expensive and painful macro-hair graft that had promised the latest laser techniques but had delivered a number of scars. Terrorized by Clive's attorney, the woman had fled to Tijuana. Perhaps she, or the drug lords that constituted her family, had now tracked him down.

Then there was Fenton. Fenton had blamed Clive for forcing him to leave the Santa Barbara fire-brigade and the divorce, after three years, had been acrimonious.

Fenton had fallen into a slow decline when he embarked on a vigorous body-building regime without the benefits of professional advice. Fenton knew nothing about perform-ance nutrition or muscle gain. He did not even know how to use the complicated equipment in Good Boys' Trim 'n' Gym. Once he had worked out how to coordinate his body with an Ab-Cruncher, for example, or Tendon-Extender, he could not then disentangle himself from the system of pulleys, weights, chains and safety belts without bruising a knee or twisting a muscle.

Refusing to acknowledge his defects, he had combined the work-outs with a terrifying diet of 'Big Man' advanced protein powders scientifically formulated to provide bio-chemical blends of metabolic intermediates.

The result of this dangerous lifestyle was that Fenton's body became distorted beyond all recognition. Once trim and perfectly adequate for spraying water over burning mansions in Santa Barbara, it blew up in all the wrong places. Cursed with a neck like a melon and a torso embarrassed by irregular swellings, his morale had finally snapped when he looked in the mirror to find that he did not resemble Mr Universe so much as a decorative gourd.

On the day that Clive had said that he could no longer live with Fenton's disorders, Fenton had put Clive's Tank watch in the Aromatherapy Solo Steam-Capsule and turned the heat up to 'full sweat'. Anyone capable of destroying a Cartier classic would be capable of assassination.

Brent's disinformation (typical) and Clive's belief in the pacifism of the British meant that he had left all equipment designed for self-defence in the bottom of suitcase number six – not that Mace or a personal alarm would have protected him. A bullet-proof vest was what was required, the only garment that he had never purchased.

Comas sometimes arrive to comfort those whose bodies have been traumatized by nervous exhaustion and long-term inebriation. Paranoia had pressed Margaret Ruthven forward and delusion had destroyed her perspective. Over-powered by the drama, the fright, the tranquillizers, the life, her body slid down the wall of the gazebo and spread all over the floor.

Clive's faculties were undermined by shock but they were not paralysed. Sensing that there had been some kind of cease-fire, he decided to sneak up and, if possible, ascertain the identity of the assailant. He jumped out of the bush, darted to a clump of trees, and crept around the back.

Silence.

He peered through the window.

Silence.

Then he saw the machine-gun lying on the floor and, beside it, a pile of old clothes that seemed to have been tipped out of a laundry bag. Easing himself through the decaying door he moved closer and, as his eyes squinted in the murk, he saw that these monstrous garments were joined by beige protuberances of human flesh. The features of the face had coagulated under an orange sprig of hair; dimpled knees lay amidst limbs that defied description and, from a foam-flecked maw, came a harsh wheeze.

He gazed down on the supine shambles and realized that he was out of danger, but, within seconds, a horrifying prospect loomed up. He realized, with a tremor of alarm, that he was going to have to touch this person. She was obviously in the throes of an overdose of some kind. Choking breath, fluttering eyelids, blue lips – he had seen the signs at parties in Malibu. She might die.

He crouched down and slapped the ravaged face quite hard. The cheeks rippled and subsided.

Loosening his cuff and rolling it up, like a vet, he gingerly reached into the pocket of the Bermuda shorts. A sensation of sandpaper met his unwilling fingertips, then the cold metal of a hip-flask. He tried the other side and produced a crumpled envelope on which the name Mrs Roger Ruthven was accompanied by Fairview Castle Hotel, Minehead.

He heaved the massy body into a vertical position.

Life had left the legs. They scattered here and there and every time Mrs Roger Ruthven fell over, so too did Clive. The tussling was more intimate than a wrestling match and just as ugly. Finally Clive flexed the muscles toned by many years spent on a rowing machine and gripped her 'waist'. Then, grabbing the MP5, he hauled her out of the gazebo.

It was now nearly dark. The grounds were closed and its attendants had gone home. Clive's only options were either to find a hospital where his unwelcome burden could be prevented from choking on her own vomit, or to take her to Fairview Castle where there might be individuals accustomed to her peculiarities.

He poured her into the passenger seat. Her head flopped forward as if dead. She was still breathing, that much he could tell from the heaving of the bosom and the gusts of beer blowing from her mouth. Quashing a strange and immoral desire to open the door and let her fall on to the tarmac, he headed for the road to Minehead which, according to one signpost, was two miles away.

Two miles can seem like twenty when the countryside is unknown and unlit, there are no freeways, everyone drives on the wrong side of the road and one can whirl round and round a roundabout for at least fifteen minutes before working out how to leave it.

He had pulled up at a crossroad and was hoping that he was going in the right direction when a headlight heralded the arrival of a motor bike. The machine screamed to a halt and waited beside him, its right-hand indicator flashing. The rider stared at the driver's window, waiting for intimation of direction. Confused, Clive was about to wind down his window in order to confirm his position when the motorcyclist pre-empted him by tapping aggressively on the glass. Unnerved, Clive let the window down.

A leather glove flipped up a vizor. Two brown eyes stared at him.

'Oy,' said the stranger. 'Where are you going with my mother?'

'This is your *mother*?' Clive sputtered.

The relationship between the snoring heap and procreation was a creepy concept.

'Yes,' said the motorcyclist.

'She is drunk and she fired a machine-gun at me. If we were in the States I would be suing for fourteen million dollars and I would be winning.'

'Oh? Well, we haven't got fourteen million dollars. Where were you thinking of taking her?'

The young man voiced this casually, as if there were infinite options – an expedition to see the Goyas in the Prado, perhaps, or a picnic in the Catskills; a walk on the beach at Denis Island, or a ceramics fair in Zamora.

'We're not on a date,' Clive snapped, 'this woman needs medical attention.'

'Nah,' said the stranger confidently. 'She doesn't need a doctor. She's always like that. Here. Follow me and we'll get her home.'

He screamed around to the front of the car, waving a leather glove as he did so.

The gloomy motorcade climbed the dark tor which rose above Minehead harbour. A jagged black line of turrets and towers sprang into the skyline like black fangs. 'Jesus,' thought Clive. 'I'm in the Orson Welles version of *Macbeth*.'

'You take the arms,' said Rupert. 'I'll get the legs.'

Margaret Ruthven hung between them like a hammock.

'She was probably running from the bailiffs,' Rupert tried to explain.

'Baliffs?'

'You know – they come to take the furniture away.'

Clive did not know whether he was speaking of removal men or repo men and he did not wish to.

'They tried to take the Austin last week but it's got a badger living in it and they're protected.'

Clive wished that he was protected.

There was a short skirmish in the hall. Rupert failed to provide adequate directions so Clive pulled one way and Rupert pulled another while his mother's body stretched out like a corpse on a rack.

They threw her on the bed.

'She'll wake up,' said Rupert. 'She always does.'

He led Clive into the kitchen and swept a pile of tin cans off a plastic chair so that he could sit down. Clive lowered himself, with grace, but little enthusiasm, and shook his head to Rupert's offer of a cigarette plucked from a row that lay drying on a radiator.

'Jesus,' said Clive. 'What *is* this place?'

'Used to be a hotel.'

Rupert threw a match at an antique gas ring and jumped back to avoid the flame that leapt out at his face.

'Always does that,' he said.

Clive yearned to be in his own kitchen, surrounded by Alessi and Zanussi and placing Tanzania Peaberry coffee beans into his Grande Café combined Expresso-Capuccino machine. The English did not know how to make a beverage. They kept offering him something called Nescafé which he had learned to refuse once he had realized that it tasted like mud-slides.

England was cute, it was quaint, it was old, but he was homesick. He missed modern lines, convenience, neon, fluff and fold, feckless TV evangelists and El Pollo Loco. He longed for his microwave oven with six power settings, two programmable memories and a child lock. He longed for his ice-box, always filled with buttermilk squash soup, aragula and bottles of Bombay Sapphire gin, chilled and ready to form the driest martinis on the West Coast. Fenton had always wanted a twist, Clive an olive. Perhaps that had been the true reason for the failure of the relationship.

A shoal of silver fish writhed on the table in front of him.

A wave of misery suddenly surged through him and, for a moment, a pulse brought scenes of old sadness.

There had been a 'bad patch' before the mission to perfect and beautify had focused his energy and absolved his spirit. Clive's father had never understood. His mother had actually wondered where she had gone wrong. So he had thrown them away, all their concepts and precepts, beliefs and adages; their irrelevant mottoes. But there had been unhealed wounds and he had found himself dressed up with nowhere to go. A depressing liberation, tainted by loss, had culminated in a panic attack in the Beverly Centre. The multi-tiered complex, once a haven for his spirit, had turned on him with vicious force.

Limitless retail options had always been a source of joy for Clive but on that day he had been suddenly and inexplicably assailed by indecision. Dizzy, he had swirled in the middle of a vortex of Levi pants, baseball hats and Nike cross-trainers. Faint, suddenly starving, he had staggered, pale and mad, around the Food Court, which became a hell of multi-national menus, gourmet salads, side orders and house specialities all with seven sizes of soft drink to go. Tempura. Tostada. Tamale. Starving but paralysed, fainting and mute, he had been faced with all the food in the world and he could not eat it because he could not make a decision – he who had grown up relishing hand-rolled pretzels in forty different flavours, who had never been undermined by a Mexico City-style taco basket and knew, from the age of seventeen, that his favourite power smoothie was a Ginseng-Fling.

He had stood at the edge of his own darkness, having been pushed there by boysenberry muffins, turkey platters and cinnamon rolls. Crazed with confusion, he had rebounded from Ham Explosions to California Krispy Stix. He had attempted to revive himself in the Jolt Connection but the ability to select was subsumed by inner turmoil. To make the wrong decision was to die and, as he experienced the true nullity of his own mortality, the tiny Puerto Rican stared, frightened, as Clive, slow and sweating, had ordered every single item on the menu – every java and mocha known to man. He had the Caffe Latte, the Caffe Mocha, the Caffe Americano, the Double Cappuccino, the Cap Royale, the Iced Cap Decaf, the Macchiato, the Espresso Chocolate and Raspberry Coffee Mocha, the Espresso Coco Almond, the Cranberry Truffle Mocha, the Tropicana (with whipped cream and Tidy-Tip Lo-Fat Choco-Bitz), the Frappuccino (with amaretto syrup), the Granita with frozen latte and mango ice-cream, and, finally, the Oregon Chai.

A procession of dark teenagers had brought the loaded trays to his table and had stood in a circle of awe as Clive gulped down the contents of hundreds of polystyrene cups. Then, speeding, high and disorientated, he had flung himself into Chilli Dogg Dog screaming that he wanted an enema flavoured pizza. A supervisor with a badge that said, 'Hullo My Name is Buttonwillow McKitrick and I Am At Your Service' assumed that this pale and perspiring customer was on PCP and, having been trained in a special programme at the Chilli Dogg Dog Institute in Des Moines, he had threatened to call the police if Clive did not remove himself.

Rupert offered him a cup of Nescafé.

'No thank you,' said Clive, struggling to bring himself back into a present that was as terrible as that particular episode of his past. 'I'll have tea please.'

'Right ho.'

They drank tea.

Clive drank his in a glass without milk and with a trace of honey found after a twenty-minute search with a torch.

Rupert drank his with six lumps of sugar dropped into a mug grasped by long oil-stained fingers. He had removed his leather jacket and was wearing a white T-shirt and motorcycle boots. He was small, thin and dark. His hair was too long, but he was quite cute if you had enjoyed *Karate Kid III*. He was also, Clive now realized, very young. Clive tried not to remember what it was like to be very young. He had gone through an embarrassing Cocteau phase. There had been a jock at Pepperdine. He shuddered. The jock had smelled of sex while he, Clive, had smelled of Joy by Jean Patou. It had never won him any friends, but it had seemed appropriate to the Cocteau obsession, that and the rings. Campus camp. Token eccentric. He shuddered again. Everyone else had been into Blue Oyster Cult.

He looked again at the calm features of youth. The boy's air of acceptance melded grotesquely with his insupportable circumstances and made Clive feel curiously desperate on his behalf. It was an unpleasant sensation. Clive always tried to avoid empathy. It hailed psychosomatic conditions and he had only recently managed to rid himself of psoriasis.

'That woman needs help,' he said sternly. 'Or she'll die. You'll have to get her into detox.'

Rupert had no idea what he was talking about.

'She is an alcoholic,' Clive continued. 'It's a disease. It will kill her.'

'A disease? What disease? She's always been like that and she's not dead yet. It's her personality. You can't do anything about people's personalities.'

'She can't always have been like that.'

'Well, she got worse when the dog died.'

'What about your father?'

'She didn't really mind about that.'

'About what?'

'When *he* died.'

Rupert tried to remember a time when his mother had not been appalling but he could not. She had been dangerous and mad since time began but chaos had somehow crystallized the afternoon that she found Ian lying in a flower-bed.

He had watched, paralysed, as she attempted mouth to mouth resuscitation. Dog and woman, blood and skin, fur and hair, all as one; breathing firmly into the black nostrils, breathing and repeating, breathing and repeating, waiting for the chest to rise, breathing and repeating, and then thumping. The chest did not rise. The body was broken, this was plain to see.

He had tried to comfort her. The dog was old, he said. He had probably fallen from the window and died of shock before he hit the ground. But she had flung herself on top of Ian's body. It was her fault, she had shrieked. She should never have left him.

Rupert still sometimes wondered why Ian had received the kiss of life and his father had not.

Brown eyes stared at Clive. There was to be no further discussion. Only the brave or the qualified would choose to trespass in this inner territory, guarded as it was by defences that had taken so many years to build that the constructor had forgotten what it was they were protecting.

Clive, like so many others before him, wondered if the hideous crone had killed her husband. He camouflaged his discomfiture by tutting impatiently.

'You all need professional help. You're obviously dys-functional. It could take years.'

He scribbled a number down on a piece of paper.

'Ring this number first thing tomorrow. Ask for Dr Dave. He's the director and an old friend of mine. He'll help you.'

The American, odd though he was, and very highly scented, commanded Rupert's attention. Rupert knew that most Americans were imbued with worldly knowledge because they were employed by the CIA. The stranger obviously worked for an intelligence agency. He had been shot at, and he had hauled Rupert's mother's body around in the dark without staining his dazzling white button-down shirt or mussing his immaculate hair. And, even more impressively, he had not been weakened by the terror common to those who were unlucky enough to encounter Margaret Ruthven.

He obediently wrote down the telephone number. The American's opinions seemed bizarre, but Rupert had, for some time, wondered if he would be forced to turn around and face his future. Now a stranger had arrived and calmly presented a theory from which there was no escape.

The next morning he rang Serenity Hall. 'Dr Dave' Loevenhart told him that his mother sounded 'chronic'. Treatment would cost some £10,000 and, he added, if Mrs Ruthven did not receive 'help', she would die a long drawn-out and painful death.

'How painful?' Rupert inquired.

'Very painful indeed,' said Dr Dave. 'In the worst cases alcoholism can grossly distort the liver's architecture causing splenic sequestration which leads to abnormal bleeding and varicose veins in the stomach. In the event of untreated cirrhosis, profound abnormalities can occur in the brain and, even if bacterial peritonitis does not occur, there can be kidney failure, not to mention swelling of the brain and death. Then, of course, circulatory disorders can bring thrombosis and gangrene which means that your mother might lose her limbs.'

'Anything else?' said Rupert.

'Isn't that enough?' said Dr Dave.

Enlightenment had been forced on Rupert but it bought no comfort. He was now faced with an exhausting problem which he had no hope of solving. There was no prospect of raising £10,000.

There was no money. There had never been any money. That was why when *they* told him that he should go to university he had not bothered to take the exams. There was no money. There was only a mad woman and a dead dog and the possibility of dismembering Loopy de Luxe with a secret slashing technique.

Now £10,000 had to be found or his mother would die and if she died it would be his fault. He would have to live with her premature demise for the rest of his days. The guilt would be as excruciating as if he had killed her himself. The money had to be found. He was her only hope. Her life had become his moral responsibility and this liability pressed down on him. It consumed his thoughts and woke him at dawn when isolation always chills the forsaken.

Chapter 6

Porlock caravan park was a model of cleanliness and order. The grass between the mobile homes was a verdant blanket of short, moist tufts. No bins spewed forth their rubbish and every window was a polished pane of sheer translucence. This high standard of hygiene was partly due to the Rural Clean-Up Programme organized by Miles Falconbridge, but it was also because, out of season, the park was empty. Only number ten was inhabited. A four-berth trailer, it had a coveted view over the cliffs to the beach below.

Neil, sociopath and gang-leader, was scrubbing the table in the kitchenette. Clouds of Vim scudded around him as he purged the formica surfaces. No gentle cream cleansers for Neil – he went for Clorox granules that scratched and abrased the stinking sediment. Neil loved Vim nearly as much as he hated dirt. He had been known to stare at the motes dancing in a sunbeam in a trance of sullen loathing. He had been known to smash a window to stop a fly buzzing. Flies deposited bacteria. They were loathsome carriers of ordure born to spread pollution and disease. Neil, like most people, could not actually see bacteria but he knew it was there, procreating in corners, a pathogenic enemy that had to be resisted with painstaking effort. The microns drove him mad. The idea that motile organisms could decompose and defile in the sanctity of invisibility meant that they were a force of insurmountable strength. Blotch and fleck were the mocking symbols of a microscopic legion over which he had no control.

Only he understood the strength of the oldest form of life. He knew that it was possessed of the equipment to swim and learn and mate. There were plasmids that could resist any variety of antibiotic and others that could travel through food, through drink and in the case of diptheria, through the simple exhalations of conversation. (Knowing this, Neil had worn a surgeon's mask until Len down at the Queen's Legs refused to allow him to wear it in the bar. Neil would have preferred not to breath in the air at the Queen's Legs which, as far as he was concerned, was as polluted with contaminants as the air around the real Queen's legs but he needed to go to this particular pub, since it was known to be favoured by London's most influential fences.) The vector could be observed but the disease could not. It lurked in air, in fluid, on every surface, waiting to blind and burn and kill. Vigilance, eternal and diligent, had to be maintained at all hours and at all costs. Only sterility brought equilibrium or what, in Neil's case, passed for equilibrium.

Neil had spent the first years of his life living in a launderette in Clapton and he knew he would never be as happy again. A premature arrival, he had actually been born in the Kwikky-Servicerama Washomat as his mother, working late, had not managed to hail a cab in time. Warmth and purity were the first sensations of his earliest minutes. Primal bliss was the whir of the dryer, the smell of Tide and the sound of public pants slushing against port holes.

He and the customers would sit in harmony on the benches, hypnotized by the circulation behind the windows and united by transcendental calm. Sometimes there was a satisfying crisis. An overloaded machine would belch out foam and water and there would be a flood, or a door would break and kilos of non-fast coloureds would be imprisoned until a pair of brown overalls arrived with a toolbox. Standpipes, drain hoses and inlet valves would then be spread all over the floor and miraculously put back together again.

He was thin, little Neil, so old women gave him peppermints. He was tall so the other kids did as they were told – particularly after he broke the nose of one who did not. There had been blood everywhere and the mother had threatened to go to the police. Her Mary's face would never be the same again, she had screamed, as nostrils overflowed onto the honey-coloured linoleum and red patches smudged into the shoes of the toddlers who came and went with the weekly wash.

Most people had something to say, some advice to impart, and Neil, at six, assumed that they knew the truth. A hippy told him about drugs, an accountant told him the facts of life, but Ray was his friend. Ray, a skinhead, came in every Monday morning with a small load, a can of lager and an illustrated biography of Dr Josef Goebbels. This he read aloud, starting with Rheydt, passing through marriage to Magda and ending with the banning of Mendelssohn.

'Who's that fat one in shorts?' the child would say as they flicked through Ray's book and studied photographs of SS officials standing in various heroic poses.

'That's Göring. He's wearing lederhosen.'

'What did he do?'

'Ur. He helped Hitler.'

'Why?'

'Because he wanted to.'

'Why?'

'He just did. 'Ere look. That's the Luftwaffe.'

Deeply impressed, Neil asked his mother if he could join the Clapton branch of the Nazi party. She told him that he was too fucking young but he could be a fucking cub if he liked. Neil did not like. He wanted a leather coat.

Then Ray disappeared. He had in fact been arrested after a Millwall match, but nobody told Neil this. Every Monday he had expected to hear the squeak of crêpe sole on lino, see the familiar gingham laundry bag containing Union Jack Y-fronts. The months limped by until it became clear that he had been disowned for no reason. At first he had not been able to believe it and then, as hope died, optimism was replaced by prejudice and an icy detachment had settled.

The decades had not dissolved the savagery created by Ray's rejection. Neil had loathed Ray when he was six and he loathed Ray now. His hatred was as resilient as a growth.

The caravan park was convenient but the cash that they had accumulated by stealing BMWs in Balham was beginning to run out and Neil knew he must find a way to make some money.

Porlock was small, very small. Everybody knew everybody and this posed many risks to the law-breaker. They needed a 'job' where their identities would be concealed and their getaway assured.

Neil had long craved the chance to commit a respectable crime, something that awarded prestige, a bank job, say, or a jewellery heist. He needed a *succès d'estime* and the empty ache of this longing was deepened by his low rank. As a career criminal he knew that he was a failure. Languishing at the bottom of the heap, he was seen as a no-hope pilferer, just above nonce and well below safe-blower.

The problem was that he did not have the connections. The recidivists of his milieu were the scum of the earth – pick-pockets, shop-lifters, bag-snatchers, and joy-riders. They were doomed to a life of petty larceny because they were content with small-time transgressions. Neil knew that he had talent but he had no entré into the genuine underworld. He did not drink with public enemies or those who were planning the ambitious offences. He sometimes thought that life would be easier if he got himself sent down. One could meet clever men in prison. He was bound to be noticed.

His brother had been sent to prison for GBH. He would have made useful friends, but who knew where his brother was now? He had walked out of the Scrubs in 1978 and disappeared into thin air. His mother had said, 'Good riddance, fucking pig,' but Neil saw it as a lost opportunity and a blow to his career prospects.

The vexation spawned by lack of professional success was sometimes assuaged by the presence of Neville and Shorty who showed unquestioning reverence for any scam Neil chose to initiate. But the effects of their acclaim were ephemeral and could not stifle Neil's lust for posterity. Shorty and Neville did not realize that their 'successes' were tiny and unimportant. Stealing stereo equipment did not earn one a place in the annals of criminology where names such as Machine-Gun Kelly and Joe Bananas were recorded. Neil had a sense of posthumous tradition. He wanted to be studied like Baby Face Nelson and respected like Jacques Mesrine. He wanted to take his place amongst 'the greats' but he never seemed to get the breaks.

Now, though, an idea was forming in his mind, an idea so brilliant that even he was surprised at the breadth of his genius.

Shorty lay on a bottom bunk. He would have preferred a berth at the top where there was more air and it was easier to avoid Neil but the process of ascending to this summit was hindered by the obstructive combination of forty unfiltered Lucky Strikes a day and a physique that, by no stretch of the imagination, was designed for climbing. He knew he would not be able to transport ladder, legs, cardio-vascular system, wank mags, beer, fags, lighter and box of Terry's All Gold to this heady summit. Plus there was a possibility, particularly after the beer, that he might never get back down again.

So he relaxed on the bottom, *Hustler* magazine open in front of him. A grotesque leer exposed sharp yellow teeth and tiny eyes darted with joy underneath the low protection of their forehead.

'Chroist,' he said, as filthy fingers the size of cocktail sausages flicked to a blonde woman in a Calvin Klein thong crawling on all fours across a farmyard. 'I feel a poem coming on.'

'Shut it, Shorty,' Neville snapped, not because he

objected to Shorty's literary aspirations but because he objected to an independence of spirit that imbued him with the courage to lie on the bed ogling at women rather than submit to the rigours of Neil's domestic regime.

Neville could not understand why someone as short as Shorty did not do as he was told. He was like an annoying child who always got away with everything while others slavishly did their duty and received no credit for so doing. Much of Neville's life was spent trying to bully Shorty into servility while most of Shorty's life was spent blissfully unaware of this.

Shorty was blessed with the greatest gift that can be bestowed upon any man. He had limitless self-confidence.

He thought that he was handsome, a grotesque delusion created by the fact that women tended to make a fuss of him. Shorty knew that this was because he possessed animal magnetism. He was proud proof that height held no sway when it came to alluring the opposite sex and this faith was not undermined by Neville's regular assertion that women only spoke to him because they felt sorry for him.

'You're tragic, Shorty,' he would say. 'You know that? Tragic. They went to mother ya, they don't want to shag ya.'

Neville was wrong because Neville, unlike Shorty, did not understand women, and they did not understand or particularly like Neville. Some sensed, correctly, that he was inextricably entwined with Neil, whose glowering presence, Satanic tattoos and staring eyes were enough to frighten anyone away. It was Shorty, not Neville, who was surrounded by giggling waitresses and thrusting secretaries. It was Shorty, not Neville, who appreciated the efficacy of conversing with every woman as if she was a dream come true which, at that moment, she *was*, for Shorty's sexual enthusiasm was unrestricted. Every female who came into his vicinity enjoyed a fleeting second as a goddess because Shorty knew how to worship.

Shorty did not discriminate. There were few aesthetic strictures (bar a preference for spandex leggings) and certainly no 'type'. Long, old, emaciated, Danish, he did not care. He would prostrate himelf before one and all.

This adventurous attitude was not reflected in his conversational skills, which were confined to simple flattery. As the night progressed he would inevitably tell his chosen target that he was a poet and that his plan was to write a poem about her. Then, of course, there would be simpering, smirking and hoping as the Muse hurled herself to the bar and bought him another drink.

'I have just met the mother of my children,' he would say to Neville and Neil and anybody else who was paying attention. The mother of his children – exuberant breasts jiggling at some distance above Shorty's head – would then experience his version of foreplay which was to allow her to divulge her life story while he sat in her lap. After the brief shuddering frenzy of the night she would write him letters outlining the rest of her life story, say that she missed him and ask if there were any other women in his life. Shorty, meanwhile, would stick the love notes on the wall with Sellotape, compose little couplets, shake his head and say, 'all this fuss over a shag in the back of 'er car'.

Sometimes he would point with comic exaggeration at his scalp, roll his eyes, and say, in his piccolo squeak, 'blondes have more fun'.

Shorty's 'romances' confirmed that some women still think that if there is honour and beauty in art it follows that there must be honour and beauty in the soul of the artist. Shorty had assumed the role of 'poet' because numerous conversations in pubs had alerted him to the truth that the opposite sex likes to stand on a pedestal, and this predilection decreed that those who pretended to creative effort were granted a licence to form limitless liaisons. These fortunate circumstances were made all the more pleasurable because Shorty was not hampered by the misery that tends to arrive with genuine aptitude.

A girl who was reading English at Newcastle University once asked him if he agreed with J. Ortega Y Gosset's contention that poetry was 'adolescence fermented and thus preserved'. She had heard Shorty boast about his 'work' in the Frog and Firkin and hoped to engage him in mutually stimulating discourse. She was in her second year. She knew all about Paul Verlaine, she could quote Hart Crane, and often did so, but she failed to understand that Shorty was not the victim of a romantic compulsion to express his innermost feelings. He had developed the ability to burst into tears, at will, at any given moment, but his image of poetic sensitivity was only an image. He had erected it solely to avail himself of sexual opportunity.

That evening, without warning, he had suddenly been asked to describe the craft that sustained the illusion. He had nearly been exposed. He had sworn, from that day on, to avoid all birds wearing glasses. Nothing worse than a clever tart, he told himself.

The girl from Newcastle had confirmed the rectitude of this opinion when she became pregnant. Shorty had been traumatized both by the possibility that he would have to pay for the abortion and by Neville's assertion that if the operation was unsuccessful and a part of the foetus' body was left behind, that part grew and grew until it became a monstrous mutant clone and the woman was forced to give birth to it.

'Yeah Shorty,' he had sneered, 'if the eye gets left behind you'll have to wheel round this 'uge eyeball in a pram. Hah! And everyone'll say, "Ooh don't it look like its dad . . .'"

Shorty had retorted that if this was the case he hoped for the child's sake that the dick was left behind, but he was unnerved, and, dwelling upon this horror, had become more and more morose.

Neil usually paid little attention to the crowds that shaped Shorty's sex life, but he relied on his equanimity, so he had intervened with the truth. 'Don't be daft Shorty – Neville's 'avin' ya.'

Neil, unlike Neville, was not jealous of Shorty. He did not wish to attract women. The idea of their juices and lubrication stimulated no excitement. He did not like their smell – there was a funky sweetness about them that made the bile rise in his throat. One could never be sure of their standards of personal hygiene. Anything could be spreading in those viscous crannies.

The others saw nothing unusual in Neil's celibacy. They assumed that his standards were high. Any woman in whom Neil showed the favour of his interest would have to be a rare construction. He was saving himself. They felt sure that he would end up marrying a Royal.

Neville, Mr Sheen in one hand, half-heartedly flicked a duster over the portable television set that he had stolen from his aunt. He did not care if there was scum or vermin, he only cared for Neil's esteem and if spraying Mr Sheen in the air was a method of obtaining it, then so be it.

Neil emerged from the shower cabinet where he had

been scrubbing his nails with Ajax and his skin with Dettol. He sprayed a cloud of insecticide around his head and inhaled the lemon aroma, enjoying the fleeting peace of one who has temporarily allayed contamination from opportunistic parasites. He was wearing a pair of newly starched jeans plucked fresh from a dry-cleaning wrapper.

'Nev,' he said, pushing a Lint Pick-Up adhesive roller up and down the lapels of his tattered dinner jacket. 'Take the plates off the bikes. We're gonna pull a job.'

'What kinda job?' said Shorty from amidst a fog of Lucky Strike smoke.

'Christ, do you have to smoke them things?' said Neil. 'Stinks the place out.'

'What kind of job?' said Neville, who dreaded these moments.

'You'll see,' said Neil.

'Well I hope it's not old ladies. I draw a line at old ladies,' said Shorty.

'What d'ya call that bint you were slobberin' over last night then?' inquired Neville.

'Charlize? She weren't old.'

'Why was her skin so big then?'

'She were twenty-six. I might marry 'er.'

'Yeah? Well. Enjoy her while you can. She's on 'er last legs. She was deaf too.'

'No she weren't, she just weren't listenin' to ya.'

'Anyway, the only reason you draw a line at old ladies is cos ya scared,' sneered Neville, who hoped that Neil's plan did involve old ladies as, in his view, old ladies represented the only risk-free criminal activity.

'Fuck off, Neville.'

'It's not old ladies,' said Neil.

'Post office?'

'No.'

'Garridge?'

'Nah. Trust me. This is foolproof.'

'I hope it's more foolproof than them credit cards Neville nicked,' said Shorty.

Neville's theft of credit cards from a handbag hanging in a pub in Clapham had resulted in their being forced to leave their Balham squat via the back window.

'We're on the lam cos of you,' Shorty accused.

'Drop it, Shorty,' Neil ordered. 'We would have had to leave anyway. The pigs were asking questions about the cars.'

'Anyway, Shorty,' said Neville, quickly cashing in on Neil's support. 'What's it to you? You ain't even got a bike.'

This shot pierced the only chink in the armour of Shorty's self-esteem. His legs were not long enough to reach the pedals and his arms were too small to grip the break or clutch. He was forced to ride pillion on Neil's 250 and this position brought an unwelcome dependency. It did not stop him telling girls in pubs that the Kawasaki was his, but the truth still rankled.

'Well, Neville,' said Shorty with the quick-fire rebarb borne of the familiar dialogue of an old fight. 'I might not have a bike but you ain't gotta woman, ya Queer!'

Neville smashed the Mr Sheen on the table, jaw stiff with hate, and glared down at Shorty, his slanted eyes glinting.

Neville carried a knife and Neil did not wish to see blood on the floor that he had just spent two hours scrubbing with New Improved Mr Muscle.

'Fuck off you two,' he commanded. 'Get out. I gotta think.'

The offenders slouched off down a trail to where the motor bikes were hidden in the middle of a wood. Neville unscrewed the plates.

'Wonder what Nil's got up his sleeve,' said Shorty.

'Ah should I know?'

'Thought 'e told you everything?'

Neil told Neville nothing. Neville did not even know his surname, but Neville did not want Shorty to know this.

''E'll tell me later I 'spect.'

'Praps it's a kidnapping,' said Shorty hopefully. Abduction held a certain frisson. ''E's always saying 'e wants to pull something big, you know, like the train robbery, or Brinks Snatch.'

'Mat,' said Neville. 'Brinks Mat ya thick git. Anyway. Wouldn't be a kidnappin'.'

'Why not? 'S a good idea. We could 'ide 'er 'ere in a mask and everythin', all tied up.'

''Er, Shorty. Would be an 'er wouldn't it!'

'We could 'ave our wicked way with 'er,' said Shorty, growing warm with the thought.

'Yeah Shorty. That would last all of three seconds in your case. What would we do with 'er for the rest of the time? Feed 'er choclits?'

Neville, who watched a lot of television commercials, associated women with chocolate. He assumed that it was the mainstay of their diet.

'Feed 'er my dick more like,' said Shorty.

'I'm sure she'll be beside 'erself when she sees that shrivelled nonentity coming at her. "Nah thanks," she'll say, "I've just put one out."'

'Very funny,' said Shorty, with the unruffled placidity of one who has never heard any complaints. This did not mean, of course, that his sexual technique was beyond criticism, but merely that he had never received reviews. Most of the women with whom he consorted were humanitarian and they saw that he had enough problems as it was – to cast aspersion on his methods would have been sadistic. Just as one did not tease babies or kick dogs, one did not taunt the genetically disadvantaged. This, anyway, was the rationale of the sober. The rest, drunk and desperate, did not notice, or were relieved when the night of passion ended in the twinkling of an eye.

'I haven't noticed anyone breaking their diet to get a mouthful of yours,' said Shorty.

'Yah!' Neville spat on the ground. 'They're afraid of getting split in half.'

'Not wot I heard . . .'

And so the afternoon passed with Neville and Shorty locked, as ever, in a dispute that could never end because both contestants were determined to have the last word.

Chapter 7

The Big Boss and Jean had taken the day off work to visit a person who, according to the Big Boss, was called Shul, as in 'Shul be cutting up something rotten'. Jean's sister had doubtless been granted an orthodox Christian name at some point in her life but this was of no influence on the Boss.

Rupert was in charge of the arcade for the day. It was not the first time he had been promoted to this position of responsibility. Shul was quite demanding and the Big Boss regularly drove Jean over to Crowcombe in the van.

The instructions were always the same. 'If there's any trouble at all, call the police. Watch the money and don't let them little 'uns do Zeke's without an adult. You won't be busy. Forecast's good. Better go. Shul be on the warpath.'

The little 'uns, in the Big Boss's view, were more trouble than the big 'uns. They were excellent customers in that they could persuade people seven times their size to spend money, but they did not understand the rules of the games and would climb over moving parts with dangerous abandon. Zeke's Shack was particularly attractive to them. Accustomed to spending long hours on climbing frames, the little 'uns would clamber over the models as if they had been designed for this recreation. Then they would crawl into boxes, peer behind plaster of Paris hummocks and wonder why they were suddenly smacked in the eye by an electronically activated effigy wearing a straw hat and dungarees.

The Big Boss had been right. The sun was out and the trickle of tourists who had taken advantage of off-season rates were striding across two hundred and sixty-seven square miles of moorland.

Rupert took advantage of the peace to read about Serenity Hall. Dr Dave or, more accurately, Dr Dave's secretary, Iris, had sent him an eighty-four-page colour brochure whose cover displayed a magnificent Palladian mansion.

The first ten pages were devoted to describing Serenity Hall's architectural heritage, which 'reflected the genius of Giacomo Leoni'. The south front was photographed with a lake in the foreground. Rusticated arches and statues of Neptune were lovingly detailed alongside the information that 'Detox units and therapy suites, set on a *piano nobile*, are distinguished by tall pedimented windows which recall the gravity of an Italian palazzo'.

The chapter concluded with a photograph of several monks holding chamois leathers and standing, on raked gravel, in front of a row of immaculate sports cars. A caption underneath this explained, 'Serenity Hall is lucky to share its thousand acres of magnificent parkland with the Order of St Rita, a community of Dominican brothers who have inhabited the estate since their chapel and cloisters were built in 1506. The Order of St Rita is known as being the owner of the largest collection of Aston Martins in the world – their most recent acquisition, the classic 1961 DB4GT Zagato, was purchased in 1991.'

A chapter entitled 'Recovery' opened with a portrait of a handsome, tanned man wearing a white coat and sitting behind an antique desk on which there were numerous gold-framed diplomas. This, apparently, was Dr Dave himself – 'an international figure' who had 'turned Serenity Hall into a globally acclaimed rehabilitation centre'. A Fellow of the Orange County Psychological Society and a consultant to the Cybernetics Foundation, he regularly received requests to speak at seminars all over the world but his aim was to 'focus on the principles of personal recovery and ensure that all his patients received individual attention as they prepared to re-enter the world'.

Rupert could not imagine a world that would wish his mother to re-enter it.

The eighty-four-page prospectus spoke much of rotundas and frescoes and transformational counselling but it did not explain how Rupert was supposed to raise ten thousand pounds to pay for what was (inaccurately) described as 'affordable' treatment, nor did it outline how Dr Dave and his team of internationally acclaimed psychologists would go about suppressing an inebriate armed with an automatic weapon.

Margaret Ruthven would not willingly surrender her person to a group of men in white coats, no matter how expert they were in holistic healing technologies. She hated and distrusted strangers on principle and, now she had the gun, would shoot at any she saw. If the doctors got as far as the front door without injury they would then have to persuade her to leave the castle which would be much the same as asking a Mediterranean turtle to leave its shell.

Fairview Castle was her domain and she moved slowly within it, bound to a rhythm which, though unconventional, was of her own composition and provided her with a self-serving omnipotence which she would not relinquish without a battle.

Rupert was still reading about the 'extraordinary range of facilities offered by Serenity Hall', when two motor bikes roared in to the arcade cutting a swathe through a group of Japanese tourists who scattered to avoid them.

The three bikers removed their crash-helmets and swaggered though a haze of carbon-monoxide.

Rupert dropped the pamphlet and gaped as the gang walked towards him. Boots clumped, heavy and slow. Leather gloves summoned.

They had returned on a Revenge Mission.

Mad with blood-lust, they had come to find the Big Boss and exert grisly retribution for the dishonours they had incurred at his hand. The Big Boss would return from Crowcombe to find his arcade littered with twisted torsos, mashed knee caps and decapitated Japanese tourists.

Rupert's eyes flickered toward the telephone. He did not have time to ring 999.

Neil's mouth pressed against the window. A breeze of Dettol whispered from fleshy lips.

'Honda a hundred?'

'Yeah?'

'Fancy a game?'

Those who have faced a life-threatening situation and walked away from it often describe how, in that instant, all their priorities change, how each minute of the present becomes distinct and how they appreciate new and subtle tones of everyday existence. Rupert had walked away from death for the second time in one day. A strange and unfamiliar sense of well-being suffused his perception and this heady spin was further enhanced by the offer of companionship from a person who had saved his life by the simple favour of not taking it.

Neil was unfathomable but his cold eyes seemed to offer indifference and, in indifference, there was freedom because those who do not care can do as they please. Quickened by danger, Rupert could not pull back. The urge to be negligent subsumed him.

'I oughta watch the money,' he said.

'Shorty'll watch it for ya.'

Rupert leaned over the shelf of the kiosk and saw a yellow face staring up from the darkness below. Dominated by the shameless eyes of a liar, the expression was contorted into a hideous smirk. This was supposed to convey saintliness but it advertised venality with as much clarity as if it had been wearing the horns of the Judas goat.

'I don't think that's a good idea,' said Rupert.

'Oh go on.'

There was £250 in the cash-box. The yellow midget would steal it. In fact, that was obviously the intention. The gang planned to divert his attention in order to allow this distorted accomplice to take the Big Boss's money.

Rupert had played arcade games for seven formative years. He had grown up in Lucky Bob's. Opportunistic goblins appeared in every skirmish and here, easily recognizable, was an opportunistic goblin. It would steal the Big Boss's money and, when it did so, Rupert would be powerless to retrieve it unless he chose to challenge two opponents to a fight which he would lose.

It was only £250.

Nothing.

A phase of his life was drawing to a close.

'All right then.'

Neil lifted Shorty on to the stool and it seemed as if the kiosk had been made for him. He stared with delight around his new manor. The height of the stool camouflaged what some might have seen as defects and created a view that he had never enjoyed before. His world had always been made up of thighs and stomachs. Now he was to be presented with an aspect of breasts that it had never been his privilege to witness. He could look down on them. Suddenly it was Christmas. Shorty settled on his seat sniggering and wolf-whistling. 'Lovely view,' he said.

Rupert noted, with little relief, that at least Shorty could not leave his post without Neil's help. If he tried to descend from the stool on his own he would probably break his neck.

'Any minge cummin 'ere?' the mouth inquired through the circular aperture.

'What?'

'Girls?'

'Sometimes.'

'Shagfest 'ere we cum.'

And so Dan the Man found himself face to face with the King of the Rotters. For the first time in his Hollywood high-kicking life he encountered an opponent of equal virtuosity.

He combated slicing blades and shredding knives and tomb fatalities. Then the King started to make mistakes. He threw high punches when he should have used low. He was slow to upper-cut at the jungle level and he wasted time attempting to attack Dan the Man's impenetrable defences.

The King finally succumbed. Three spikes appeared from the ceiling of the Cell of Despair and impaled him. Dan the Man pulled down both joysticks. The body of the dismembered monarch slid off the spikes and crashed on to the floor in a flood of blood.

'Good game,' said Neil in his monotone. He watched politely as Rupert's initials flashed into their rightful place on top of the electronic scoreboard.

'Comin' for a ride?'

'Better close up first.'

Shorty was air-lifted from his position on the stool. The cash was still in the box. Rupert could not count it to make sure that it was all there because this would have been seen as an insult, and insults were the stuff of friction.

Neil and Neville wheeled their bikes out on to the pavement.

'How's it go off-road?' Neil said, indicating the Honda 100.

'Never tried.'

'The exhausts burn out on the Japanese.'

'Yeah.'

'Cruise speed?'

'Sixty.'

'Ever fallen off?'

'Course not. You?'

'Skidded once. Goin' round a corner. Too fast I 'spose. Broke a leg!'

Neil did not say where this accident had taken place. It could have been a European round of the Supersport 600 at Hockenheim for all anyone knew.

'Comin' to the pub then?'

'OK.'

A pub reputed to be the tavern in which Coleridge once drank away the memory of the man from Porlock took pride in its authenticity. Its traditional scrumpy (made from a recipe dating to 1693) collected notices, as did the pies from its Country Fayre counter. Such a pub did not wish to see its antique oak door slammed back off its hinges as if it were a prop in a spaghetti western. Nor would its authentic atmosphere welcome the arrival of low-life trouble-makers in leather jackets. Such a pub did not care if they came from broken homes or not, and it certainly did not wish to hear Shorty's screeching voice describe the night that he drank a pint of Cointreau.

Shirley behind the bar did not mind if she had an ode dedicated to her or not. It made no difference to her whether her eyes were like lakes twinkling under the Northern star or if her hair was the burnished gold of a cornfield at sunset, although she might have been more appreciative of these descriptions if her husband Ken had not been sitting at a table twenty-five yards away.

'Yes?' she said, with the expression of one who has just been stung by a bee.

'Eighty-four quadruple gin and tonics,' Shorty squeaked.

'Yes?' Shirley repeated, ignoring him and looking at Neil, who had the money.

'I'm married,' she said, before Shorty could open his mouth again.

'We could have an affair.'

'My husband is over there.'

She indicated a figure moulded by long hours working on a building site.

Rupert drank a pint of Watneys, Neville had a rum and Coke, Shorty draught bitter, Neil bitter with a whisky chaser. Rupert usually ordered halves when he was out with the Big Boss. He wondered if he would be able to get the bike home.

'Got a girlfriend?' Shorty asked him.

'No,' said Rupert, with magnificent insouciance.

'You can 'ave a go on one of mine if you like.'

'Thanks.'

'Blimey,' said Neville. 'Give the lad a break. 'E's a bit young to die of gonirear.'

'That barmaid's got 'er eye on you Nev,' Shorty replied. 'Ha Ha Ha!'

Shorty's grating cackle caused two members of the Anti-Angling Association to stare at him, alarmed and then angry. Shorty, ignorant as always of the nuances of atmosphere, continued to convulse with hysteria, slamming the table so that glasses jiggled and coasters fell on to the floor.

'Ere!' he snorted. 'She's lookin' atchya!'

Shirley was indeed looking at them, partly because the sound of an animal being strangled had reached her ears and partly because she was keeping an eye on the box which contained money for the Lifeboat Fund.

At last Shorty subsided.

'So d'ya live 'ere?' said Neil.

'Yeah,' said Rupert.

There was a silence. Neil struck a match and, as it flared up, he, Neville and Shorty stared into it, as if hypnotized by one memory.

Neil liked fire. After leaving school he had enjoyed a short but lucrative career as a professional arsonist, a period that he still thought of as the happiest in his life. He had started by setting fire to BMWs for no reason other than he disliked the idea of their owners. His 'work' had been noticed and he had taken on commissions for men who needed to defraud insurance companies. Employing Shorty as a 'lookout' he had successfully burned down five warehouses, three launderettes and a Thai take-away when a gust of wind had blown in the wrong direction and a housing estate in Hackney had been reduced to rubble.

He and Shorty had been lying low in Lambeth when Neville had approached them in a pub and attempted to sell them a pirate copy of a Chinese porn movie.

'I am "A Hanging Blue Lantern",' he had whispered.

'Oh yeah?' Shorty had sneered. 'Who are they when they're at home?'

'I cannot disclose the secrets of the Hung family or I will die by a myriad of swords.'

'Then you wouldn't be so well Hung,' Shorty had retorted, shrieking with laughter.

Neville had not understood the joke but he was buying the drinks so they had allowed him to stay. Then he followed them back to their squat and showed them his melon knife used, he said, to cut those who wouldn't pay up to the Triads' demands. After that they had not been able to get rid of him.

Neil concluded that Rupert could be of use to them. He

knew the locality, he might have access to resources and he could probably lend them money. Neville, meanwhile, saw a new opponent, one who threatened to attract Neil's attention and who could join forces with Shorty, thus casting Neville back into the social wasteland with which he was painfully familiar and to which he did not intend to return. Shorty, however, saw no reason to disbar Rupert. His personal looks presented no competition. Shorty, as the most attractive member of their set, would still have first choice of the women and that was all that mattered.

'So,' Rupert said. 'What are you doing here?'

There was a longer silence. Neville and Shorty did not speak because secrecy was their only bond and the truth was a liability. They did not know why Neil had chosen to befriend this person but past experience told them that the complex workings of Neil's mind always became clear with time. They would have to wait for an explanation – any attempt to bestow their own ideas would be seen as an attempt to appropriate leadership and would, consequently, incur the punishment of his disregard.

Neil, fleshy-lipped, calm, inscrutable, looked into Rupert's eyes with unblinking primacy. His inanimate presence spoke of nothing and everything. Unnerved, Rupert stared at the cigarette burns on the table. He knew that he was being assessed. He tried to visualize the true nature of everyday amorality. He wondered if the boundaries of Neil's depravity were imaginable. And then he wondered how far he would go for this man.

'We're on the run,' Neil said.

Neville's mouth tightened. Neil trusted the stranger. He had initiated him and, by so doing, he had abandoned Neville. He felt like slashing the usurper's face but he knew, even as the pain surged through him, even as his life drained away, that patience was to be his most important weapon.

'Yeah,' said Shorty. 'Burglary 'n' stuff.'

'We're gonna pull a job,' Neil continued, casually, as if he was talking about the weather. 'Good dosh. We could do with another rider . . .'

Rupert gulped from his glass.

'Good dosh?' he said.

'Yeah,' said Neil.

Shirley called time.

Rupert thought of his mother.

'Ten thousand quid?' he asked.

'Could be more,' said Neil.

Rupert drank the last draught.

'I'm in,' he said.

Chapter 8

Grace lay on her bed listening to a cassette of Vagina Dentata Organ and reading the copy of American *Vogue* that Clive had left behind. There was an article entitled STILL FAB AT FIFTY in which a pop singer explained that pink had become her favourite colour after she had been run over by a bicycle. 'I was walking back to the projects, after school, and it was dark you see, and I could not be seen. I came home, with all bruises and my hair mussed up and my Daddy said to me, "You know Diana, people won't notice you if you wear dark colours. Browns, navies, leave them right out! *You gotta stand out!*" And from then on I wore eye catchin' shades like oranges, silvers and pinks. Sometimes I think my Daddy should take the credit for all my success because, thanks to him, I have always stood apart from the crowd. Pink is the colour of love – it's a lucky colour. Janis Joplin never wore pink and look what happened to her . . .'

Grace's father interrupted her. He was flustered. Tony Torrible had dropped out of the pageant and someone had to be found to play Arthur Haslerigg. Kenneth Hertzel had contracted impetigo which meant that the BBC had no secretary, and the chef had failed to order the meat for Saturday night which meant that people from all over the county would travel to the Blackmore Hotel's world famous carvery to find themselves facing a meal bereft of bovine presence.

He wavered in the doorway, surveyed Grace for a few seconds, tried not to remember her mother and tried not to ask himself why his curious offspring sat in a cell-like room with bare white walls, rush matting, candles and incense sticks. He tried not to think about these things and he tried not to ask himself why she had no friends. One friend even. He was sure he had had friends at her age. Everyone had friends at the age of eighteen, didn't they? He seemed to remember a time when most women had husbands at the age of eighteen. In his heart of hearts he would have liked Grace to marry rather than attend Art College. Art College would cause worry. She would make friends at Art College but they could only be drug addicts and deviants.

He resolved to ask the Beckinsales round for a drink, perhaps they would bring Amos. Perhaps he was still single. Miles had seen him working behind the counter in the cheese shop. He was a very nice young man.

'Christ, what's that noise?' he said.

'Hard-core ambient.'

'Sounds like road-works. You'd better take that horse down to Marvin. It needs bloody shoes.'

Grace looked at Diana's shoes. They were silver mules with a kitten heel and a white fur trim.

She wondered if shoes gave Diana's life a meaning.

The people who scattered themselves about American

Vogue were semi-naked. They ate muesli parfaits and bought hats for $85,000. They lived in houses where all the walls had been painted Mediterranean blue. They were incomprehensible but they seemed to know things that she did not and she was beginning to feel excluded. What were their secrets? Did 'sleek synthetics' and Chris Izaak's trousers hold answers to the questions she spent hours asking herself? Was she missing subtle messages because she did not understand? Grace looked at her own existence. She knew that she had no answers. Exciting moments were marked by a slight twist in the stomach as a mood passed from dull depression to the fury of boredom.

She often studied the magpies who nested in a tree outside her window, day in and day out. She saw their whole cycle, from twigs and nest to eggs and feeding. It seemed to be an automatic thing, winding round and round, as if on a mobile; an eternal cycle of pointless eating and feeding propelled by biological urge and certainly not by love, for where could there be love in a bird's body? The birds were propelled by the perpetual motion of biological urge, that was the simple secret of the animal world, but how could one explain those who must wear unitards and admire Lenny Kravitz? Their instincts were undoubtedly the same but, unlike Grace, when the urges with which they had been born united with conscious thought, the result was not ennui, the result was the ability to find joy in a gilet and meaning in a handkerchief hem.

There was a conspiracy of sorts. All these figures seemed to be friends, and these friends were trying to persuade her to become like them, unitarded and free of inner doubt.

'It's dark,' she said.

'I know. It's taken Robert two hours to get him in the trailer. Nearly lost an eye. Be careful . . .'

Grace did not like driving in the dark. Langford Budville was at the opposite end of Exmoor and meant navigating murky roads whose web did not seem to be reflected on any map. If you got lost on the moors you could circle for hours; if the car broke down you might die out there in the maze of deserted shrubland. She considered arguing but her father would simply say, as he always did, 'It's *your* horse.' Marvin was expecting them and Miles Falconbridge wished to maintain relations – he was the only blacksmith in Somerset with the courage to go within two hundred yards of Charger.

'You better take some cash for Marvin,' he said, and gave her £200.

She drove slowly, the trailer swinging at the back. There was a mist, visibility was poor and the road was deserted.

She had turned a corner and was crawling into a tunnel of darkness when the glowing orbs of three headlights jumped out in front of her. They were stretched across the road, in a row, as disembodied discs, and they did not move as she drove slowly forward. There was no alternative but to stop.

She braked.

Her eyes were blinded by the lights. Then a leather glove thumped on the driver's window with aggressive urgency.

She jumped and her heart began to beat. She wound down the window with trembling fingers.

'Has there been an accident?'

The voice inside the black crash-helmet said something.

'I'm sorry, I can't hear what you're saying.'

The leather fingers flicked the tinted vizor up and pale blue eyes examined her.

'Get out the fuckin' car,' said the mouth.

'Why?'

'Just get out.'

Grace had grown up in a hotel so she was accustomed to bizarre behaviour. Rude men did not frighten her, on the contrary, she found them entertaining. She climbed out of the driver's seat.

The crash-helmet slammed her up against the car. He seemed angry about something. Perhaps they had broken down.

Another crash-helmet appeared. He held a knife.

'What are you doing?' she said.

'We're muggin' ya, ya silly bint.'

'Mugging me?'

She wondered if they wanted the horse.

There was an exasperated groan. Then, 'Just give me the bag.'

The tall figure rifled through the recesses, but his search was obstructed by his motorcycle gloves and by the number of items in the bag. He flung paintbrushes, tubes of acrylic, a bicycle pump, an orange, a chocolate rabbit, and a pom-pom hat on to the ground. Then, as he came across a sticky substance that had congealed at the bottom, he became angry and punched the satchel, now flaccid, into Grace's stomach.

'*The money! Give me the fucking money!*'

Marvin's £200 was in an envelope in a side pocket. She handed it to him. He opened it with difficulty as the gluey mass from the handbag had stuck his fingers together.

He was shovelling the notes into his pocket when the air was split by a loud roar, a volley of stamping, then a crash as Charger's body banged against the sides of the trailer. The horse had been mishandled when young. Grace and her mother had coddled it. It had eaten Alpen. Consequently the stallion was now unmanageable. When roused it could be lethal.

There was the sound of wood splintering as hooves crashed against the door.

'Bloody Hell!'

The youth with the knife shrieked and dropped the blade. As he did so, Grace stooped down to retrieve the contents of her handbag. The tall man violently pushed her over into the road then stood over her looking down through his black vizor. She could not see his face, but he seemed triumphant, to have won some unknown battle.

He leaned over her and, with one finger, he mockingly beckoned, motioning her to stand up and come towards him. As she struggled to stagger to her feet, his metal-plated motorcycle boot pulled slowly back and she realized that he was going to kick her in the stomach.

'That's enough,' said a third voice.

A figure she had not seen before moved out of the shadows and passed into the beam of the headlights so that his silhouette was illuminated from the back. His vizor was up and, in the recesses of his helmet, Grace saw dark-brown eyes that spoke of a sadness so fundamental, but so familiar, that to see them was to yearn to know his secrets.

He strode forward.

'That's enough,' he said again.

There was a short silence, then, without a word, the leader swivelled around and walked towards the motor bikes. The second biker snatched his blade from the ground and ran after him. They remounted their machines, turned them, and screamed down the dark road until the break lights dissolved into the night.

Grace drove to Langford Budville and told Marvin what had happened.

'Jesus Christ,' he said. 'Are you all right, darlin'?'

'Yes.'

'They could have killed you.'

This had not occurred to Grace. Murder was not a part of everyday life. People might be butchered in London but they were not butchered in Somerset. She realised that Marvin was right. The gang could have killed her if they had wanted to but the man with brown eyes had saved her life. She was not particularly grateful to have been saved, her life was expendable, but he had cared enough to protect her. Passion emerged with these thoughts and she began to lose herself in his mystery.

Once she would have wept as the cart clattered to Tyburn and she would have watched as the crowd fought over the corpse of a beloved outcast. Who cared that this stranger came from an old line of thugs who would slit a man's throat and then go out for a laughing drink in an alley alehouse? They were loved because they did not care and they boasted and they bought the drinks. Turpin with his pock marks. Plunket pretending to be a gentleman. William Page caught on Shooters Hill.

Only the strange is truly erotic and only the unknown offers transcendence. Now Grace was guarded by the perfect creation. The Highwayman was unavailable and unobtainable. He was the perfect man. He would turn her into all the things that something deep inside her told she could be, for somewhere, very hidden, someone was trying to get out, someone beguiling and brave and ready to love.

'You better ring your dad,' Marvin said. 'He'll tell the police.'

Miles Falconbridge was appalled.

Highway robbery would kill the American market as surely as if an IRA bomb had exploded on Dunster high street.

Guidebook, brochure, pamphlet, map – all described heathery uplands and wildlife enjoyed by Wordsworth. West Somerset was known as an unspoilt area of peace and quiet for the 'connoisseur of the countryside'. Connoisseurs came expecting to find fields full of withies. They looked forward to viewing the 'old life' of the noble countryman as it was represented by the Cider Mill or Gypsy Folklore Collection. They wanted to witness pagan rituals such as wassailing, egg shackling and Punkie Night.

Anarchy had no place in Picnic Areas. Gangland was not a Natural Attraction. The visitor wanted cot and stream and gorgeous purple headland. If families felt they could not ride or ramble or camp without receiving a knife in their necks they would take the children to Devon instead.

If the connoisseurs of the countryside deserted Somerset, picturesque villages would turn into ghost towns and, as deprivation escalated, so too would the crime level. Shifty shadows would haunt the streets while responsible home-owners would peer from their windows, afraid to go out. A ghastly procession marched across Miles Falconbridge's mind's eye – this was not a parade of cavaliers and roundheads dressed up for tourists, but of junkies, scroungers, travellers, layabouts and losers.

It was as if the Doone family had returned to haunt their birthplace. Congenitally delinquent, the clan had once spent their days torching homesteads, plundering crops and carrying off farmers' daughters. Now they had re-emerged from their valley at the bottom of the River Lyn. The very legend upon which West Somerset depended had reincarnated and was bent on bringing mayhem.

Miles Falconbridge had devoted much time and energy to tending and protecting the peace. Now lawlessness had come upon him and he took it as personally as if he had been visited by a degenerative disease.

He called an emergency meeting of the Bed and Breakfast Corporation and about twenty of the most conscientious members collected in his Private Function Room.

He told them the details of the incident and asked them to raise any points that they thought relevant, stressing that this was an unscheduled, informal meeting but their comments would be noted and included in corporation records.

The Rubbish Ranger voiced concern about the dropping of litter.

The Noise Warden voiced concern about the volume of noise from the motor bike engines and the effect it would have on the lambs which, as everyone knew, were already dying because of the weather.

Len from the Travellers Rest (Coach Parties Welcome) said that his customers had been accusing him of highway robbery for years but he didn't consider £76 with full Somerset breakfast to be an unfair price.

His friend Chris from Lorna's (sixteenth-century

licensed restaurant) suggested that they dress up as high-waymen and do a stand and deliver re-enactment for the tourists.

Mrs Prink (non-smokers' holiday flat in Bossington) moved that the meeting put it on record that it disapproved of the motocyclists' flagrant violation of the country code.

Miles Falconbridge suddenly leapt to his feet and thumped his fist angrily on the table.

There was an embarrassed silence. Everyone looked into their glasses. Len from the Travellers Rest noticed that his was empty.

'I think,' Falconbridge shouted, 'that you are missing the point here. I have called this Extraordinary meeting because I consider the mugging of my daughter at knifepoint to be very serious indeed. Please consider the implications of this incident. The Easter Break is coming up. If news of this gang leaks out the effect on trade could be devastating. Ladies and Gentlemen, *there is no guarantee that our roads are safe*! We don't know when this gang are going to strike again – it could be anywhere at any time! Next time it could be your daughter! This gang are armed and they could kill – if they kill we may as well all shut up shop and file for bankruptcy.

'Now. At the very least I recommend that we draft a letter, signed by us all, to the police, emphasizing the absolute necessity for discretion on this matter. If news of this robbery leaks out at a local or national level we are done for.'

This motion was passed with silent speed.

Two days later a headline appeared on page three of the *Daily Mail*. HIGHWAYMEN IN EXMOOR! was accompanied by an artist's impression of the gang. They were illustrated wearing metallic breast-plates, and sitting on top of customized choppers.

'Blimey,' said Shorty when he saw it. 'They've turned us into *Robocop*.'

Rupert laughed but Neil and Neville did not join in; to laugh would have been to engage in relations and Neil's patronage had dissolved when Rupert stepped in to protect the woman on the moor. He had challenged Neil at a moment when retaliation was impossible and, by so doing, he had forced him to submit. Neil would not forget this. If he wished to kick somebody, then he would kick them. Gainsay could never be granted, not even as a favour. Neville, in silent support, knew that Neil's authority was immutable and only death or a jail sentence could destroy it.

They related to the present with the intensity that arises from rootlessness. They needed now because now was all they had. This would always segregate them from Rupert, from everyone. And Rupert did not understand that the moment on the moor had displaced him – to seek approval now was a waste of time.

Easter bookings were cancelled as a result of the *Daily Mail* story but members of the Donga Tribe of New Age Travellers told each other that Somerset looked like a cool place to spend the weekend. The Donga Tribe did not, of course, read the *Daily Mail*. As some people believed they could contract AIDS from kissing, the Donga Tribe believed one could contract fascism from reading the *Daily Mail*. However, one member came across it while searching for cigarette stubs in a municipal dustbin.

Fleet Street was mobilized by the *Daily Mail*'s description of the 'Somerset Highwaymen'. The savoury odour of the picaresque wafted under the nostrils of those manning news desks and forces of 'writers' were dispatched with instructions to find out more.

Business was brisk in the pubs of Porlock and Dunster as the media convened and foisted their expense accounts on grateful landlords. They were all too willing to help because they knew that helpful interviews often meant a gratifying 'name check' and the reward of nationwide attention to the services they offered. So alert were they to this encouraging trend that scarcity of facts posed no obstruction. Poetic licence coloured the grisly aspects of 'the gang', the terror they were inflicting upon the community and general speculation as to the possibility of the episode ending in a Greek tragedy bloodbath.

The words 'Marauding' and 'Menace' poured forth as easily as beer gushed from the taps.

Only Mrs Prink (non-smokers' holiday flat in Bossington) missed out on the free publicity. Accosted by a lady reporter from the *Daily Express* she had assumed from her desperate and dirty appearance that she was selling white heather and had slammed the door in her face.

The song of an exaltation of larks celebrated the news that the Highwaymen had 'struck again'. The gang flagged down a farmer named Hippisley on the historic toll road between Porlock and Minehead. The car, swerving to avoid them, had crashed into a tree. The bounty was £50, a car radio and a niblick belonging to the farmer's wife.

One newspaper's Weekend Section devoted two pages to HIGHWAYMEN – THE MYTH AND THE REALITY. This included a picture of Mr Hippisley wearing a neck brace, a map showing the tree where the car had crashed and an outline of the legend of Tom Cox, the Somerset highwayman whose execution had been celebrated in a poem by Jonathan Swift.

Readers learned that Tom Cox was the ne'er-do-well son of a gentleman who, having been bailed out of jail by an heiress, married her and spent her fortune on gambling and whoring.

He robbed travellers on the road between Somerton and Castle Cary until he was arrested after a holdup near Chard. He escaped from the county jail at Ilchester (stealing a tankard from the turnkey as he did so) but was caught and sentenced to death.

This interesting tale was juxtaposed with a cautionary leader column which berated an 'irresponsible press' for pandering to a public whose thirst for 'lovable vagabonds' was unquenchable. It warned the reader to remember that the 'Somerset Highwaymen' were not robbing from the rich to give to the poor – they were little more than petty crooks, willing to maim innocent members of the public for the sake of a golf club. Although in this way they were similar to most members of the Government, they should nevertheless be discouraged. The exposure that the 'highwaymen' were receiving would foster a sense of self-importance and encourage them to commit further felonies which would jeopardize the tourist trade on which so many livelihoods depended.

Righteousness held no sway. The Somerset Highwaymen gripped the nation's imagination and became a symbol of inspiration to the dispossessed.

Miles Falconbridge's fears materialized. Somerset began to be visited by people of no fixed abode who dragged their children along on a piece of string and trapped rabbits for their dinner.

Free-thinkers and situationists set up camps on common land, sat round fires, passed pipes from hand to hand, and exchanged personal theories on natural theology. Underground magazines were made on public library photocopiers. Songs were written and hummed to guitars late into the night and a straggling incoherent philosophy evolved as the troupe of mysterious outcasts became what each individual wanted them to be.

Unshapely nubiles wearing Highwaymen T-shirts made a shrine where the farmer Hippisley had been robbed and could be seen walking up and down the toll road hoping to find traces of the gang, much as, years ago, devotees would search for remains of the saints – a finger perhaps, or a knee, that could be authenticated by the Vatican and then subjected to eternal worship.

Some, wishing to promote themselves to places of importance, claimed that they were bearing the Highwaymen's children.

Grace was known to be one of the few people who had actually seen the Highwaymen and strange strangers came to the Blackmore Hotel to hear her account. She found herself amongst women who had rings in their noses, chains in their labia and eagles on their backs. They had, they told her, claimed back their bodies and, by letting their own blood, they had expunged the pain of their oppression. They lived in tepees and trailers and they could mend things – doors, shoes, cars, musical instruments, anything. Grace became a show for them as they courted and encouraged her, and she, who had never been encouraged by anyone (except the art master) and had never really been seen, drew towards the leather girls who did what they liked.

One of them, Denzel, shaved Grace's head. Denzel wore an old army jacket with gold epaulettes on the shoulders. Her own head was not bald, she had a short Mohawk dyed violet, but she had once worked in a barber shop in Wandsworth so she knew how to operate an electric razor.

'Baldness is a good look for women,' she told Grace. 'To have no hair is the best way to make our own statement in the male culture of beauty – it's the best way to say "bugger off, we don't care what you lot like, we're going to do what we like and you are going to have to accept it".'

Grace had never really thought about what men liked and did not like because she did not care particularly, but she knew that, somehow, she was being excluded by an omnipresent confidence trick in which all women were brushed and teazed and curled into *au courant* conformity. An extreme measure would be pleasing if it managed to advertise dissimilarity as well as irritate others.

Grace loved the soft grey skull-cap; she loved the fact that she was barely recognizable and that a part of her old self was disintegrating. Later, in the middle of the night, when Denzel had returned to her tent, Grace sat amongst the feathery remains of a discarded persona and plucked out every single hair on her eyebrows. She picked obsessively, in a mirror, by the light of a candle. It was a ritual of a kind. So now, grey eyes stared from a skull and a forehead as hairless and smooth as every alien of popular culture.

Her inner landscape had changed after the night on the moor, its tones were now bright with possibility. She was venturing out, supported by a fantasy man who would love every aspect of her and would understand all the personal adventures encapsulated in her appearance.

She knew that she had met the truth of her destiny, that he and she would unite. Sustained by longing, her idea of love was only fettered by the limits of her imagination.

No aspect of reality flawed this happy optimism; the problem of finding the Highwayman, for instance, was not a difficulty. He would appear, walk into her life, and, when he did, she would not be shocked because she was always expecting him. Indeed, there were many evenings when she was surprised to realize that the day had passed without evidence of his physical presence.

She was never disheartened. He was with her anyway. She knew him as well as she knew the external landmarks of her environment – the photograph of her mother on the dressing table, the clump and thud as guests walked down the corridors of the hotel; the waft of their *coq au vin* being cooked in the evening.

Now, wherever she went, whatever she did, she was never alone. He was always there, observing her actions and in her thoughts. She woke up with him, spoke at length with him as the sun fingered through the wooden shutters of the bedroom. He watched her in the bathroom, he watched her at breakfast and she dressed for him. Sometimes his disinclination to leave her alone was burdensome. He would not leave her mind and she could not make him go, even though she had so much control over the dance of their mutual life.

As the full force of his personality occupied her attention, she became less and less aware of the bric-à-brac of everyday life. Her father, shocked by her shaven head, told her 'For God's sake keep away from the guests. You'll put them off their food.'

But Grace, the new Grace, the Grace evolving in romantic illusion was invulnerable because he was always there saying what she needed to hear, taking her away. And he looked as she wished him to look. He was never fickle or undermining or dull. He had courage and wit and the strength of the single-minded.

Every day became a ritual of preparation for his arrival, every moment a speculation. Slowly she made herself ready. She knew that she was not quite right; although he said, in her mind, that she was fine, she was not sure.

Lex, leather chaps, leather jacket and breasts, found Grace alone behind the bar. She wore the stare of one who is powerless until she receives orders from an authority existing in a different time zone. Lex, once Alexandra, had the swagger of a cowpoke and the manners of a gentleman but she did not, nowadays, have much to do. She was good at tying knots, which had been useful on the bondage scene in San Francisco – but there was limited demand for these talents in her native country. Now she was wandering. She did not know what she hoped to find. Sex was always of interest; drugs and rock and roll had not lost their promise. She was thirty-two. Perhaps she should marry and settle down, get her dinner cooked. But she wasn't ready. The predator in her was still breathing. Boredom could kill.

Breasts and leather bore down on Grace.

'A pint of Smithwicks,' she said.

Grace pulled slowly into the present, a dull space where colours grew more muted and where there was not, as yet, the presence of the Highwayman. She focussed lazily – a huge individual with a circular face was staring at her chest.

Her blonde hair was cropped and her studs said 'Terror Crew'.

Grace watched, fascinated, as she drank beer like a man, throwing her head back, throat vibrating.

Lex, with the charisma of experience, smiled the smile of self-assurance. Grace felt as if she had been punched in the stomach.

'I'm Lex,' she said. 'A friend of Denzel's.'

'She shaved my head,' said Grace.

'I know. Looks good,' said Lex. Then, after pausing, 'Do you wanna see my bike?'

'OK,' said Grace.

Lex rolled forward like a man. She smelt of oil, meat and two veg. She was so big.

She opened the door for Grace and ushered her through.

'It's a Norton Commando,' she said, when they got outside. '1971.'

Grace stared at the bike politely. It was not as interesting as Lex.

'I got paranoid about gearbox layshaft bearing failure so I replaced 'em with a lipped roller. The outer cover was modified to accept oil seals for the gear change and kick-start shafts.'

'Oh.'

'Yeah. Crankshafts as good as new and all I done is piston rings and valve replacement.'

'Oh.'

'Wanna ride?'

'OK.'

''Ere 'ave these.'

She took a huge pair of filthy sneakers from her rucksack and gave them to Grace.

'For protection.'

Grace put them on her bare feet.

Lex knelt down and tied up the laces. 'Jeez you must be cold,' she said, wrapping a hot hand around Grace's naked calf. 'Don't you ever wear shoes?'

'I have got some,' she replied. 'But I don't like them. I was thinking about mules.'

'Mules?'

'I saw them in a magazine.'

'What magazine?'

'Fashion.'

'Fashion?' The child was wearing a filthy grey shift and an over-sized leather jacket. 'Fashion huh? I don't know much about fashion I'm afraid.'

They rode the bike to Baker's Wood where they sat cross-legged and passed a bottle of vodka between them, drinking it straight from the bottle.

'Like the bike then?' asked Lex.

'Yeah,' said Grace, thinking of the Highwayman and how it would be when she sat on the back of his bike.

The vodka kicked in. She was quite calm.

'I had a new tattoo done last week,' said Lex. 'Do you want to see?'

'OK.'

Lex took off her T-shirt. There were snakes all over her white breasts. They writhed and disappeared into her cleavage as she moved.

'I got this one in New York,' she said, pointing to a viper. 'You should have one done. Would suit ya.'

They were beautiful, the snakes, with their green and blue stripes and their dead little eyes. Grace giggled.

'That's fashion,' said Lex. 'Tattoos. Everyone's tribal now. Yeah, that's what you need, a tattoo.'

Lex stared at the tiny waif in front of her. God, she looked about twelve.

'That and a square meal.'

Grace knew that Lex was right. She should have a tattoo. She was restless now, provoked by transformation. Nothing was going to stop her.

'Where can I get one?' she said. 'In London?'

'There's Jo,' said Lex. 'She works in Glastonbury – she's famous. All the pagans go to her. I'll take you if you like.'

'OK.'

Jo's studio was advertised by a square sign that said 'Body Art' in irregular hand-painted letters.

Jo was also painted. Her neck and arms were covered with lilies and tigers and, underneath her right eye, there was a permanent blue teardrop. She wore a shawl, a dirty floral skirt and a pair of Doc Martens that had once been silver. Two curtains of long raven hair were divided by a streak that shone, thick and white, down the centre of her scalp.

Jo and Lex hugged each other, kissed on the lips, then punched each other on the upper arms.

The tattooist showed Grace a book in which there were photographs of technopagans with Celtic insignia, gangsta rappers with scorpions, bearded sailors with galleons and a grotesque penis on which Popeye had been stamped for ever.

'I am a creative person,' said Jo, whose voice was as soft as a whisper. 'I am an artist and I am a Leo.'

Grace told Jo what she wanted. It was not in her book. It was not in any book. The idea came from an article, in

American *Vogue*, about how makeup should be applied to give the face more definition.

'That,' said Lex, with genuine admiration, 'is radical.'

'Sit there, Darling,' said Jo. 'Just there, in front of me, let me take a look at you.'

Grace sat on a small stool so that she was lower than Jo. The older woman held her chin with her hand and scrutinized her face with a lamp. Her hands smelt of antiseptic; her breasts, in gypsy blouse, rose and fell rhythmically, and her body and breath exuded heat.

'This won't take long,' she said. 'It's very simple, one colour only, but it will be painful because it's near the bone.'

She wiped Grace's forehead with antiseptic and marked it with a felt-pen.

'All right?' Jo asked.

Grace nodded.

'Let's go.'

Lex handed her a small wet joint and a mug of warm wine milked from a box. Then she lit a sandalwood joss-stick and put a tape into the cassette player. As Grace Jones' mannish tones filled the room she undulated in a belly dance, hands above head, hips swivelling, feet doing a two-step. *Feeling like a woman, looking like a man ... walking, walking, in the rain.*

And as the incense curled in a smoke signal above the burner, with the light shining into her face, the shadow of Lex undulating, Jo took the electric drill-shaped device, which, huge and heavy, whirred with a hum that signalled pain.

'Don't move,' whispered Jo, who now stood above her

and clasped her face with a firm grip. 'If you move you could lose an eye.'

Walking, walking in the rain. Come in all you jesters, enter all you fools, sit down no nos, trip the light fantastic, dance with swivel hips, button up your lips, walking, walking in the rain . . .

The agony shot through Grace's head. Her body jolted, then tears sprang to her eyes and rolled down her cheek. Jo, static with concentration, wiped away some excess ink.

Dance with swivel hips, button up your lips . . .

And now Grace entered a small world where there was only pain and the bodies of Lex and Jo, their breath, their faces, their arms, their bodies pressing in, a fleshy wall of tyrannical affection. She surrendered to searing excruciation, she was nobody, just a person to be decorated by an unknown woman in whom she was forced to have complete trust, and with the burning came an odd love, creeping in, sideways, unexpected. As the wine and grass calmed her, she wondered if she would ever be able to leave this enclave with its perfumes and inks and symbols of sentiment and dishonour. Attempting to divert from the pain, away from the face of Jo, she stared at the photographs on the wall – the Mudmen of the Asaro River with masks made of dried clay, the red-nosed Wapenamunda dancers and the naked Kandeps with blue faces and white eyes. And as her eyes swam with tears and her body vibrated with the shock of suffering, the tribesmen seemed to come alive in front of her.

Finally the whir, the burning and the wiping stopped. Jo placed her machine back on the table, wiped for the last time, and stepped back to admire her canvas. Then she held up a mirror. Grace, dazed, looked into it and saw a strong redefined woman staring back. Euphoria, warm, sensual, delicate, trickled slowly from her face to her neck to her stomach and to her thighs.

Jo had neatly tattooed two thick black eyebrows in straight lines across her forehead.

'They're beautiful,' said Jo. 'They're beautiful because they are you.'

'It's certainly different,' said Lex.

'The scabs will heal in a week,' added Jo. 'Don't pick them. Dab with antiseptic and pray to the Moon Goddess for a healthy life.'

'Here,' said Lex, handing her two Anadin Extra on wide dirty palms. 'For the headache.'

Later, when the shock had worn off, Miles Falconbridge told his daughter that she looked like Mr Potato Head.

Chapter 9

The air in the mobile home in Porlock, tinged with Pine Smell-U-Like air freshener, was as invigorating as that breathed by Heidi and her goats.

A new press cutting was attached to the front of the Mini-Freeez with a magnet in the shape of a pizza. HIGHWAYMAN HYSTERIA SWEEPS THE COUNTRY. EASTER CHAOS!!! The article described how a Volvo estate had been stopped outside Dunster and the Simpson family had been forced to hand over a leather backgammon set worth £500. A side-bar noted that this was the gang's third crime in six weeks and a map illustrated the locations of the robberies, each of which was marked with a black skull and cross-bones.

These details were embellished by an 'expert opinion' from Arthur 'Bicycle' Jones who hailed from a Woolwich-based crime family. The photograph showed 'Bicycle' with his eyes covered by a black patch in order to conceal his identity. A casual observer might have remarked that this was not an efficient way to protect 'Bicycle' since his distinguishing characteristics were not his eyes, but his bald head and flat nose, neither of which were camouflaged.

Interviewed at home, a fortified council flat, 'Bicycle' said, 'These muggins are the work of a criminal bloody genius.'

Fame had settled on the outlaws and it affected each individual differently.

Neil was as taciturn and as impenetrable as ever but his violent scrubbing was now combined with assiduous cutting and filing of press clippings. These were dated, colour-coded, sealed with plastic and kept in order in a black box (with a lock) shop-lifted from Ryman's in Taunton.

He designated an hour a day to his 'paper-work'. Lovingly fingering the stories of copycat crimes he luxuriated in the knowledge that the gang was receiving credit for doubling the crime figures in the West Country.

Neil had long known that extremism bought notoriety. He had learned it when, as a teenager, he had briefly attended a crowded comprehensive in south-east London. Some individuals had distinguished themselves by puffing on forbidden cigarettes. Neil had not smoked Number 6. He had carefully burned his skin with their lighted tips and incurred a reputation whose evil renown still lingered as frightened whispers behind locker-room walls.

Some of his contemporaries had graduated from football and fascism to dealing Ecstasy in Raffaella's nightclub in Stoke Newington. Others had gone into protection and extortion. Neil had never wanted to wear gold jewellery and he certainly did not wish to mix with prostitutes. He enjoyed violence but he was not motivated by it. He was a showman and a maverick and he knew could never be one of the crowd. The crowd was ordinary and dirty. The crowd had no class. The crowd got caught.

Neil planned to become as big as any Mr Big in any Essex villa and as respected as any Satan Slave, Yardie or Yakuza. He had waited a long time for his opportunity and he planned to exploit it. Now was the time to present the final show.

He started to disappear during the day and, returning to the caravan after dark, would spend the evenings studying maps, scribbling in notebooks and whispering into his mobile clone phone.

Neville's emotions usually fluctuated to synchronize with Neil's moods. Now, though, his temperament was independent. Tormented by fear, he had the puffy eyes of one blighted by insomnia. His stomach had twisted into a walnut of tension which meant he could not eat and he was losing weight. Every newspaper headline edged them towards prison.

He paced. He pulled his fingers. He ground his teeth. He was woken up by the sound of his own screaming.

Sometimes he would stare, dazed, out of the window, and he would almost hope to see a squad of police cars for at least then the unbearable tension would cease.

He spent hours sitting in front of the portable television set where, communing with regional programmes, he successfully detached himself from the uncomfortable suspicion that Neil was planning a raid of horrifying proportions. He could not, however, distance himself from Shorty who had been laid low by a respiratory condition.

It poses something of a philosophical conundrum that the Maker should feel the need to expend so much energy creating a specimen such as Shorty and then, having done so, wish to take him back a full sixty years before the normal allocation. One would think that anyone who had released Shorty would wish to leave him alone in the hope that, like an antique, age would beautify him and bestow some value.

This was not to be. Shorty's condition was deteriorating and he seemed destined to be ripped prematurely from his mortal coil. His constitution, already weakened by chips and poisoned by alcohol, had long been blighted by a weak chest. Now he suffered all the symptoms of a collapsed lung.

He lay on his bed hacking, hawking, shivering and (when he could find the breath) screeching for an oxygen tent. Palpitations, nausea and dry heaving had merged with a high temperature and, at night, frenzied by fever, he would shout the names of the many women who had staggered through his life.

During the day, exhausted by the barbs of fire burning his body, he lay on his bunk limp and weak, warning, in a stertorous whisper, that he would 'soon be gone' and then 'you'll be sorry'.

Shorty thought that it was particularly unfair that he could not have a nurse – preferably one from the Benny Hill Show, although he would have settled for nice Jane Seymour with her lovely soft hair and gentle manner. Why couldn't Jane come and mop his brow with a damp cloth now that he was dying?

He wondered if anyone would miss him.

Not Neville. Neville kept telling him that he wished he would die so that he and Neil could 'clear out of here before the filth gets us and that's only a matter of time, Shorty, and when we get nicked it'll be *your* fault!'

Rupert, surrounded by ghastly scenarios, studied them

with the calm submission of one who has been desensitized by horror. Neil detailed him to bring daily food packages to the caravan. 'The filth'll be looking for strangers,' he explained. 'You're local, they won't suspect you.'

Rupert initially limited the supplies to sausage rolls, samosas and Kit Kats, but the menu soon stretched to include plastic bottles of cider, pills stolen from his mother's bathroom cupboard (antibiotics for Shorty, tranquillizers for Neville) and the *Sun*. Neville would highlight the television pages with a felt-pen, Shorty would flap one weak wrist to communicate that he wished to look at the Page Three Girl, and (when he returned in the evening) Neil would scour the pages for references to their activities.

Rupert knew that celebrity was no friend to undercover operation. They were fortunate that no accurate description had been circulated. Blinded by headlamps and confused by shock, the victims had not seen their faces. No one even knew what kind of bikes they were riding. He realized that Neil's fixation with their image could undermine his judgement and endanger them. But Rupert's agitation did not stem from fear of discovery so much as practical consideration. The three 'jobs' had only bought £230 for each gang member. This was not enough to pay for one morning at Serenity Hall. If they continued at this rate it would be years before his mother received the necessary attention, years in which her liver would blow up and her blood would slowly poison every organ in her vast body.

Neville intimated that Neil was working on 'something big', but did not encourage more precise speculation.

Rupert's optimism was dwindling and he carried out his duties with little enthusiasm. Life in a gang was not the glamorous spree that he had envisaged. He had hoped for camaraderie and conversations about adjustable push rods. He had imagined tech tips, kicker kits and buffalo grips. He had smelled WD40 and seen exhilarating drag races on the open road, dust blasting into goggles, throttle open, easyriding. Then, when night fell, they would rumble noisily into towns where people would stare, envious of their freedom and afraid of their unity.

The possibilities should have been endless because those who cannot go back are forced forward to embrace limitless options. There should have been deserts and mountains, coyotes and camp fires and lonely gas stations manned by women who begged to be taken to Reno.

He knew that these things existed, and he thought that he had found a way to experience them. He had not imagined that he would spend hours watching Ken Hom's *Hot Wok* and listening to Shorty's whine, repeated as a rote – 'I should be under the doctor y'now. I haven't got long. Who's going to be my literary executor? There's all me poems. Who's going to manage my estate when I'm gone?'

Rupert was still cold and poor, and now, for the first time in his life, he was also bored.

Perhaps he should have gone to university, like they had told him to. The head of the English Department had even offered to speak to his mother about it. He had not realized that Margaret Ruthven was going through an unpleasant phase where she thought that if she took her clothes off it made her invisible. Rupert, panicking, had made excuses, and managed to save the man from an experience that would have caused sorrow to all.

One day he arrived to find Shorty lying in silence on his bed. A flush had spread over his face and neck. A moist sheen covered his brow and his eyes, half closed, were flickering. His chest shuddered as each breath fought to leave his body. *Randall and Hopkirk (Deceased)* shouted at each other from the television set while Neville threw his melon knife against the wall, retrieved it and threw it again while muttering 'I don't care if he does fuckin' die, fuckin' dwarf.'

Rupert, heart beating, dropped the package on the floor, knelt down by the lower bunk and lifted Shorty's head. It rolled limply on to his hand. He choked. 'I'm goin',' he whispered. 'This is it. Stay with me, Rupe.'

Neville grabbed the bag from the floor, threw out packets of cigarettes and fell on the pill bottles. Shaking, he poured out a handful of Ativan, unscrewed the bottle of cider, threw back his head, and swallowed. Then, without acknowledging Rupert, he sat back in front of the television and said to Shorty, 'I'm not taking you to the hospital you bastard. They'll ask questions and we'll all git arrested.'

'I'll die,' wheezed Shorty.

'Good.'

'I'll die and it will be your fault.'

'Good. Least I'll 'ave achieved somethin' in my life then.'

'Murderer.'

Neville turned up the volume of *The All New Popeye Show* so that the voices drowned out Shorty's whining. He tried not to worry about Neil's disappearances or why he was not being told about 'the job'. Soon it would be *Rainbow Days* and *Scoopy Doo* then *Neighbours*, *Noel's Telly Years*, *Capital Woman*, *Watchdog*, *Talking Telephone Numbers*, *Wowser*, *Stunt Dawgs*, *Rosie and Jim*, *Silvester and Tweety*, *Mork and Mindy*, *Jonathan Dimbleby*. He tried to look forward to a programme about the Dandie Dinmont terrier. He tried not to think about 'the job'.

'You're not dying,' said Rupert. 'Come on. We're going out.'

Fresh air would revive him and it would remove them from Neville, which was a priority until the Ativan kicked in. He wrapped Shorty in a tartan travel rug, lifted him up, and carried him to the bench which stood on the outskirts of the caravan park and looked out to the grey sea below. A sign announced that they were in a Designated View. The public were welcome to take photographs, free of charge, courtesy of the Bed and Breakfast Corporation of Somerset County.

A cloud floated disconsolately across the sky.

Shorty gazed at the horizon and, after a moment, a tear rolled down his cheek.

Rupert shifted in his seat and opened up the *Encyclopedia of Unusual Sex Practices*. This would cheer Shorty up. It always did.

They had reached Q. 'Queening,' he read, 'refers to the European practice where a dominant female uses a man's head as her throne . . .'

'I am going to die,' said Shorty, rocking in his blanket cocoon. 'I am going to 'ell. 'E's goin' to pay me back for all them . . . them . . .' He thought for a moment. What would he be paid back for? '. . . snatched purses.' He paused, reflecting on his life of crime – the siphoned petrol, the car radios, the tea sold as grass, the time that he stole fifty quid from Freddie the Fence. 'I am going to go to a deep dark horror place where there's no women and no booze and no mates and I'll be made to do gardenin' or something. I'll be made to trim the parks, like my brother, he did that. Trimmed the parks when there was nothing to trim. Then I'll get a disease and me winkle'll shrivel up slowly and drop off and be left on the ground for huge boots to trample on. If I'll 'ave no dick then where I'll be?'

'You'll be dead, Shorty. It won't matter so much.'

'Yeah. But I won't be dead will I? I'll be in 'ell, I'll be burnin' in a special 'ell, specially chosen for me personally, Shorty, to give me gip for eternity.' He paused. 'Mind you,' he added gloomily, looking over to the caravan, 'anythin' would be better than livin' with that Antichrist.'

'That's nothing,' said Rupert. 'You should see what I have to live with.'

He outlined the atrocities committed by his mother, and Shorty calmed down. His wheezing abated and he looked impressed as Rupert described a thickset dipsomaniac armed with a sub-machine-gun.

Shorty suddenly felt much better. His sufferings seemed to have been cured by the mere description of this wonderful woman. A pleasing lightness traversed his brow. His nose and throat felt clear for the first time in a month. The pain left his chest. He could breathe. It was a miracle. He nearly threw off his blanket and ran around the field as he felt the poetry rush back into his bosom – the old poetry that was the sign of love. He fired up a filterless Lucky Strike and smoked it with growing excitement. He had not seen this vision of wild abnormality but he knew that when he did he would be consumed by the heat of desire.

'So,' he said, as calmly as lust enabled. 'No boyfriends then?'

'No,' said Rupert. 'She's got no boyfriends. Too old really. And too dangerous.'

'Perhaps she'd like to come over and look after me. I wouldn't mind the danger. You're lookin' at a man who once kissed Big Alex.'

'I don't think so,' said Rupert. 'She passes out a lot.'
This, in Shorty's view, was an advantage.

The holiday-makers who queued to see the caves at Wookey Hole did not know that they were being watched by the most wanted man in Somerset.

Neil spent long days weaving in and out of the groups of tourists. They took photographs of each other, dithered around the Mr Whippy ice-cream stand, bought postcards, enjoyed themselves. The clack and clamour of pleasure was an ugly sight with grating sound-effects. Neil scrutinised them with distaste. His only release from aversion was the prospect of grabbing the prizes that he had chosen for himself. He would take what he wanted when he wanted it because, frankly, *he was owed*. Families. Straights. The public. Where was the pleasure in doing what was expected rather than what one wanted? And what was there to enjoy, here in these grey hours, in the drizzle and cold, shuffling and paying to see geological growths? What was there to enjoy? They were like sheep, buying tickets. Little men. The little British man, a sheep and a slave. The worst. Neil, confident in his superior intelligence, despised them and he hoped that they despised him because to be despised by the little men was an honour. If he was despised then he knew that his energy was not being wasted.

He developed a range of disguises because, loitering every day, he might be noticed by those who were paid to notice, or picked out by a surveillance camera. He did not realize that disguise was unnecessary because his own appearance was disguise enough. A pale, balding male slips easily into a crowd. He can be as invisible as he wishes for there are many like him and the few who do notice him will forget about him an instant later. But Neil, mind always at work, always one step ahead, sometimes loitered in a subtle hair-piece, sometimes in a pin-striped suit, sometimes on a skateboard. Once he attempted to wear a moustache but, during lunch in the cafeteria, it had fallen into a cup of tea and the children on the table next to him broke into a loud round of applause.

Neil could not risk causing a stir. He needed to be able to watch as the families shuffled towards the cash kiosk, paid for their tickets, and ushered their children to the entertainments – the penny arcade, the Victorian carousel, the Hall of Mirrors and the holes themselves, dark and low and distorted with stalagmites.

Neil never followed the lines into the caves as he was claustrophobic and, anyway, stalagmites were not the point of his presence. Robbery was the point of his presence. He concentrated on calculating the numbers of £5 tickets purchased in an hour, on observing the till and finding out what happened to the bundles of notes when the complex closed.

Dogged surveillance revealed useful facts, not least the advanced age of those hired to look after the takings and the punctuality of their schedules.

The 'run' was usually undertaken by one Bert Slade, a man who had banked the Wookey takings for seven years. Neil estimated that at 8.30 am on the morning of May 30, Slade would leave the office with some £45,000. This would be locked in his briefcase and placed on the passenger seat beside him, a habit that he had practised since Neil had started to tail him. Neil knew Slade's routine from the time he left his house, to his ploughman's lunches, to the long hours spent playing darts in the pub. He had traced Slade's route to the bank many times. He knew every hedge and every corner of the A371 to Wells. He knew them better than Slade himself.

May Bank Holiday was the time to strike. There would be three days' worth of cash and it would not be banked until the following Tuesday.

'Oh yes,' the woman in the cafeteria told him. 'May Bank Holiday is our big weekend all right. We get thousands of people, *thousands*! From all over the place, far as Scotland and I don't know where. We broke the record last year. Mind you, the weather was nice.'

She looked at the lad in front of her, she saw manicured nails and tattooed fingers and a shirt as white and as clean as the driven snow, but she did not see an evil genius committed to carrying out the Crime of the Century.

Neil knew that he could have performed the robbery on his own but he was lumbered with three impediments.

Neville and Shorty's flattery, once pleasing, had grown into a cumbersome dependency that was beginning both to compromise his career and endanger his personal safety. Rupert was also of limited use. They were millstones and they would have to be dropped, sooner rather than later, but they would have to be dropped with care and diplomacy. He did not wish to incur their disloyalty – rejection could turn into hatred and hatred could turn into helping the police with their enquiries. But Neville and Shorty had long expended their few advantages. He did not need their pandering. Now he had a larger audience to play to. He had a reputation to live up to and the British people were waiting for show time.

Neil prepared to go to the very top.

Chapter 10

Life at Lucky Bob's Amusement Arcade changed on the day that Jean burst open a bottle of Pomagne and announced that she was pregnant. Anyone who found themselves in her vicinity was now forced to dedicate themselves to all the aspects of her 'condition'. This involved disgusting monologues in which Jean outlined the various mutations her body was experiencing. These, apparently, included the loss of the use of the legs. Rupert spent all day opening and closing doors, drawing curtains, shutting windows 'just a crack'. Jean always seemed to be too hot or too cold and 'shouldn't be getting up and down all the time'.

Her dictatorship was complimented by dreadful commentaries on natural childbirth ('I think I should have some nice music, like Roger Whittaker or something like that'), on the unique genes engendered by the Big Boss's lineage, on the dangers of being scarred and shaved and strung up and sliced open.

Rupert had found Jean unnerving enough when she was

merely frosted and flirtatious but now he was forced to listen to hideous intimacies pertaining to those regions of Jean's body which could only be of interest to paediatricians and Jack the Ripper.

He tried to be polite but her descriptions of crowning made him feel dizzy and he was afraid that he would smash his motor bike into a bollard.

Jean's 'condition' was, as yet, only in its fourteenth week, but she was already eating enough for three people. 'If you can't eat when yer up the spout when can yer eat?' she had enquired from behind a pyramid of danish pastries.

This nutritional stance had caused her to blow up to twice her normal size and she looked as if the birth was imminent.

Pastries did not provide Jean with enough strength to work 'in her condition', to the covert fury of the Big Boss who wandered around muttering that he wished he could take a nine-month holiday.

'You'll be running the place soon,' he told Rupert one morning. 'With Jean in her condition, we'll be busy, not sleeping and everything and Shul be on the warpath makin' us buy carseats and God nose wot. I don't know where the money's goin' to come from, I really don't. She's gone shoppin' mad the woman and she's eating six meals a day. Look at the size of 'er!'

'She'll lose the weight,' said Rupert.

'I dunno,' said the Big Boss. 'At her age – it'll be difficult. I tell you. I've 'ad enough and It's not even here yet.'

'It,' said Rupert. 'What about a name?'

'Shul be going on about calling it Albertine after their mother. Jean wants Sean if it's a boy. I'm not enterin' into it. I tell you, I'm worried sick as it is. What if It looks like *her* side, poor little blighter?'

He stomped down to the basement to unpack a delivery of souvenirs.

Rupert was sitting in the kiosk when Neville slouched in. He placed his thin lips at the hole in the window.

'We need a gun,' he hissed.

Rupert stared. They were going to kill somebody. He hoped it wasn't going to be him.

'And we know your mother has got one.'

'It'll be difficult.'

Rupert knew, in fact, that stealing the Heckler and Koch from his mother would be a simple matter of timing. She passed out regularly and, during these hours, was so deeply comatose that one could have removed her head without any hindrance. Nevertheless, she had become more dangerous of late. She was insisting that an American had stolen Ian's remains from his grave and was using them to conduct medical research. She claimed that it was only a matter of time before the American would need a human body and, driven by ambition, he would come for her. She had read a book entitled *Advanced Mantrapping Techniques* and now she spent every day standing at the window, like a sentry, gun at the ready, waiting for the fictitious research scientist to arrive. Then the Special Brew would overcome her and her body would suddenly slump to the floor.

The gun would be easy to take.

'Neil planning a big job?' he asked casually.

'Yeah.'

Neville did not know what Neil was planning but he was not going to admit this to Rupert.

'Anything tonight?' Rupert said.

'Nah. Bank Holiday Nil sez.'

'Shorty better?'

'Better than wot? A dose of the clap?'

'You know what I mean.'

'Nah. Worse if anythin'. 'E escaped last night, to get chips he said. Rained on him and now 'e's coffin and spittin all over the shop and course I get it from Nil.'

Rupert tried to look sympathetic.

Neville's lips clamped tight.

'So you'll bring us the gun then?'

'I suppose so.'

'I'll tell Nil you'll bring it then.'

'Right.'

Neville slunk out, glaring at anyone who made the mistake of catching his eye.

Three days later Neil unveiled his masterpiece to Neville and Rupert.

They were sitting around the formica table in the kitchenette. Neville, uncomfortably situated on a collapsible camping stool, was taut with anxiety. Hundreds of television wars were coming to life. He saw mud and mad colonels and guerrilla 'gooks' creeping about in the shadows of the jungle. Neil was about to involve them in a massacre.

Neil lovingly caressed six pounds of lightweight, air-cooled, cold-hammer forged metal. This would transport him to the realms in which he was destined to travel. He shouldered the machine-gun, looked through the telescopic sight and swung it around the room. Neville ducked. Rupert laughed.

'It's not loaded,' he said. 'I couldn't find the ammo. She must've hidden it somewhere.'

'Not much good without the ammo, is it?' Neil sneered, fiddling with the selector lever. The strip-light cast shadows under his eyes and exaggerated the unhealthy pallor of his skin. His mouth, pink and fleshy, relaxed into its customary grimace of disapproval.

Rupert did not answer but he disagreed. The MP5 was perfectly good without the ammo. It presented the threat that would be required by any robbery but it did not present Neil with the means to murder anybody. He drummed his fingers on the table, stared into space and hoped that the plan did not involve another backgammon set.

'How do you clean it then?' said Neil.

'Lord knows,' said Rupert. 'Never seen her do it.'

Neil placed the gun gently on the floor and flicked an invisible particle of dust from the ordnance survey map of the A371 that he had spread over the table. He indicated the spot where Bert Slade's Ford Escort could be stopped. 'Neville,' he said, 'You'll park yer bike there, about four hundred yards behind, and signal if there's any oncoming traffic. Rupert, you'll do the same from the front. That way we'll be covered . . .'

'What about Shorty?' said Rupert.

He knew that neither Neil or Neville would consider Shorty's welfare and he felt that someone should look out for him. He was as helpless as an animal wounded in the middle of the road.

Neil suddenly glared at him with undisguised loathing. As his jaw stiffened with hostility, Rupert was reminded of Loopy de Luxe's second-in-command, the putrified Mask of Id. Frank emotion rarely unsettled Neil's features. This abrupt appearance of a personal vendetta was disturbing but

Rupert knew, as Dan the Man always knew, that it was only a matter of time before this new demon showed his fatal flaws, and when he revealed them, the mighty Man would overcome and ensnare him. *Kick. Kick. Thrust. Forward.* The Mask of Id would fall under a sophisticated strategy of attack, and when he fell, he would have nowhere to go.

A pathetic utterance, somewhere between a sob and a croak, emanated, as if on cue, from the bunk-bed at the back of the trailer.

'Fuckin' defect,' Neville muttered.

'What about Shorty?' Neil rasped. ''E'll 'ave to stay 'ere *obviously*, unless you wanna hang 'im on yer charm bracelet.'

'What you gonna do, Nil?' Neville said in the reverent tone of one who wished to convey that they were aware of Neil's eminence.

Neil held up the Heckler & Koch, his face an expression of triumphant moral insanity.

Neville felt the chill of the slab in his own morgue. He poured a shot of whisky into a paper cup and lifted it to his lips with trembling fingers.

'I'm gonna grab the cash,' Neil said in his bored monotone. 'Peasy.'

Peasy it was.

Even Neville was surprised at how easy it was to earn £45,000 in two minutes.

There was no traffic on the road. Bert Slade appeared at 8.36 am, driving at 30 mph, as Neil had said he would. The old man stopped the car the instant that he saw Neil in the middle of the tarmac. Faced with the twenty-six inch barrel of a weapon capable of firing eight hundred rounds a minute he handed over the brief-case as quickly as he was physically able.

Neil blindfolded him and handcuffed his wrists to the steering wheel. Then he strapped the briefcase on to the back of the Kawasaki, signalled to the others, and they returned, by separate back roads, to a copse in the middle of a forest. They hid the bikes, split up and, using different routes, walked back to the caravan park.

Bert Slade was released some thirty minutes later when, by banging his forehead against the horn, he managed to attract the attention of a passing motorist.

He was unable to provide the local CID with many details. He had not seen the gang's faces, or their motor bikes. He suspected that the leader was in his twenties, and he thought that he had smelled a leather jacket, but he had been confused. 'So would you be,' he told DI Rexroat, 'if you were driving along minding your own business and some maniac jumped out and threatened to murder you.'

He did not even know how many there were, there could have been two, there could have been ten, all he knew was that the gun looked like one of those 'on the telly' and that he was looking forward to his retirement.

Mrs Slade later went on the *News at Ten* expressing gratitude that her husband had not attempted to 'be a hero'. Forty-five thousand pounds was all very well, she said, but it wouldn't buy her a new husband, would it?

The *News at Ten* edited out Mrs Slade's further details about her daughter (Kylie) and length of time in Weight Watchers (eighteen years).

The following day the 'Wookey Snatch' appeared on the front of the quality newspapers and on page five of the tabloids.

Miles Falconbridge called an emergency meeting between the Bed and Breakfast Corporation and representatives of the police department. They agreed to print a thousand 'public information' posters warning drivers that 'an armed gang known as the Highwaymen' were operating in the locality. Drivers were advised to keep their doors locked and report all hitchhikers to the police. A reward of £2,500 would be paid for information that led to an arrest.

That evening the mobile clone phone rang in the trailer and a voice informed Neil that he was head-hunting for a London 'business man'. There were chances of promotion and the money was very good – $12.3 million to be exact.

Neil knew the 'business man'. Fatty Baba had once employed him to burn down a café on behalf of the Kurdish Workers' Party. Now he was the head of a Turkish syndicate and one of the ten Euro-Villains most wanted by Interpol.

Neil had arrived.

Neville knew that something was up because a contortion embraced Neil's features and he realized, with a shock, that it was a smile. It revealed a melange of uneven broken teeth that he had never seen before.

They counted cash late into the night. Neil sat at the head of the formica table. Spurting mists of apple-scented room spray into the air, he gingerly doled out the money. A pair of latex surgeon's gloves protected his hands from the dirt engrained on the limp notes but they did not prevent his mind wandering to all the filthy fingers that had touched them.

In Neville's opinion Shorty's absence from the job negated him from a share of the proceeds. Neil, however, knew that granting Neville and Shorty financial independence was necessary if he wished to escape from them. Shorty knew too much. His silence had to be bought.

'We're all in this together,' he told Neville. 'Shorty's done other jobs wivus and it weren't 'is fault he couldn't come on this one.'

'Yeah. But he dint take none of the risks,' said Neville sulkily. ''E should get less.'

Rupert had wrapped Shorty in the tartan blanket and placed him at the table so that he could enjoy the sight. The yellow bristles on his huge head had collapsed and now lay flat on his scalp. His skin had turned grey and thin lines had appeared around his mouth. His eyes, half-closed, had lost the glint that so many women had misconstrued as courtly love. His head lolled. He was exhausted.

'Why?' he wheezed. 'I'm an accessory. I could go dahn for years just for sittin' 'ere and lookin' at your ugly mug.'

'Yeah!' said Neville. 'Look at ya – no good to anyone sitting there with yer big 'ed and no legs – ya look like a Pez dispenser.'

'Shut it, both of you,' Neil snapped. 'It goes four ways and that's final.'

There was a silence as each mind engaged in private thoughts. The caravan was small, it pushed them together, forcing them to converge and be close to one another. Now they all sat, elbow to elbow, leg against leg, foot on foot, breath on breath, but the distance between each individual was immeasurable.

Neil focused on his promotion. He had been instructed to put on a suit and go to Surrey as soon as possible. Mr Baba wanted a meeting. Neil knew that if the planned operation was successful it would forge links with crime syndicates all over the world. As Mr Baba's representative, he would become part of a network that stretched from New York to the desert emirates.

Neville did not know how much longer he could carry on. Southern Comfort and Temazapam had helped him through the Wookey 'job' but he had had enough. The stress was killing him. The money meant nothing. It did not buy peace of mind and it did not buy Neil's trust. Neville had become accustomed to succumbing to the whims of a higher intellect but now exclusion and secrecy were beginning to wear him down. His only pleasure arose from the thought that Shorty might die which would mean that they could leave this bastarding hell-hole for ever.

Shorty was still wracked with symptoms but he was most excited. £11,250 in used fivers was a lot of money. He heaped up the piles, made them into rolls, and tied them with elastic bands. There were fifty in all, fifty pleasing paper cylinders that could be worn with ease around his body. They poked through his clothes and gave him a lumpen look, like an old sock full of walnuts according to Rupert, but they rubbed against his tiny crevices with a stimulating sensory intimation that spoke of many fantasies and brought him hope.

Shorty knew that his life would be enlivened by this easy win. Big wads attracted high-class totty – proper totty of the type one saw in magazines and on the arms of old men.

Now he could buy the perfect love-life full of genuine nymphomaniacs. There would be dream beavers, Latin beauties, hard thighs, exotic strippers and nineteen-year-old centrefolds. There would be topless hostesses and 36DD breasts. A tanned and flawless playmate would beg him to ram her cave and a Scandinavian fantasy dancer would let him rub her until she was on fire. Mud wrestlers would perform privately. Highly creative schoolgirls would roll about on rubber sheets. Samantha would do it any place any time. Bianca would be kinky and flexible. They would all be open-minded, wild, willing, young and playful. Money could buy pure sex and no commitment. Money, in other words, could buy happiness.

Rupert had already pledged his share to Serenity Hall. A duty officer had told him that he had done 'the right thing' and that an Intervention Team was on its way to collect his mother.

And so, his purpose fulfilled, Rupert resigned from the gang.

'I'm not suited to life as an outlaw,' he told them. 'I'm going to accept the Big Boss's offer of promotion and become manager of Lucky Bob's Amusement Arcade.'

Neil pursed his lips, stood up, and started wiping surfaces with Mr Kleen.

He was offended, and to offend Neil was to ignite a range of abreactions.

He slowly removed the latex gloves and studied his nails which, square and white, were, as always, free of particle and pollutant.

Rupert had transgressed. Neil had permitted his inclusion and Rupert had not observed the codes introduced by this privilege. He seemed oblivious to all the undercurrents of Neil's authority. Respect was the currency that counted in Neil's realm. He should have been courted and flattered by his employee, courted and flattered and asked for permission. He should have been the one to sever the alliance – an announcement presented as a *fait accompli* was as respectful as a kick in the groin.

Neil tossed his head in the air and flounced from the caravan. The door shut behind him with a cold click.

Rupert's announcement afforded Neville a pleasure that he had not experienced since Shorty contracted crabs from an aromatherapist in Dollis Hill. The creep was out. Out of grace, out of the caravan, out of their faces. He would have cheered out loud if it had not been for the sight of Neil's displeasure.

Rupert shrugged his shoulders, put his share of the money in a pocket in his leather jacket and picked up the machine-gun.

'Well,' he said. 'I'm off.'

'You fuckin' borin' git,' Shorty panted, his small chest heaving up and down. 'We were just gettin' goin'.'

Chapter 11

Karl Künterbunt was German. This was not his fault, but it was his fault that seventy suitcases were piled on the narrow pavement outside the Blackmore Hotel. None of these (except the camera cases) belonged to Karl himself. He did not need luggage because he wore clothes, bought in Gap, that he threw away as he travelled from country to country. He rarely visited a place where there wasn't a Gap so his attire (white T-shirt and white chinos) was always assured. He could stroll from immigration desk to limousine with the relaxed gait of one who pays three boys to carry his equipment.

Today Karl's entourage numbered fourteen individuals, two thirds of whom were semi-hysterical and all of whom were telling Miles Falconbridge exactly what they wanted, when, and, because they were in analysis, why.

Some were named Chip, others would become 'less creative' if they did not have a window that looked on to that 'cute sea'. Some refused to share with Vendela, because she was only an assistant, others would lose a $1.5 million cosmetics contract if they were not provided with a fax machine. Everyone wanted to know 'what money you use in this country?' and whether the water was safe. There were questions about low-sodium diets and caffeine-free beverages and the location of the restrooms and ice-making machines. One gargantuan woman told Miles, quite unnecessarily, that her folks lived in Kansas and her pop had started an incest survivors group. A shrill Jamaican asked where the nearest leather bar was.

The fact that they had all been allocated rooms prior to their arrival held no sway. The domiciles had to be reshuffled to coordinate with a self-contained infrastructure, bizarre and incomprehensible to any member of the outside world, but of inestimable significance to those who worked in 'fashion'.

Miles Falconbridge was confused. Everybody seemed to think that they were more important than everybody else and there was no way of judging who was correct. A man with a quiff and a trunk full of mascara seemed to hold exalted status judging by how many people were offering him chewing-gum, but a magnificent Adonis dressed in an Armani suit was 'only a model and hadn't even done *GQ* yet'.

Struggling to conform to the rites of this tribe, he was relieved to see Clive's tanned features. At least a mutual language could now be spoken,

Clive's status was complicated but it was understood by those around him. As Karl's Number 2 he was in charge of administration, which created the impression that he was possessed of both influence and prestige. This image was misleading. The most powerful men were the three who represented Hatch Hamstone – his vice-president, a vice-president of the advertising agency, and an Art Director. The first two were paying the bills and the third had to be satisfied if any future jobs were to be forthcoming.

Confident that they would be handed the most beautiful suites, the trio stood apart from the wrestling crowd and waited to be handed their keys.

Clive took over the allocation of rooms as he always took over the allocation of rooms. He had allocated rooms in the Aliki Hotel on the Greek island of Symi and he had allocated rooms at the Georges V in Paris; he had arranged suites in the Masai Mara and penthouses in Gstaad and he had fought foreign nabobs for a view over Lake Pichola in Rajasthan. The technicalities of these arrangements fell into the whimsical load that formed his job description – they defined him and validated him.

He followed the rule that had saved him many times and in many different countries. Karl, the Hatch Hamstone vice-presidents and himself were placed on a floor above the lower orders thus creating a concrete symbol of the hierarchy. Hair, Makeup, Styling, models, assistants and Brent were placed on floors below them so that they were, in every sense of the word, beneath them.

Finally everybody installed themselves and, after a blast of calls for room-service, the silence of the jet-lagged descended.

Clive lay on his bed with a lavender scented towelette on his forehead.

He had a bad feeling about this shoot,

The auguries of disaster had already manifested themselves.

Hair was definitely on smack.

A vice-president had overheard Styling describe the peasant collection as 'Beyond Hidierama', setting up a relationship that was still strained.

Karl (flustered after a meeting with his accountant) had informed Clive on the plane that he did not wish to talk to the Art Director at all. If there had to be communication he would write handwritten notes which Clive would have to deliver.

The models, Tythe and Storm, refused to speak to each other which was a sign that they either wanted to sleep together or once had.

Brent, meanwhile, had taken to wearing a full Native American costume that included chamois leather with tassels, feather head-dress and a small tomahawk.

He told everyone who would listen that his grandparents were pure Oglala and that his ancestors, who came from the buffalo plains, hailed from the Teton tradition of honour and spirituality. They had fought for their rights with Crazy Horse himself. Enacting the suggestions outlined by Handsome Longhair in his book *Unleashing the Medicine Man* he now carried a suede bag which contained seaweed and caused a smell of rotting fish to hang around him.

The customs officers at Heathrow had held them up for two hours while they examined Brent's sacred equipment, a suspicious selection of dogwood, hawk feathers, masks, smudging bowls, prayer-sticks, beads, bells, and animal tails.

'Your father manages a Thrifty superstore in Albuquerque,' Clive observed acidly. 'You've never even been on a reservation. What do you need all those, those ... acorns for?'

'My totem is the squirrel,' Brent explained. 'Symbol of good-nature, curiosity and reason.'

'Burning sage-brush in the non-smoking section of a Boeing 707 is not the sign of reason,' Clive retorted. 'And neither is telling people in the first-class cabin that they stole your land.'

'The white man is a thief,' Brent replied. 'I am a direct descendant of Rain-in-the-Face and my destiny is to unlock the secrets of my forefathers, enhance my personal identity, and spread *Hokshichankiya*, the spiritual power of the Oglala.'

Clive wished that Brent's ancestors had been Canadian Blackfoot – at least then he would be forced to perform their practise of attaching skewers to their bodies and pulling until they tore themselves to shreds.

'Ver is the girl?' Karl enquired the next morning. 'And ver is the nearest Gap?'

Clive dispatched an assistant to Taunton to ascertain the answer to the second question – to the first he lied.

'She'll be here tonight, Karl.'

'Vell I hope so. Ve should start shooting tomorrow and I don't like that ... that ...'

He waved his hand as blue eyes rolled above a golden beard.

'Storm?' said Clive.

'The girl?'

'Storm.'

'She's no good. The eyes ...'

Karl crossed his own eyes to indicate that he was under the impression that one of the most beautiful girls in the world had a squint. She did not have a squint; if anyone

169

needed to see an oculist it was Karl, but Clive did not voice these observations.

'Ve need a better girl. A girl without (Karl shivered) eyes . . .'

'We could always put them out,' Clive muttered under his breath, 'with red-hot pokers.'

Miles Falconbridge shrugged evasively when Clive asked him to specify the hour of his daughter's return. The hotelier did not feel up to explaining that Grace had disappeared two days previously on the back of a Norton Commando motor bike.

'Ur. She's not here at the moment,' he said. 'She'll be back soon.'

He knew that he should tell the American that Grace had turned into a freak but words failed him. There were no adjectives to describe her.

Sometimes he saw the flicker of the little girl who had been so easy to please; sometimes he saw his late wife, but mostly he saw a woman that he did not recognize at all. She spoke tongues that he did not understand. Sometimes he would come upon her unexpectedly and her face would register shock, as if she was surprised to discover that he was still alive.

The circle of grotesques who had become her friends did not seem to notice abnormality. They would gather in the bar, wearing Kangol golfing hats and Doc Martens, drink too much and talk about the significance of their past lives.

Her eating and sleeping habits had become erratic. He would hear her rise at dawn and talk to a man who did not exist. She was fixated by minutiae. One day she had seen a pigeon lying on the pavement, half alive, with a broken wing. Collecting a box from the pub, she had returned to the street to find that the bird had gone. Tortured by the possibility that it had been run over, or that it was dying a slow, painful death, she felt the creature's despair as if it were her own. This scene had been followed by a phase of walking barefoot through frost-covered fields in order to look for the pigeon that had escaped her unconditional love.

Now she was bringing cats into the house. Strays. Filthy, thin, semi-wild, limping, blind. Asked where she had found one dusty orange-coloured specimen, she said, 'I got it from a skip – you should be pleased it's only a cat. Some people live in skips you know. Perhaps I'll start bringing them back as well . . .' The more furious he became, the more cats arrived. Everywhere he looked there were whiskers and eyes and noses and tails. When they were not whining for food they were lined up on his best sofa watching reruns of *Miami Vice*.

If this was not enough, he was being blamed for the fact that Somerset had turned into the crime capital of the country. Everyone had forgotten that it was he who had predicted mayhem. Now that mayhem had come to call, fingers were being pointed at him. Bitterness and rancour were beginning to pervade the meetings of the Bed and Breakfast Corporation as hoteliers reported that they were losing business and what did he, as President, plan to do about it?

Grace still had not appeared at lunchtime and Clive began to panic.

He made the mistake of confiding in Brent.

'Don't worry,' he said with sickening serenity, 'just let go.'

'I'll be letting you go if the hag doesn't turn up,' Clive snapped. 'I'll be out of a job.'

Ignominy was crawling closer. He had to bring forth the star of which he had boasted so loudly. If the girl could not be found, Clive knew that he would be held personally responsible for the dissolution of a multi-million dollar campaign and he would be sued by hundreds of people. Faced with a life spent in litigation, he turned to the Somerset Yellow Pages and noted down the numbers of a couple of private detective agencies. Then he dialled a twenty-four-hour Psychic Prediction line (Quality Clairvoyance promised), gave an Irish woman his credit card number and stated the nature of his problem. Clive did not, in fact, believe in the sixth sense. Sixth *non*-sense he called it, but he was desperate. Grace Falconbridge had to be produced and he was willing to examine any clues to her whereabouts.

The Irish woman informed him that he was, without doubt, a typical Virgo. Then she asked for the star sign of the young colleen. Clive put her on call-waiting and rang down to reception.

'What is your daughter's star sign?' he asked Miles Falconbridge.

'I have no idea,' replied the hotelier. 'She was born on February 2.'

'Aquarius,' said the Irish woman.

There was a long silence at the price of £10 a minute then, 'I see a little river trickling by?'

'Jesus. She's drowned.'

'No. She is there and she is all right. There are trees.'

'That sure narrows it down,' said Clive. Where? Where is it?'

'The spirits cannot say specifically, but it's not far . . .'

'Thanks for nothing!'

Clive slammed the phone down.

The Irish woman rang back and asked him out for a drink. She liked masterful men, she told him.

'How did you get this number?' Clive shrieked.

'I'm psychic,' came the smug Dublin burr.

'Well if you ring it again I'll call the police.'

He dropped a Kalmeez herbal sedative, spent four minutes on his facial exercises, and opted for a black ensemble to coordinate with his mood – a pure new wool suit by Cerruti, a lilac shirt and matching tie by Richard James, black wraparound shades by Kirk Originals. Leaping down the stairs to reception he drew himself up to his full height (six foot one) and stood staring at Miles Falconbridge, hoping that the combination of the suit and shades would frighten the hotelier into submitting the full truth.

'How long has Grace been gone?' he said.

The landlord, momentarily overpowered by the smell of Eau de Guerlain, sneezed and then pursed his lips.

'Ohh,' he said, whistling. And then again. 'Ooh . . . Two days?'

'Two days!' Clive's life passed in front of his eyes. 'Two days! She could be in New Zealand.'

'Oh I don't think so,' said Falconbridge. 'Why would she want to go there? She may be with her friends at Robbers Bridge, they've got a camp there in the Oare Valley.'

'Do you know what any of them are called?' asked Clive. 'The, ur, friends?'

'There is one named Lex,' Miles answered. 'I don't know the surname.'

Miles Falconbridge still found it difficult to believe that

people like Lex were real. He would have been less surprised to look out of his window and find that an ostrich was living in his garden. 'Hi Dad,' Lex had said when Grace introduced them. Then the disgusting woman had kissed him on the mouth. He had managed to show no surprise at this revolting gesture but, after they had left, he had drunk three straight whiskies and cleaned his teeth. An ostrich would have been preferable to Lex. Characters like Lex bought a shift to the status quo and the last few months had seen more shifts than Miles Falconbridge wished to entertain.

'What does he look like?' Clive asked.

'She,' corrected Falconbridge. 'She is big.'

'How do ya mean?'

'You know . . .' Miles swung his arms to indicate bosoms. 'Big,' he repeated.

'Anything else?'

She has a knife scar on her neck.'

Clive began to feel the need for another Kalmeez. Grace had been kidnapped by some kind of Riot Grrrl and this dingbat had simply let her go.

'Anything else?'

'Leather jacket.'

Robbers Bridge had become a popular site for those attracted by the legend of the Highwaymen. The tribes had gathered. There were children, dogs, ghetto-blasters and litter.

Clive hopped and ducked through an obstacle course of washing lines and camp fires.

'Do you know Lex?' he asked a dreadlocked youth who

was wearing a Skunk Anansie T-shirt and sitting cross-legged outside a tepee.

Bloodshot eyeballs stared at the ground.

'Who wants to know?'

'A friend.'

'Lex ain't got no friends. You from the council?'

'Don't be absurd. This suit cost fifteen hundred bucks.' Clive took out his Gucci wallet and removed a £10 note. The traveller took it.

'She's not here. Be back later probably.'

'Well tell her,' said Clive, through lips so tight he could hardly breathe, 'tell her that £250 goes to the person who delivers Grace Falconbridge to the Blackmore Hotel by 7 pm this evening.'

'Grace huh? £250? Well. Shouldn't be difficult.'

The traveller's sunken face creased into an expression of unaffected delight and, suddenly, he laughed. The shrill squawk of a tropical bird pierced the air. It was still piercing the air as Clive walked, with as much dignity as a muddy field would allow, back to his car. He heard the nasty shriek all the way back to the hotel – it was as if the grimy refugee was sitting in the back seat. Clive almost thought he saw the sallow features mocking him in his rearview mirror.

'Jesus,' he told himself sternly. 'Geddagrip.'

There were three hours left and Clive spent them ingratiating himself with Karl. They talked about light and clothes and concepts and then they joined the whole team to tour the area and view locations.

Styling (who could not see that much since she was wearing a veil) announced that everything was neat. Makeup initiated a row with Brent by proclaiming that, 'The Indians weren't that smart. They sold Manhattan to that Dutch arsehole for two beads and they wouldn't have even had trousers if the Eskimos hadn't taught them tailoring.' Hair stuck up for him. 'The war bonnets were cute though. Ah lerv the look with the buffalo horns. Comanche Queen me in!'

The assistants wondered how they were going to get the tripods over a mile of marshland.

At dusk Clive led them all back to the bar and, as he entered, he saw a figure standing in the shadows under the low wooden beams. The silhouette told him that it was Grace. Karl noticed the shape at the same time.

'Is dis hur?' he enquired.

'Yes.' said Clive.

But the apparition that materialized from the gloom was one that he had never seen before. A shrivelled spectre floated before them – a gargoyle that made the skin crawl and the legs want to run for cover.

It was bald, it was grimy and its grey eyes rested calmly underneath two thick black lines that moved in a gruesome morse code over a once beautiful forehead.

Clive could not have felt more brutalized by this ruination if somebody had forced him to smash a Fabergé egg.

He had promised a faery and produced a gremlin.

Tact, diplomacy, dissimilation – all his skills honed by years of use were obliterated by distress.

'Christ!' he shrieked. 'What the fuck have you done to yourself? There's eighteen million dollars riding on this campaign.'

'Is dis hur?' Karl said again.

'Yes.' said Clive.

He saw his Spanish adobe in Laurel Canyon disappear

into the hands of his bank manager. He saw his Ford Explorer driven away by repo men. He saw himself living in a shack in Sun Valley and wearing clothes bought in downtown thrift stores. He saw his Nieman Marcus credit card cut in half and thrown into his face. He saw his skin grow wizened and grey, his hair and teeth fall as one into the gutter and a life in which he would stumble from portal to shelter bed carrying his possessions in an old Tiffany carrier bag.

No one spoke.

The auditorium of artistes and visagistes gazed in silence as the tragedy of Clive's final act was played before them. The curtain was about to fall. Moved by the drama they would pick themselves up and carry on, but the protagonist on the stage before them would not. He was dead.

Clive remembered that he had health insurance. He could arrange to have a serious operation and a long term in hospital.

'She's great.'

The Teutonic tone seemed to echo from beam to lattice window, from rows of beer mugs to shuddering hat stand.

'But Karl . . .' (the Art Director) 'you don't think she's a little, er, wild to be a peasant.'

Karl pretended he had not heard this but he had and it confirmed the instinct upon which he so often relied. All art directors were blind and talentless and to do the opposite of what they said was to assure oneself of originality and creative progress.

'But Karl,' (Hair) 'The hair! There is none!'

'But Karl,' (Makeup) 'The makeup! Those eyebrows! I'm not going to be able to do a Thing. There's no time for laser treatment, you know. Those . . . those . . . what are they? Whatever they are they should be told to stop. Karl! *They will show!*'

'She's not quite as perky as we had hoped,' said one of the vice-presidents.

'Or as pert,' added the other. 'Hatch likes pert. Pert sells in Idaho.'

'There's always touching up,' said the Art Director. 'It's in the budget.'

'She's great,' said Brent.

Brent's opinion could not have held less influence, but he was oblivious to this, as he was oblivious to the truth that his automatic acquiescence was the sole reason that Karl had requested his presence on this trip.

They had to conform. Clive could see Karl's logic. The girl was a Looney Tune but a grungey wild child in Hamstone's pioneer frocks created an interesting juxtaposition that would steer attention away from the dullness of the clothes. It was not beautiful, but it was weird and it was eye-catching. They might (he told the Art Director) get away with it. In black and white.

'But Clive,' the Art Director whispered, 'these pictures have to go in *Vogue*. We're not talking *The Face* here.'

'Do them good,' said Clive. 'About time magazines stopped lying around doing nothing. Time they got up and said something.'

'Yes,' said the Art Director sadly, 'but what are we saying?'

Later, Lex roared with laughter when Grace told her what had happened.

'Well,' she said succinctly. 'That's fashion for ya.'

But Grace was dismayed. She felt humiliated, as if she had tripped on her own shoelaces. She had been sure that her guise of non-compliance would be deprecated by those she disdained. She had hoped to be snubbed and dismissed. But her new self had turned against her. It had been accepted. Now it mocked and danced and told her that she had become the latest uniform. Do not bother to stigmatize yourself, it jeered, do not try to be disowned. No matter what you do you will never be different. Mr and Mrs Mall are out there and they will buy you.

The Hatch Hamstone team rose at 6 am to take the first photograph in Porlock Weir, where the sea was silver with the crystalline cloak of dawn and where the ancient fishing village, bereft of life, looked as it had a hundred years ago.

Makeup asked Grace what she used to wash her face.

'I don't wash my face really,' said Grace.

Makeup applied a thick matt finish to her flawless skin and topped it with the light correcting pigment contained in Chanel's *poudre lumière*. Then Hair created a tall muslin turban and wrapped it around her head so that it stood in a whorled point, like an ice-cream. Styling gave her a simple cotton nightdress and a basket of onions and the German man told her to go and stand in the sea, which was freezing.

The effect cast a silence on the crew. Karl had perverted the landscape to his own decree and produced a singular image with fantastic content.

He was a genius.

Then Karl strolled to the water's edge and, without saying anything, pushed Grace. She fell backwards into the wash and, as she sank down into the cold mud, she stared up at him, the spray dashing her face. Now she had been pushed twice. Two men, two bullies. One man wearing a glass mask, one man wearing a beard. But to be pushed by a man you do not know and to be pushed by a man you know you dislike are two different things. Grace, disconnected, unafraid of death, had not resented Neil's show of force. In Karl, though, she saw the symbol of the trap which she had set for herself – and now she was walking into it, ready to have her stomach torn out.

Hot hatred blazed from her grey eyes and she wiped her hand across her mouth, leaving a smear of lipstick. And so the photograph changed from a lovely mysterious country girl to a wet semi-naked waif crouched like a beaten animal.

Karl walked back up the beach declaring that it was one of the most powerful portraits he had ever taken. He would use it on the cover of his next book.

He was a genius.

Only the Art Director experienced shivers of non-conformist uncertainty. He gathered the Hamstone vice-presidents behind a stone wall for a whispered conference concerning the turban which, he felt, was not in keeping with the simple agrarian effect that Hatch was hoping for.

'He wants clean rustics not punks in weird millinery,' he said. 'I'm not sure that this interpretation of the noble savage is communicating the plain charm of the country-side. It's a look, but is it the look we want?'

The Hamstone suits knew a lot about money. They could draw a graph describing the corporation's gross turnover and they knew exactly how much the scent had brought in last year, but they knew nothing about fashion. Furthermore they were jet-lagged and disorientated and terrified of Karl, who had single-handedly put the Hamstone name on the global map for reasons that neither of them could understand. The symbiosis between Karl and profit was a fact, but it was a fact whose tenets were beyond their ken. They could only accept it and hope that it would continue.

'It's not just about the turban,' the Art Director explained patiently. 'Even if we took the turban off we have a hairless child with tattooed eyebrows. If *Vogue* won't take the ad we've had it. It's curtains for all of us.'

'To my knowledge *Vogue* have never turned down an advertisement,' said the older suit.

'And think of the publicity if they do,' said the other. 'It'd sure be cheap.'

'Let's hope they don't take it,' said his colleague, after a few seconds of mental arithmetic.

The Art Director sighed. Money men were so literal – so unable to sensate the concept and envision the tangibility of its effect, but he relinquished his position on the turban. To fight against it would have been to risk a dramatic exit by Hair who would be followed, in sympathy, by Makeup and Styling. An 'atmosphere' would settle on the shoot and relations with Karl would deteriorate further. The whole group would be on the photographer's side and the Art Director would be left in the lonely desert of the lowly worm. It was not worth it, not on the first day when there was so much to lose.

The turban stayed on.

There were other days. Perhaps one of them would be turban-free. Perhaps one of them would involve a haywain or apple loft or something in keeping with the original marketing strategy that had been brainstormed over a period of four weeks around the conference table in Hatch Hamstone's penthouse suite overlooking Central Park.

'We should use Storm in some pictures,' the Art Director whispered to Clive, 'just in case your girl is too, er, cutting edge.'

'Karl hates Storm,' Clive hissed. 'He says she's got a squint.'

'I doubt somebody costing $30,000 a day would have a squint for Chrissake.'

The Art Director could feel the beginnings of an attack of hypoglycaemia. He wondered if he was contracting diabetes.

'The girl is up for a Yardley campaign. He only hates her because she usually works with Bruce.'

This was true. Karl resented any model that he had not 'discovered', and if this job had been for editorial pages, he would have turned Storm down flat. Only advertising lucre brought a shift in his artistic prejudices and a lowering of his standards.

'I think this new girl is great,' said Clive.

The Art Director knew that Clive was protecting his discovery as well as his own position with Karl.

'The suits aren't sure,' he lied.

But Clive knew that the suits did not have opinions. Their thoughts, if that is what they could be called, would be the result of input from the Art Director. 'Well the suits can tell Karl then,' he said, knowing that they would not dare. 'We can't freak him out now – it's the first shot. Let's see how it goes. The Polaroids are fine.'

He touched the Art Director's arm. The man was alone and British and heterosexual and under pressure. He couldn't help feeling sorry for him.

'Chill out. Hair thinks it's fabulous.'

'He would. He did it.'

'Makeup thinks it's fabulous.'

'She's not paying for it.'

They looked out to sea. Hair, Makeup, Styling, Karl, three assistants (one with a silver light sheet) were all in it, grey water swirling around their knees.

'The dress will be ruined but I suppose that's the least of our problems,' said the Art Director, and stumped off to find someone who wasn't underwater to go and buy him a box of Jaffa cakes.

And so the days rolled into each other. Day after day in which Grace found herself surrounded by those who spoke of the importance of the patent leather pump, the Chaumet necklace, bugle beading, fish-tail pleats, effort dressing, piqué, Uberta Camerana, Arthur Elgort, strappy sandals, accessories in high shine plastic, bolero jackets, body buffing, chunky ribbing, body-moulding, glazed linen, streamlined sportswear and, of course, *The Sixties*!

Grace could not care about these things. She could not comment on the new Calvin Klein clutch. She knew it was nothing and she could not understand how it had come to be something. Aweless, she was now forced into a small place in which she was the only inhabitant and in that small place she was bent double with need because she was subsumed by physical longing and the Highwayman was still absent. The ache made her clasp herself and moan out loud. Emptiness was stretching before her, an emptiness into which she could not step with the optimism with which some are blessed, knowing that uncertainty can support them, because she knew that if she was pushed forward to vicissitudes where the Highwayman did not exist, those vicissitudes would annihilate her. The Highwayman, her vision, was becoming the sum of her inner life and Grace did not know the difference between her inner life and reality, she just waited and waited and wanted. And so, of course, she was never really connected to the hour, or the place, or the Estée Lauder tinsel lip-gloss. She was never really there. Everyone thought she was thick, like all models are thick. They thought she did not speak because she was too stupid to speak. She did not have anything to say.

The photographs were good. Karl soon realized that she was more interesting when she was angry and so he spent hours mocking and insulting her. When they were not working he did not speak to her and because Karl treated her like this, so too did the pack. She was ignored by everyone except one or two of Karl's assistants. They knew the truth about glamour – it was heavy and it rained and the muscles ached. Further, they were younger, they saw the street and they knew that it was full of people like Grace.

One afternoon she drank three beers and said to one of them, 'I do not want to be like these people but I feel as if I should be like them if I am to join the world. But why should I join the world when it's easier not to?' 'I know what you mean,' he said. 'Why do you do it then?' she asked. 'Because it is leading me to do the things that I want to. I have hope.'

There were moments when the hours of withdrawal crazed her and something inside her wished that someone would notice her and like her, love her even, and if someone had been kind to her during these moments she would have compromised and nodded with interest when they talked about their friendship with Cher's acupuncturist.

Creating beauty is a stressful process requiring dedication, stamina and blind optimism. As everyone's nerves began to suffer from the anxiety of artistic effort an air of free-floating angst descended on the team.

Hair and Makeup finished the drugs and became ill-tempered. Makeup started to wear 'Seizure', a new unisex scent whose label insisted that it was composed of orange blossom. Hair stimulated a rift by saying that it was a biohazard, an accusation that Makeup met by doubling the application so that everyone could smell her four streets away. Hair started to screech for mercy every time she appeared and claimed that her fumes were making his eyes bleed. Makeup threatened to take the next plane home.

Clive, the scapegoat for all the ills and angers, found himself in the middle, like Solomon. He managed to introduce the idea of strategic dabbing that would not offend Hair or compromise Makeup, but he knew that Hair was mutinous because he was bored. Grace was bald and there was little for him to do except occasionally 'groom' Tythe and wage a forceful campaign on Karl to allow him to use wigs.

Then Karl suddenly and inexplicably requested a hundred hedgehogs.

Why he had to have hedgehogs and not something easy (and available) like a cow was a question that Clive knew, from long experience, was not worth asking.

He spent long hours on the mobile telephone and eventually tracked down Hog Heaven, a specialist company based in Builth Wells.

'They don't have diseases, do they?' he asked the woman.

'They do,' she said. 'Sometimes they get maggots in their eyes – but don't worry, I'll only bring the healthy ones.'

'I'd be very grateful.'

Brent managed to avoid the crossfire. His only job was to agree with Karl so his days were relatively free. He pottered about, experiencing his authentic Self and surrendering to aliveness. One afternoon, intending to meditate on the ways of the Ancient Ones, he put a tape of didjeridoo and click sticks into his Sony Walkman and set off for a walk down the beach.

It was odd, he thought, how much he had changed. He had once been consumed with a desire to model. He had thought he would die if an agency did not sign him. Now he was satisfied with rituals, dreams and release through drumming.

He wandered away from the water's edge to prevent the salty droplets from spraying his moose-skin moccasins. Immersed in shamanic vibrations, he failed to notice the figure in the leather jacket until he was six feet away from it.

It was hurling stones into the sea but it was not plucking small flat pebbles and flicking them to make them skip gracefully over the water's surface, it was launching boulders.

Neville lifted the rocks with two hands raised above his head and heaved them so that the missiles dragged his body forward. They crashed into the sea ejecting a spray like the explosion of an underwater mine.

His life, to date, had been rough, nomadic and hungry, but, in a curious way, it had also been sheltered, for the boundaries surrounding it were tight. In the absence of any education, his knowledge derived entirely from the programmes he watched on television. He had seen little except sitcoms, pubs and the edges of nameless roads.

These narrow experiences had not prepared him for the sight of a Red Indian walking along the beach.

There was no time to run. The Indian had seen him and it would have looked suspicious to leg it.

He hoped fervently, since the empty beach stretched out for miles, that the Indian would respect his privacy and give him a wide berth. He hoped that he was not one of those people who sat next to you when the rest of the bus was empty.

He was.

The Indian walked straight up to him, as if drawn by a magnet. Neville could hear the muted buzz of his Walkman and almost feel the brush of his feathers on his face.

The Indian removed the headphones from his ears.

'Hi.'

He put out his palm face up in the traditional greeting of the Oglala tribe.

Neville's face folded into a horrible scowl.

'Ya look like a cunt,' he sneered.

'How fabulous,' thought Brent. He hadn't seen anything so attractive for weeks – the straggling mane, the oriental features, the studded leather jacket. He felt swept away.

'Do you want to have sex?' he said.

'Pardon?'

'I said, do you want to have sex?'

Neville had imagined that one day he would probably be persuaded to engage in physical intimacy, but he had not imagined that it would be with a Red Indian.

He looked nervously around for a camera crew. He had seen this kind of practical joke played on people on the television.

'Are you joking?' he mumbled, flushing.

Brent had always been stimulated by timidity.

'No,' he said.

'But I don't even know you.'

'So?'

The Red Indian lifted his chin and kissed him on the mouth.

Suddenly Neville wanted sex very much indeed and sex is what he got – full-throttled, rigorous, uninhibited, beautifully paced, there on the shingle where the whisper of the sea finally mingled with the vast cheer of his first mutual orgasm.

'I'm Brent,' said the Indian, doing up the tassels on the front of his suede trousers. 'Let's go for coffee.'

They bonded in a teashop in Porlock.

Brent lit up a hand-crafted prayer pipe and disappeared behind a billowing cloud of acrid smoke. Waving away the waitress who bolted towards him with a fire-extinguisher, he talked about himself for a full hour. His soliloquy covered a booger mask he had made out of a hollowed-out hornet's nest, the misery of working in a Thrifty superstore in Albuquerque, why two hundred Miniconjou tribesmen had died at the Battle of Wounded Knee, his various auditions, Geronimo, peyote, bourbon, and the quest to find the purpose of his soul.

He said he had spent many evenings calling out to Underwater Panther until, finally, he had been blessed with a vision. His late Aunt Soo had appeared carrying a (symbolic) stick topped with eagle feathers and followed by Tsistu, the rabbit spirit.

'She bought the Band of Hope, the bracelet that she left me in her will, and do you know what she said?' Brent asked.

'No,' said Neville.

'Why aren't you married yet?'

Clive would have described this narrative as pathological narcissism, but Neville was mesmerized by these revelations. Here was an individual who could scatter secrets without fear of retribution. His candour was awe-inspiring. He did not seem to care what anybody thought. Neville was entranced. As the American breezed on and on, knowing it was his inalienable right to do so, Neville's defences began to fall away. Intoxicated by the joy of love and liberated by sexual expression, it was as if a plug had been removed. His life began to shoot out in a geezer.

He told Brent things he had never told anybody. He told Brent everything.

Slowly (at first) the depressing saga of Neville's life emerged through mouthfuls of organic scone. How he had (unsuccessfully) tried to rob the till in his father's Take-Away, how he had slept rough in Leicester Square. Then, gathering momentum, he 'confessed' (and exaggerated) the details of his activities in the Soho underworld. Now, he whispered, he was hiding from the Law. He could not (for Brent's own safety) reveal his mates' identities but Brent was led to believe that 'Nil' was Sam Giancana, while the other members of the gang were 'fuckin' wallies who do what me 'n' Nil tell 'em'.

Tales of illegality were novel to Brent. Novel and sexy. He wondered if Neville had ever been on the game. He wondered if he smoked crack. He wondered what he would look like in a dress.

By the time Brent returned to the hotel at 5 pm he was 'in a relationship'.

And Neville was in love.

'Where the fuck have you been?' said Clive.

'Getting laid,' said Brent.

'Typical!' Clive spat. 'Jesus. Why can't I get laid?'

He looked murderous.

Brent described the drama to Hair (swearing him to secrecy as he did so) and Hair immediately told Styling. Styling told her assistant, adding a few details of her own, and, within hours, the murmur of a confidence swelled to the whisper of gossip and thence to the full shout of a story which bore little relation to the original revelation.

It quickly got back to Brent via Makeup that the whole crew was talking about his gang-bang on the beach with seventeen local Hell's Angels.

Brent did not resent being the centre of a mini-scandal. He liked being talked about. It made him feel as if he was providing entertainment and thus serving a purpose. He would probably be famous one day and attention was useful in practising to cope with this destiny.

He had asked Hair to be discreet not because he thought he would be but out of loyalty to Neville who had been so nervous as, whispering his life story, he had looked about the teashop as if enemies were all around.

Dinner at the hotel that night was a convivial affair ennervated by two photographs that everyone (except Grace) thought were fabulous. Everyone felt touched, to some extent, by this fabulousness because they had all contributed to it.

The Art Director felt calmer because Karl had agreed to shoot Storm in a pink pie-crust affair the next day.

Karl was confident that in Grace he had a new 'star'. She simply had 'it'.

Clive had placed £120 worth of serum ampoules on his eyes and the effect had been to make him look five years younger.

Hair, Makeup and Styling had found some Ecstasy and would have had a good time in Rwanda.

The assistants and Grace excused themselves from dinner. The former, exhausted from heaving and placating, lay in a heap on one bed where they rolled joints, made long-distance telephone calls, played with the trouser press and flicked the remote control pads.

Grace sat alone in her room staring into space and thinking about the Highwayman. The knight errant. Every hour until his arrival was only a waiting period in a semi-lit room full of people to whom she could not speak and who would never understand. *'Please* give him to me,' she shouted out loud. 'I want him.'

Floating about with mineral water, salad platters and the mien of one who offers a personal service, Miles Falconbridge could not help overhearing the talk of Brent's gang of bike boys and their mysterious headquarters.

He rang the incident room at Minehead police station and told the inspector on duty that he had information that the Highwaymen were still in the area, possibly in Porlock itself, and it would be worth their while keeping an eye on a young man dressed as an Apache.

If the CID inspector had not been familiar with the voice of the President of the Bed and Breakfast Corporation he might have dismissed the tale of Red Indians as a hoax. But he thanked him for his call and the next day, when Neville picked Brent up on his motor bike, neither noticed the presence of an unmarked police car following them as they walked, hand in hand, through the dramatic purple headland.

Later that evening, Neville returned to the caravan to discover that Shorty had died.

The body lay on the bottom bunk. It looked, at first, as if it was asleep rather than absent of life. But the mouth gaped open and the face lay to one side with the neck twisted at an unnatural angle.

Neville knelt down and listened to the chest because he had once seen Stratford Johns do it on *Z Cars*.

Neil was ironing.

'He's dead,' he said. 'Died about an hour ago.'

'You couldn't revive him then.'

'Didn't try.'

'Good.'

Neville noticed that the small coils of cash that once stuck out of Shorty's clothes had been removed.

'We'll have to get rid of the body.'

'Yeah. Early tomorrer.'

'What about his, er, effects?'

'Dint 'ave any did he?' said Neil. 'I found a book full of writing and crap, looked like shite so I threw it out with his dirty magazines and fags. It's just the body now . . .'

'We'll have to stay the night wivit then.'

'Yeah. Well at least there won't be that bloody coffin' and racket all night. We might get some kip at last.'

'Well. 'Es not heavy. We could just throw him over the cliff inter the sea. Or chop him up into little bits, put him into rubbish bags and put it in the . . .'

Neville was beginning to enjoy himself but Neil interrupted him.

Might arouse suspicion. We'll bury the body first thing tomorrer. I know a place in the woods – near where we hide the bikes.'

At last they were free. Shorty's illness had incarcerated them, they could neither desert him or move him, but now they could leave. Leave Somerset, leave the heat, do as they wished. Neville, new to the decision-making process, floundered for a few minutes as options spread before him. He could not see his future exactly, and would not have been able to describe it, but Brent was his life and Neville would follow him wherever he went. This would mean leaving Neil and he did not know how to break the news. Neil needed him. He would be gutted.

Neville had spent three years ensuring the Neil was never inconvenienced. He had managed to prevent distress, but now he was going to cause it. Neil, in a clean environment, surrounded by beer and flattery, was calm, but, jealous and wounded, he presented a dangerous prospect.

As Neville tried to find the words that would describe his departure in the least offensive way, his perspiring fingers closed around the knife in his back pocket. He was ready to defend himself.

There was a short silence marked by the creaking of the ironing board. Neville noticed that Neil was pressing his best shirt.

'Whatcha gonna do in the, er, future?' he asked.

Neil would have liked to have been able to boast to Neville about the sophisticated counterfeit operation with which he was about to become involved. He would have liked to drop hints about Mr Baba and the Turkish syndicate, but he knew that the risks were too high.

'Er. I've got some plans.' He pushed a button and a

geyser of steam shot into the air. He brought the iron carefully down on a pair of silk socks.

'I'm going to London,' he said.

'I might stay 'ere,' said Neville.

Neil put the iron down with a thud and looked at him. He was genuinely surprised.

'Not 'ere in the caravan, 'ere in town,' Neville continued.

'Why?'

Neville blushed.

'Ur, I've met someone.'

Neil did not like Neville and he hoped that he would never see him again, but he was accustomed to his unquestioning devotion. He had assumed that Neville and his complicity were permanent. He was relieved to hear that they were not, but he was curious to know how he had been so easily displaced. He had never seen Neville talking to a woman unless she was in some way connected with Shorty. And here he was, suddenly in the throes of passion.

'Christ,' he said. 'That was quick.'

'Yeah.'

'Well watchyaself down 'ere, the heat'll be around.'

Later, Neville fried some samosas and they finished a box of white wine that Shorty had stolen from Tesco.

'Only useful thing 'e ever did,' said Neville.

'Yeah,' said Neil, pushing the Lint Pick-Up roller up and down his sleeve, where there was no lint.

'Knowing 'im, 'e'll haunt us,' said Neville nervously. 'Perhaps we should leave the light on.'

'Don't be thick,' said Neil.

Neil did not relish the idea of sleeping with a decomposing health hazard but they could not risk leaving the body outside. They would have to live with it for eight hours and risk contamination. This was quite a high risk considering the state of Shorty's health. His blood had been so full of toxins and his skin so alive with hives, they would be lucky if they were not attacked by any one of a number of vermin. He scrubbed himself down with Heavy Duty Ultra Pine-O-Sol (with anionic surfactants and hypochlorite bleach) and wrapped himself in cling film. Then he put a gauze mask on his mouth and the latex gloves on his hands, took one of the sleeping pills provided by Rupert and passed out.

Wincing and wide-eyed, Neville lay on his bunk listening to Neil's breath and the faint crackle made by his protective outer garments. He envied his ease.

The dark hours did not bring respite. As he cringed and trembled he thought he could hear Shorty mewing for help. He was sure that Shorty was not in fact dead but had achieved a realistic coma in order to con them. The stunted creep planned to savage them in their beds and then steal the money. Shorty had always been cunning. At dawn, when inertia did finally arrive, Shorty appeared in a nightmare. He was standing on a podium surrounded by women wearing jewellery. He was wearing a dinner jacket and reciting his poetry in a loud deep baritone with which he had never been equipped in real life.

I met you in the Queen's Head
And then we went to bed.
I found it ironic
That you only drank tonic.

The women stood up, clapping and cheering. One ran up on to the stage and kissed him and, as she did so, Shorty's face fell apart into a congealed mass of rotting flesh and Neville ran screaming from the auditorium.

The police department decided that a 'flaming dodgy girls' blouse' riding a Yamaha without a number-plate constituted enough evidence to stage a raid.

To this end two CID inspectors, twelve uniformed officers, one Alsatian, two police cars and a van arrived in the caravan park at 8.30 am.

DI Rexroat found himself in the front of the queue and rapped firmly on the door. Then he kicked it in while several of his colleagues circled the caravan site shouting at each other through megaphones.

The fresh smell of pine that wafted into nine pairs of nostrils did not signify heinous activity.

The policemen bundled into the neat caravan. Their bodies, constricted by space, rubbed uncomfortably against each other and it was difficult to discern visual detail as each man's line of vision was impeded by the massive shoulder in front of him. However, it quickly became clear that the unnaturally lustrous atmosphere did not exude innocence.

DI Rexroat and the Alsatian noticed the lump on the lower bunk at the same time, but the dog (who was younger and more intelligent) acted first and leapt on the body in a frenzy of excitement.

'Christ!' said DI Rexroat, 'the bloody animal is trying to eat the corpse. When did you last feed it, Sergeant?'

'He had his Choppy Chews this morning, sir' said the dog-handler, 'but flesh is flesh.'

After a fierce tussle the policeman managed to pull the

dog off. He peeled back a tartan blanket to reveal the small stiff shape of one dead poet.

Joy and relief met this welcome sight. The department had not been blessed by a murder for eleven years.

The pathologist was called but, after a perfunctory examination, delivered a disappointing conclusion. There had been no evidence of violence, he said, as far as he could tell (without post-mortem). The young man had died as a result of a chronic respiratory condition possibly complicated by pneumonia.

'Not choking on his own vomit then?' said DI Rexroat, who had hoped that at least a drug overdose might be involved.

'No,' said the pathologist.

Neil and Neville, who had gone to steal a spade with which to bury Shorty, returned to the caravan park to find that it had been cordoned off with yellow police tape and that the entrance was guarded by panda cars with flashing lights.

'Christ,' said Neil.

'They'll find the money,' said Neville, 'and Shorty.'

'Fuck,' said Neil.

Neville started twitching in a way that was guaranteed to attract attention. A spasm, a few seconds, and Neville would destroy them both. Neil clasped his arm, gripped it as if he meant to break it, and muttered in a tone cold with the menace that was his weapon, 'Turn around. Walk slowly. Follow me.'

He walked away from the entrance, down the road, and, in silence, led Neville across a field to the copse in which the motor bikes were hidden.

Neville fell to the ground gasping for breath and shaking.

There would be road-blocks and APBs, torture and interrogation. He had seen it all on *The Man from U.N.C.L.E.* They should walk out now, walk out with their hands up. It would be better for them, better to cooperate. They would do less time. Did Neil have any *idea* what happened to people in prison? Neville did. Neville had heard people describe it on *NYPD Blue*.

Neil stared down at him impassively.

'What about the money?' said Neville. 'It's all in the caravan. Shorty's. Yours. Mine. The filth'll get it all.'

'We'll have to leave it there,' said Neil.

'They'll find it.'

'We'll have to leave it.'

'What are we going to do? There'll be helicopters, road-blocks . . .'

'Shut the fuck up,' said Neil.

As the police must align themselves with the criminal mind, so the criminal mind must imagine the workings of the police. Neil knew it would take some time to discover their identities and that as long as they did not ride the motor bikes escape would not be difficult. He was not worried. They had long planned to leave Somerset.

The sun was moving into the middle of the sky. He saw sheep and flowers and flies. Soon it would be his birthday. He swallowed down three dull decades in which he had been worn down by anonymity, surrounded by stupidity and oppressed by mediocrity. Mundane conspiracies had offered fleeting escape from being a nobody. Bursts of cash had briefly bought better booze, better beds, less hustle, but that was all.

Neil's dreams were not of trappings, they were of administrating global operations and of being known by those who mattered. He did not want Ferraris, he wanted to be feared. He did not see champagne, he saw himself giving orders. And he saw a reputation, cast in magazines, described on FBI files and talked about in high-security prisons. His name would be known but his face would never be documented. There would be biographies. And now, as he was poised to gain all this, life had betrayed him yet again.

Birthdays promised gifts but Neil had never got what he wanted. That was the story of his life. Missing out.

He flicked a millipede that was walking up his scrupulous jeans and crunched it slowly beneath the sole of his motorcycle boot. Revolting thing. He hoped it felt the pain.

Loathing, fierce and sour, jumped from his stomach into his throat.

'Somebody grassed on us,' he snapped at Neville. 'The pigs must've got a tip-off – there's no way the filth could've found us on their own.'

Neville remembered his confession to Brent in the teashop. Brent had sworn on the grave of his great-grandfather (Mad Elk) that he would take Neville's secrets to his grave. He had made an arcane Native American sign and stared piously up at the ceiling. 'I am known as a confidant,' he claimed. 'There is something about me that people trust. Everybody tells me things. Michelle Pfeiffer has told me things *you would not believe*! Trust me.'

Surely Brent had not betrayed him? Brent loved him.

Keen to hurl suspicion away from himself, Neville said, 'Ruthven! He's grassed to save 'is own skin . . .'

Neil addressed the feasibility of this. Neville was right. Ruthven had somehow been caught and he had grassed to save himself. It was the only explanation.

Neil spat violently on to the ground. He had even begun to trust that loser. He had never trusted anyone before, an instinct that was now, too late, confirmed by experience. Misjudgement was new to him. He had always been so right. Now he had to sicken himself with the knowledge that he had been deceived by simple duplicity. He had miscalculated and by so doing he had helped to manufacture his own downfall. This realization galvanized the lethal malevolence that squatted, cold and dangerous, at his core. Ruthven was going to pay.

'Plus,' Neville continued, "'e's got his share of the cash and I reckon he should give us some of it. How else are we gonna get out of here?'

'Give me your knife,' said Neil.

Ruthven was going to have to be visited. Visited, questioned, and forced to hand over his share of the Wookey job.

Seeing that his theory was working to his advantage, Neville calmed down and began to address his own future.

'You should come to Los Angeles,' Brent had said.

Television had told Neville something about Los Angeles and he had concluded that, like Somerset, it was full of policemen and coast guards. He was not sure that he would love it. But Los Angeles contained Brent and wherever Brent went, Neville knew that he must go too. Scenes of domestic bliss scudded across his mind's eye. He saw himself frying samosas, brushing the chamois leathers with a suede brush and kissing Brent on the lips as he returned home after a long day in fashion.

But had Brent betrayed them? As Neil was impelled to confront Rupert so Neville knew he must find Brent; he must know the truth because without the truth he had nothing.

'I'll go up to that castle,' said Neil. 'Ruthven can give us 'is cash and 'e's got some explaining to do.'

Neville nodded.

Neil took the path through the wood that led up the hill to Fairview Castle. Neville made his way towards the village. There were police and police cars everywhere. A uniformed officer stood on every corner, talking into his radio. White vans with tinted windows patrolled up and down every side street. A riot van containing six men with shields had parked outside the library.

Neville navigated a route through narrow alleys, over walls, through back gardens and across the rooves of garden sheds, a method of travelling that he had learned from Neil during their brief and unsuccessful career as house-breakers. Eventually he reached the hotel, climbed a wisteria, and entered Brent's second-floor bedroom by the window.

Brent was standing in front of a long mirror. He had ceremoniously adorned himelf with porcupine quills.

'Oh hello,' he said. 'You look awful. Take a beverage from the mini-bar if you like.'

Neville ripped open the tiny fridge and grabbed two miniature bottles of Kahlua.

'What the fuck are you doing,' he snarled.

'This is full dress,' said Brent, twisting the quills and enjoying the beauty of his reflection. Full dress is worn when preparing for death. Every Indian wants to look his best when he goes to meet the Great Spirit. The idea arose from the danger of battle, but nowadays, of course, it is symbolic, to accompany momentous decisions, walking towards the unknown and so on.'

Brent collapsed on the candlewick bedspread and swallowed the Kahlua.

'The voice of the Great Spirit is heard in the twittering of birds, the rippling of mighty waters and the sweet breathing of flowers.'

Neville was suddenly and horribly reminded of Shorty's poetry.

'From Wakan-Tanka, the Great Mystery, comes all power. It is from Wakan-Tanka that the holy man has wisdom and power to heal. Man knows that all healing plants are given by Wakan-Tanka, therefore they are holy. So too is the buffalo holy because it is the gift of Wakan-Tanka.

'Everything on the earth has a purpose, every disease an 'urb to cure it and every person a mission in life. That is the Indian theory of existence, so says Mourning Dove of the Salish.'

Neville, for the life of him, could not imagine what his own purpose might be, but he was sure that this Wanking Tankard bastard was not going to help.

'You will have noticed that everything an Indian does is in a circle and that is because the power of the world always works in circles. Everything tries to be round. The sky is round, the wind whirls round, birds make their nests in circles, and so too the war dance is round.'

Brent proceeded to demonstrate this by throwing himself into an interpretation of the steps performed by Sioux warriors before going into battle.

In the room below, Miles Falconbridge was attempting to take a rest before serving lunch. He had hoped to enjoy silence but he was, instead, subjected to a thudding for which the structure of the hotel was not designed. He looked up. The ceiling was old and thin. Dust began to fall from it. A piece of plaster dislodged and landed in his eye. Then, as suddenly as it had started, the noise stopped.

'We do not want riches,' said Brent, burying his face in Neville's groin. 'We want peace and love.'

'The feathers are getting up my bloody nose,' said Neville.

'Sorry,' said Brent.

'I'm gonna have to hide out with you for a while,' said Neville.

Brent looked at him.

'Problems with cops?' he asked.

'Yeah. *Somebody* grassed on us.'

Neville stared at Brent to detect signs of shiftiness and guilt. There were none.

'How exciting,' he said. 'An HBO True Life Special.'

'I'll probably have to leave the country.'

'*Fabuloso!* You can come to the States,' said Brent.

'Could do.'

'We can get married in Vegas.'

Brent leapt up and grabbed his medicine bag from a chair.

'This,' he said, brandishing a bracelet made out of brass beads and woodpecker scalps, 'is Aunt Soo's Band of Hope – the one that appeared in my prophetic dream.'

He placed it on Neville's wrist.

'We will die in each other's arms.'

Neville, consumed with love, knew that Brent was innocent.

They would die in each other's arms.

Chapter 12

The 'Intervention Team' were a tight group of highly-skilled individuals trained to confront the suffering addict and transport him safely to Serenity Hall. Over the years the more experienced members had seen the chemical dependant's range of resistance and they knew that anything could happen. Even the captain, who had taught counter-insurgency tactics in the Honduras, was continually surprised by the savagery and cunning of this opponent.

Sobbing was the norm, verbal abuse was regular, but the 'I' team (as it was known) had also seen flight (leaping out of loo windows and jumping out of moving limousines) and excuses ('I am the Minister of the Environment') as well as simple violence. Dame Hyacinth Holyfield, for instance, had jumped out of her bedroom wardrobe and had nearly killed an operative with the Oscar that she had won for the comedy classic, 'Don't Call me Noddy'.

Over the years the 'I' Team had been attacked with fists, swords, watermelons and Habitat plates. It was a dangerous job and it called for a knowledge of unconventional warfare. To this end members of the team were required to attend a training course in a secret camp in Scotland. Here they were taught land-navigation, strategic reconnaisance, abseiling, river-crossing (with poncho and rope) and basic ambush. At the end of the first week each individual was sent (alone) to spend three days on a moor equipped with only a Swiss army knife, a box of Swan Vestas and a live rabbit.

The Fairview operation, like all Interventions, was a high security mission planned in a specially designed, cork-lined office that could only be accessed by a computerised voice printout. A 'safety briefing' conducted by the team leader (a former Green Beret) outlined the potential hazards which, in this case, of course, included the presence of a semi-automatic weapon known for its accuracy in close-quarter combat and respected for its flexibility in a wide range of tactical requirements.

The 'I' Team were then shown satellite pictures of Fairview Castle and a black and white photograph of Margaret Ruthven. Correct identification of the target was particularly important. In the early days, when the team were less experienced, innocent people had been forcibly removed from their homes and driven away to detoxification before anyone realized that they were not the target, but a relative or neighbour whose sole indulgence was to take a couple of soluble Disprin at Christmas.

The 'I' team considered the possibility of landing by black parachutes at night, but the Civil Aviation Authority would not give them permission. Some operatives, trained in explosives, suggested that entrance should be made by blowing up the north wall, but this too was dismissed.

Access to Fairview Castle could be gained by two doors (front and back) and any number of windows. It was decided that the raid would be a two-pronged attack from the back door and Margaret Ruthven's bedroom window (which would be entered via a rope from the roof). The front door would provide an escape route should the strike have to be aborted.

On the morning of the raid the 'I' Team were given Mission Orientated Protective Apparel which included gasmasks, insect repellant, flare-guns, morphine syrettes, penlights and booby traps. On top of kevlar body armour they wore white coats on which the Serenity Hall motto 'Live and Let Live' had been embroidered in red thread.

They arrived at 1300 hours precisely.

Parking the ambulance outside the castle gate in order to retain the element of surprise, they poured from the vehicle like sugar.

Margaret Ruthven stood behind the curtain at her bedroom window. Her Para-Ordnance Opti-Viz binoculars, as always, were trained on the terrain below and she saw the diversion team jog into the front garden.

Picking up the sub-machine-gun she unlocked the safety catch, switched the selector to 'auto', shouldered it and peered through the scope. She had the advantage of observation but the range of the MP5 was limited – a hundred metres at the most. She would have to wait until the enemy drew nearer and then fire a warning volley.

Concentrating on her defence, she failed to hear the footsteps as they walked up behind her. But then, suddenly sensing a presence, she swung round and blindly peppered bullets into the room.

'Jesus Christ!'

Neil flung himself out of the door and hurled himself down the stairs as the Intervention Team was filing up them. Rupert, at the back, felt himself pushed over. He somersaulted to the bottom where Neil landed on top of him.

Neil, torn between the compulsion to kill Rupert and the instinct to escape from the mad woman in the bedroom, staggered to his feet. Shocked and dazed, he surrendered, briefly, to confusion. Then the moment for choice disappeared. He knew he had to run for it.

'I'll get you, you *fuck*!' he rasped, mouth hot on Rupert's ear. Then he kicked him violently and bolted.

Margaret Ruthven did not have time to reload.

Rupert watched as the Intervention Team overcame her, sedated her, laid her on a stretcher and carried her (with great difficulty) down the stairs.

As the red brake-lights of the ambulance disappeared down the hill, Rupert wondered if his worries were over. He felt sure that they were not. His mother could, and probably would, escape. Neil could, and probably would, return.

He trudged back into the castle. Deprived of Margaret Ruthven's dreadful presence it was a different place. Bigfoot had left the mountain and now there was nothing to watch or avoid. He thought he had been alone for years, in that he had lived a life of self-reliance, but now he was genuinely alone. No Mother. No Neil. No Gang. No side shows. No demands. Only him. He did not know if he was supposed to be on holiday or if he should be on guard for the next attack. Certainly it was difficult to drop his guard as it was as much a part of him as his teeth and hair – and likely to be more permanent.

He shuffled through the hall where his mother had once enjoyed long conversations with a reproduction suit of armour, and where there was a photograph of his father wearing a Barbour and holding a trout. He slouched into the kitchen and gingerly tried to clear the debris. He collected up her pill bottles, removed the dead vermin from the bread bin, piled up her beer cans, and tore up her survival manuals. He did not think that it was necessary to hold on to titles such as *A Practical Approach to Propellants*.

He shouldered the Heckler & Koch, looked through the view finder, and wondered whether he should keep the gun or not. He might need to protect himself against Neil. Then, in the new stillness, insights began to come to him, and he saw his choices. He could go forward armed and ready to become like his mother, or he could equip himself with common sense and make his own present. But how best to cast away this black thing, heavy and lethal and probably stolen. The garbage disposal unit would not be able to take it; the compost heap was useless. Eventually he succumbed to the obvious and threw the gun in the bin.

Neil escaped from Fairview Castle with his life and with £250 cash that he always kept on his person in case of emergencies. He could have returned to take Rupert's money and maim him for life, but this would have meant missing the meeting in Surrey with Mr Baba and Europe's leading executives of organised crime. The choice between business and pleasure is an easy matter for a careerist. Neil filed Rupert in the back of his mind where he took his place with all the other enemies who he would not forget, and to whom he intended to return. Refreshed with the prospect of opportunity, Neil disguised himself with a baseball hat onto which a nylon pony tail had been sown. The latter proved to be an efficient deterrent – he was avoided at the railway station and no-one spoke to him on the train to London.

Chapter 13

Serenity Hall was a Grade One Listed Palladian mansion set in a hundred acres of Capability Brown estate outside Axbridge.

Men with beards who ate in Kensington restaurants and had connections with British Heritage said that the Rotunda that formed the entrance hall was more 'satisfying' than the double cube room at Wilton.

Serenity Hall recommended that 'guests' stay a minimum of three months but this suggestion had become obsolete because once people crossed the graceful Ionic portal very few wanted to leave. The clinic would have had no effluence at all if its prices had not been so high.

Those unfettered by financial restriction – musicians, for instance, and arms dealers, had made Serenity Hall their home. It looked very much like their homes and was full of nicer and more interesting people so there seemed little reason to leave it. Dependants and accountants could only visit by appointment, one was not harassed by the press, there was a Deco swimming pool (heated), a cuisine created by a Parisian chef and the freedom to talk about oneself, without guilt, for between six and eight hours a day. It was difficult, if not impossible, to divest oneself of these perfect arrangements, and, since departure was voluntary, many patients had not departed. Cosmo Quist and Clive Overdiek, of the legendary Sixties progressive rock band Dr Pimlott's Acid Experience, had both arrived in 1974; Morny Stannit the newspaper baron had lived in 'the bungalow' since 1981; Dee Skiddly (the former model) and Dave Dark (the impressario) were amongst the many long-term residents who had known Brion Gysin in Morocco, who had seen The Floyd play in The Underground and who had slept with Nico. They knew how Kennedy and Brian Jones had really died. They knew why 'opel' had not appeared on The Madcap Laughs and who broke the butterfly on the wheel.

And so Margaret Ruthven learned to play Boggle with what had been the best minds of their generation.

'Detox' was a relatively painless experience thanks to a black box that had once belonged to Keith Richard, and the attentions of the Beverage Liaison Officer who brought her refreshing cups of mint tea. After three days she sprang out into the lustrous land of the sanitorium with the joyful skip of a new-born lamb.

Her private recovery room, designed by a world-famous interior decorator, was painted white and mint. There were snacks packed in raffia baskets, fresh-smelling linen laundry bags, mineral waters, fruits, and a line of shampoos in postmodern packaging. White muslin curtains drew back to reveal a view to a patchwork of lawns and, beyond this, lush fields and blue skies.

The garden, designed along Tuscan lines, stepped into a series of parterres where hedges had been cut into geometrical cubes and where gravel pathways wound around classical grottoes. Behind one wall there was a gymnasium with sauna, exercise studios, gym, tennis and squash courts, all designed to encourage physical awareness and develop stress management.

Margaret Ruthven hung out of her window, breathed in the warm June air, and felt happy for the first time in her life. It was an unfamiliar sensation and it took her by surprise. Her legs buckled and, suddenly confused, she wondered what year it was. Where had she been? Did it matter?

She walked to the first floor where she was to meet Dr Dave and receive her personal recovery programme.

She entered a long white office where the sun shone through mullioned windows on to one of the most attractive men she had ever seen in her life.

Dr Dave.

Dr Dave's youth caused animated controversy amongst his patients. Some people claimed, swearing with their right hands on the *AA Big Book*, that he was twenty-five. Others insisted (correctly) that he had had a face-lift.

Dr Dave was not a doctor of medicine, he was a doctor of Economics. His interests had switched to the personal growth movement after he had seen the size of the vegetables at Findhorn. Having received a diploma in integrative psychotherapy, he had founded a successful practice, but had been unprepared for the challenges of transference. His female clients mistook him for someone they could trust and always fell in love with him. He had tried to be fair and sleep with all of them but there were so many. A seraglio had flung itself at him, a dipping frenzy of disappointed hopes, slack breasts, incurable neediness, fleshy arms, Nina Ricci scent bottles, gold lipstick holders, infertility, menopause, villas in Ascot, gin and dreams of romance that, in Dr Dave's opinion, every woman should discard the same year that she discarded her student union card.

His evenings had once been a riot but his health had suffered and exhaustion had forced him to close down his clinic. He wrote a book on Quantum Molecular Rejuvenation that made him famous. Having established himself as a highly-paid public speaker in California, he rose rapidly through the ranks of the human potential movement thanks to a mixture of avarice and sex appeal. He arrived at Serenity Hall in the autumn of 1990, bringing with him some of the ideas that had appealed to him when he was travelling and which were based, by and large, on his belief that it was possible to get away with practically anything.

Dr Dave looked at Margaret Ruthven's notes. He had not had enough time, or interest, to appraise himself of her entire medical history, stretching, like a Russian novel, over many decades and pages, but he had read enough to assure himself that Ruthven, Margaret (Mrs) was an obvious lunatic.

'Ah Mrs Ruthven, please sit down.' He paused. 'May I call you Margaret?'

He looked into her eyes.

She looked into his.

He saw years of over-medication.

She saw a person of mesmerizing loveliness.

'I wish you would call me My Only,' she thought as she nodded silently.

'How are you feeling?' he said.

Suddenly she could hardly speak and a flush had started to bleed from her face to her throat. She swallowed and cleared her throat, a manoeuver which evolved into retching and a painful explosion of choking. Dr Dave came out in a cold sweat and wondered if he had chosen the right profession. Sometimes the money wasn't worth it. Sometimes he wished lobotomy had not gone out of fashion. He mentally kicked himself back into reality. The woman seemed to be saying something.

'Fine, thank you.'

'No compulsive urges?'

'I don't think so.'

'You don't want a drink then?'

'Well, if you're having one I'll join you . . .'

Dr Dave sighed and wrote 'Step One' down in his notes.

'Do you know why you are here?' he asked patiently.

'I don't think anyone does,' she said. 'Either our actions are our own and we can't help but perform them or they are not ours in which case we cannot be held responsible for them. The position on this dilemma depends on the position one adopts with regard to the mind-body problem. How is a mind or will free while the body in which it is apparently lodged is causally determined and subject to the laws of science? Or, if the mind is psychologically determined, how can this be reconciled with the bio-physical determinism of the body? As a fatalist I have to insist that the inevitablity of the future event is more than a tautology. Thus everything, including my freely chosen actions themselves, is predetermined, which seems to make my freedom an illusion.' She paused for breath.

Dr Dave was not in the mood for Cartesian dualism.

'No, Margaret. Here. *Here*. In this clinic.'

'I didn't realize it was a clinic. I thought it was a spa.'

'No, Serenity Hall is dedicated to caring for chemical dependants with a view to providing them with a bridge to normal living,' he said.

'Oh.'

Margaret Ruthven did not know what on earth this film-star was talking about but she kept silent, hoping that time would produce clarity.

'You were brought here by our team of qualified medical carers.'

'Oh. Is it on the NHS?'

Dr Dave nearly laughed out loud.

'Your son Rupert is paying the fee.'

'Rupert? Rupert?' She looked vague. 'He must be twenty now.'

Dr Dave wrote down 'possible senile dementia' with a question mark, crossed the question mark out, and added 'pre-morbid personality'.

'You could do with losing some weight,' he said.

Margaret Ruthven looked down at herself. She was wearing the Serenity Hall 'complimentary', terry-cotton track-suit distributed to all clients on arrival and paid for if they wished to take it when they left. Most people were given white ones with the words Serenity Hall (Centre of Sober Living) written on the back. Those who were attending the clinic as a result of a court order (in lieu or in the place of a prison sentence) were given orange track-suits. This meant that, in the event of escape, they could be easily identified.

Margaret Ruthven had always thought that her body was

perfect the way that it was. She had no intention of going on a diet.

'I am fine as I am,' she said. 'I do not wish to eat Ryvitas.'

Dr Dave wrote 'denial' down in his book.

'Now, Margaret,' he said with the mixture of authority and humanity that had destroyed so many women. 'It seems to me that you have never benefited from a holistic approach to your health problems. We here at Serenity Hall believe in providing tools for self-exploration so that you may find the wisdom of your inner self.'

Margaret Ruthven nodded.

She still had no idea what this man was talking about.

'We match each client to the most appropriate treatment, creating a personalized plan of recovery in a safe, private and therapeutic setting.'

'I see,' she lied.

'We try to resolve the traumas of old wounds,' he went on. 'Some children, you see, were not loved.'

'I'm not surprised,' she said. 'Some children are very nasty.'

'Here is your Beginner's Chart. It lists the classes that I think will help you personally.'

He gave her a white card. Serenity Hall was embossed on it in gold letters over the motto 'Sobriety is Us'. Underneath Dr Dave had written *anger management*, *sprituality enhancement*, *therapeutic craft*, *headstand workshop*.

'You will find details of the class times and places on the notice-board in the main hall, the Rotunda,' he said.

Margaret Ruthven remained in her chair staring at him, mouth agape.

Dr Dave got up wondering, as he did so, if, like his grandmother's Yorkshire puddings, Mrs Ruthven had become stuck in her pan. He dislodged her and guided her towards the door.

'Good luck,' he said, 'and remember to breathe.'

In the Rotunda Margaret Ruthven came across a lot of things besides the time-table of activities. A glass display cabinet showed a wide selection of recovery gift items that included anniversary medallions, deluxe jewellery, stamps, neck chains, key rings, ceramic wall plaques, stoneware mugs and bumper stickers, all beautifully crafted and adorned with the platitudes of AA philosophy.

Another corner housed an exhibition to advertise a forthcoming visit from a London-based Phobia Programme. A patient, having recovered from arachnophobia, had built a vast spider out of papier mâché, and fun-fur. It was modelled on a tree-dwelling species, found in Brazil, that crushes snakes with its jaws and then sucks their bodies dry.

The artist, unfortunately for the onlooker, had an eye for detail that was almost obsessive and had constructed each ghastly component of the carnivore with loving realism. Each leg was divided into six hirsute joints, complete with tarsal claws. The head was a threatening arrangement of palps and maxillae. A row of huge eyes had been made out of cricket balls wrapped in PVC; fangs were cut-glass and a jaw was complete with half-eaten prey and realistic blood. The creature, some four foot across, stretched over the floor and, thanks to wires attached to the ceiling, shivered as if it was alive.

The many Serenity Hall patients who did not have phobias about spiders were beginning to experience panic attacks at the sight of this monstrous arachnid. There had been letters of complaint to the director's secretary and members of Father Dominic's anger management group had threatened to stamp on it.

'Why a spider, I'd like to know,' a tall man in a stetson was saying to an obese American woman. 'I had a cousin who was petrified of pigeons. He couldn't go out of the house. Finally he took a night job. But it can be anything, you know, phobias. Buttons, tomatoes, tennis, Bertrand Russell, you name it.'

Margaret Ruthven went to the Headstand Workshop.

Yogi Jon, a pert Mancunian, had a shock of thick white hair and a tight body of which every muscle could be seen undulating beneath a smooth brown skin and, in particular, around his groin. This, scarcely concealed by a green loincloth, offered a message of protuberance that could only be described as exhibitionist and, when involved in the Lotus position, was barely legal. Yogi Jon had spent many years turning himself into a module of firm perfection and his muscles did not intend to avoid company. They intended to go out and be seen and it seemed that they were fighting amongst themselves in order to do so.

'Welcome to all new aspirants,' said Yogi Jon, putting down the Veena, on which he had been plucking out a personal interpretation of 'Feelings', 'and welcome to the first step towards Brahman.'

He walked into the middle of the room, curled his body forward, placed his fingers flat on the floor, smoothly lifted himself into a handstand and took one hand off the floor so that his body, vertical, was balancing on one palm. Then, slowly, smoothly, without gasp or groan, he let himself down again and stood with his palms together, as if in prayer.

'I do that not to show off,' he said, 'and certainly not to

suggest that you do it, especially you Mrs Tilbury with your sciatica dear, but to show you the miracles that can be achieved in the process of *Antaratma Sadhana*. The *asanas* bring health, they help us overcome the *chitta viksepa*, and they calm the turbines of the mind in order to achieve *Isvara pranidhana*, or devotion to the Lord. This is not my body, you see, it is the body of The Creator.'

He paused

'I am forty-three.'

He paused again as if waiting for the gasps of surprise that greet a conjuror who had just pierced his wife with swords. Gasps did not arrive. Yogi Jon's face looked forty-three, it was only his body that was bizarrely divorced from the rigours of degeneration.

Yogi Jon forcefully exhaled so that the muscles of his stomach contracted one by one, like a collection of balletic giblets. 'The ancient books have called the *Sirsasana* – the headstand – the king of all *asana*,' he said. 'When we are born, the head comes first. The skull encases the brain which controls the nervous system and the organs of sense. The brain is the seat of intelligence and wisdom and it is also the seat of Brahman, the soul. A country cannot prosper without a constitutional head – so also the human body cannot prosper without a healthy brain.

'The Bhagavad Gita says harmony and mobility stem from the brain. Regular and precise practice of Sirsasana develops the body, disciplines the mind and widens the horizons of the spirit. One becomes balanced and self-reliant in pain and pleasure, loss and gain, shame and fame, in defeat and in victory.'

Margaret Ruthven managed to stand on her head for seventy-five seconds, which was approximately twenty-five seconds more than that achieved by Mrs Tilbury whose legs rotated like a windmill before her body crashed to the floor.

Her brain thoroughly stimulated, Margaret Ruthven went to have lunch in the self-service restaurant – *Le Café Delicieux* – which overlooked the Italian garden and was already crowded with people. She helped herself to a *tartelette a l'ancienne*, (a tartlet with provençale sauce,) a *feuilleté de legumes cressonnière* (vegetables in filo pastry served with watercress) and a *parfait de pamplemousse épicé* (grapefruit with a ginger and orange coulis).

Yogi Jon, still semi-naked, came over with his tray. 'Hullo,' he said, 'How are you feeling?'

'Fine, thank you,' said Margaret Ruthven. 'I'm having a very nice holiday.'

'Goodo,' he said and sat down opposite her with his yogic lunch. Designed to sustain those attempting to achieve the *niyama of saucha* (purity of the blood), it consisted (thanks to *Nos Plats Végétariens*) of a hot roulade of cheese, peppers, nuts and tomato served with a mushroom sauce.

Yogi Jon cleared his plate, lit up a Marlboro and settled down for a chat.

'Dr Dave is very beautiful,' she told him.

The Yogi's face looked as if it had bitten into a disappointing peach. His eyes narrowed and his lips pushed themselves into a nozzle. He stabbed the Marlboro butt into the remains of the roulade.

'Dr Dave?' he declared, 'A shallow man, you know, a very shallow man indeed. He is full of *pramada*.'

'Pramada?'

'Self-importance. To gratify his selfish passions and dreams of personal glory he will deliberately and without scruple sacrifice anyone who stands in his way. Such a person is blind to God's glory and deaf to his words.'

'Oh dear,' said Margaret Ruthven and went to Therapeutic Craft where a range of creative suggestions were brought to her attention by a woman named Sorkina who believed in wearing the things that she made. To this end she was sporting an orange crochet skullcap and a long pair of batik harem pants. 'This is Dez,' she said, 'One of our out-patients.' A stout youth in combat fatigues was sticking pressed wildflowers on to cartridge paper. 'Wild nipplewort,' he said. 'Lovely with Japanese anemone.' Margaret Ruthven did not feel inspired by flower-pressing, neither did she feel drawn to origami (too annoying), tie-dyeing (too ugly) or the pottery wheel (too difficult). She sat down at the knitting machine.

'That's been broken for ages,' said Sorkina. 'Look. I've been trying to make this.' She indicated a half-finished cape knitted in grey mohair wool and still attached to the carriage in a misshapen tangle of bales and strands. 'It's stuck in the machine and I can't get it out – it's been in there for months now. It's a disaster.'

There are many people who will argue that a naturalistic explanation can be found for every documented 'miracle'. There is no such thing, they will say, as a transgression of the law of nature by the volition of a deity or the interpolation of some invisible agent. They will speak of hallucination, mass hysteria and the hypnotic states induced by religious ritual or mood-altering substances. However, even those of the most scientific bent would have been hard-pressed to explain what happened next.

Margaret Ruthven sat in front of the latch needles, springs, masts and levers and, without saying anything, adjusted the tension disc. The Purly-Knit Whirly Wonder buzzed into action. The carriage slid smoothly up and down and needles shot back and forth. As she pushed the yarn through the antenna spring, a cone spun round and smoothly fed the fluffy gimp into the knitting. The cape expanded, as if by divine intervention, into an artwork of extravagant open-mesh lace. Sorkina's garment was finished within ten minutes. There was a brief mechanical expostulation of bells and the machine shuddered to a halt.

Sorkina, a superstitious woman, was slightly frightened. The rest of the patients looked on in silent admiration.

'Perhaps this is me,' Margaret Ruthven thought. 'Knitting.'

Sorkina was convinced that it was the work of the Higher Power. No human hand could have caused the Purly-Knit Whirly Wonder to behave in such a way. Old and temperamental, it had long spewed out unsightly knots. It had been introduced to help clients develop patience and tolerance but it had only incited rancour. Even Mrs Frogley, a professional seamstress, had given up after a simple chenille scarf had taken her two years.

Later, Sorkina related the incident to her colleagues who had gathered in the staffroom for tea. 'That woman will surprise us all,' she said.

'I must get her into my group,' said Gerald, who supervised Growth Through Gardening. 'The melons could do with some help.'

The staffroom, on the first floor, was light and bright. A book shelf displayed liturgies that stretched from Krishnamurti to L. Ron Hubbard and, on a mantlepiece over the fireplace, Celtic deities jostled with joss-sticks, an AA newcomer's card, a biro from the Theosophical Society, an old pamphlet illustrating the techniques of Rolfing and a framed parchment that read, 'He that is born with tendencies towards the Divine is self-controlled and truthful; he has a tranquil mind with malice towards none and charity towards all for he is free from craving.'

The Divine, no doubt, has many different aspects, but if any one of them had chosen to manifest in the staffroom that afternoon, they would have found an atmosphere stiff with acrimony as members of the Serenity Hall 'teaching community' indulged themselves in the excitement of mutual contempt.

Sorkina had hated Gerald since she had spent four weeks making a quilted waistcoat for him and, visiting his cottage (to deliver a signed copy of her book *Natural Dyes for Home Weavers*), she had seen the garment lying on the sink where it had been used to polish Gerald's size eleven boots.

Gerald thought Sorkina was a Monster of Compassion – she tortured him with kindness, controlled with gifts and suffocated with sympathy in an attempt to manipulate him into the mould of her desires. He was not an unkind man but she had driven him over the edge and his favourite fantasy now involved throwing her corn dollies on the fire.

Father Dominic hated everybody.

Dr Dave distrusted Yogi Jon and, in particular, his pledge of celibacy which he thought was both unhealthy and sinister. Devoted to Vedic lore in order to move in Brahman, Yogi Jon often boasted that he was in the state of *santosa* (contentment). He feared no man and was joyful in who he was. This perverse detachment made him free of the rules that bound others to Dr Dave's authority. He was a maverick and he would stare at Dr Dave with a patronizing air that made the doctor want to punch him in the face.

Yogi Jon, for his part, detested Dr Dave. As he had renounced sensuality, he had also renounced materialism. In an effort to train his mind not to feel austerity he possessed only a mattress and a copy of the Bhagavad Gita. But adherence to the *yama* (ethical displicine) was harsh when faced with a man who indulged in all the pleasures and vanities that Yogi Jon had surrendered in the interests of communion with the Creator and in the belief that those who could not detach themselves from these things would never achieve the bliss of Samadhi. While Yogi Jon lived in an attic and wore a loincloth, Dr Dave was rich, greedy, sexually promiscuous, vain, self-centred and, to the yogi's fury, he was happy being all of these things. His carefree amorality was like a slap in the face. He was contented and unpunished while clothing himself in enjoyable vices. This shook the yogi's faith and forced him to wonder if he was on the right path.

Dr Dave was combing his hair carefully while studying himself in the mirror.

'Keep that Ruthven woman away from me,' he said. 'I have read her notes and she is very dangerous. Not only is she a drug addict, she is also clinically deluded.'

Rupert did not particularly enjoy his visits to see his mother at Serenity Hall. He was confused by the facilities and did not understand the language. The inmates all seemed to be seriously ill. Strangers sprinted up to him, smiling and shaking his hand and welcoming him to unity consciousness. One man even hugged him and he had to sit down for ten minutes until the shock and physical revulsion abated.

He could not work out what the money was being spent on and his mother seemed just as confused. Her vocabulary, once confined to monosyllabic abuse, now included phrases such as 'enriching', 'healing energy', 'cosmovision', and, 'Carlos Casteneda'.

She told him that she now realised that the finitude of mundane existence cannot satisfy the human heart, then she gave him a lilac and cream striped V-neck pullover which was both worrying and depressing – worrying because it was tight and ugly and he would be forced to wear it when he saw her, and depressing because it represented how little she knew and how little she saw. He tried to remember that she was old and ill but it should have been obvious that he would not wear lilac. He did not play golf and he did not present children's television programmes. He wore a leather jacket. He was a modern isolate who, thanks in part to the demands of her instability, had come to understand that the outlaw was not a sage, transience was mundane and escape was impossible.

He tried to steer her away from speeches about primordial energy and towards the topics more common to conversations with relations in hospitals – to the food, for instance, the weather and the infirmities of the other patients.

She did not seem to remember the trauma of being abducted by the Intervention Team, nor did she ask where the money was coming from, but then she had never asked questions about money. Practical concerns had never existed for her. Rupert felt that he had done his duty and saved her life, but she seemed no less mad. The difference now was that she wore more makeup and said that she was happy, whatever that was.

One afternoon she asked him if he hated her.

Taken by surprise, Rupert drained his cup of tea in one short, hot gulp that blistered his throat and brought tears to his eyes.

'Course not,' he spluttered. 'Christ, is that the time? The Big Boss'll kill me.'

He sprinted out of the cafeteria and slammed the motor bike to Lucky Bob's.

'All women are barking,' the Big Boss told him when Rupert presented a simplified account of some of his difficulties. He could see that the boy was upset and he felt sorry for him. Jean was right. He didn't have anyone looking after him. They should ask the lad to be a godfather.

'Why doesn't she feel guilty?' said Rupert.

'There is no explanation for them, Mate, we just have to accept it. And mothers are the worst.'

'What's that about mothers?' said Jean, who had made a rare appearance to help with the stock-taking but who was hampered by her attempts to chain-eat fairy cakes at the same time as unpacking a Mothercare bag full of breast-shaped objects whose function was a mystery to both Rupert and the Big Boss.

'Need I say more?' said the Big Boss, rolling his eyes. 'I swear she was in the garden yesterday eating worms.'

'I was not,' said Jean. 'Don't annoy me. Doctor says I mustn't get stressed. It's bad for baby.'

'Fairy cakes dropping down on its head day and night can't be good for it,' the Big Boss couldn't help commenting.

'I'm goin' 'ome,' said Jean, suddenly hormonal and tearful. 'I've 'ad enough of you bloody blighters.'

'I'll finish up 'ere if you like,' said Rupert. 'You go home as well if you want.'

'No thanks,' said the Big Boss. 'Me kitchen's full of Shul going on about folic acids and the price of Pampers. Let's 'ave a beer.'

The Big Boss was a comfort but Rupert could not help fretting about his mother's future. She would soon be forced to leave paradise and wander undefended amongst the thorns of the outside world. This was a landscape that she had not seen with sober eyes for many years. He feared that the shock might propel her towards new forms of deviance and he did not think that a newly acquired ability to sing the lyrics from *The Soft Parade* was adequate protection against the disharmony that would inevitably occur when brutal reality reasserted itself.

The Serenity Hall 'Real Life Acclimatization Officer' assured him that their 'One-Day-At-A-Time Out-Patients' Programme' was highly effective. Based on a scheme developed in a Texan penal colony, it allowed the client out gradually – shopping for an afternoon with a Designated Buddy, and so on.

Rupert was not convinced.

Chapter 14

The history of poetry has long described the necessity of dying young. If the artist is carried away before the age of thirty, insignificance will undoubtedly be replaced by undeserved prominence.

Shorty's untimely end stoked a lurid biography far removed from the truth of years spent under-achieving and under investigation. Here was a biker, a thief, a poet, a dwarf, a genius, an *idiot savant*, and no one knew who he was. This was glamorous enough but there was also the matter of his body which, it was said, had been half-eaten by a wild animal and bore teeth marks that the police officially attributed to the Beast of Exmoor. In life Shorty had won no prizes. As an unidentified corpse the rewards of artistic success were his. It was as if Rimbaud had passed on in the farmhouse at Roche.

A torn notebook containing cryptic couplets had been found underneath the trailer. Various professors agreed that they represented a genuine breakthrough in terms of poetic structure and Shorty's reputation swelled in a milieu where those with the loudest waistcoats also have the loudest voices.

The poetic remnants were auctioned for a ridiculous figure and, as the publisher made ready to print a limited edition with a hologram on the cover, the publicity department 'leaked' the theory that the verses had, in fact, been compiled by a group of students as an amusing hoax.

The furore doubled when Norman Mailer flew in and announced that the unknown poet was to be the subject of a magnificent true crime opus in the manner of *The Executioner's Song* and *Oswald's Tale*.

Miles Falconbridge reported these details to Grace at breakfast.

'Mr Mailer's presence is very timely,' he said. 'He'll be a tremendous tourist attraction. People will come for miles to look at him. He'll be more popular than Pick Your Own Fruit, I can tell you that ...'

It was 7 am. Early. Grace had had two hours' sleep after a long night drinking vodka and cherry liqueur chasers with Lex, who had decided to spend the summer on the road. 'Perhaps I'll go to the Angels' rally at Dymchurch,' she said. 'Swell hard.' Then she had grasped Grace to her musty bosoms and, macho unveiled, begged her to go with her. 'Just you 'n' me and the Norton. We can go anywhere you 'n' I – the Dutch TT in Assen, Speed Week at Daytona, the Italian world trials in Bardonecchia ...'

Grace thought of the moon face, flushed with vodka and zeal, the eyes bright with encouragement and need. She knew that Lex would look after her, that she offered an escape of sorts, but she could not leave without knowing the truth.

'What happened to the rest of the gang?' she asked her father.

'The police think they have left the country,' he said. 'They think they were tipped off about the raid. Good riddance, I say. Now at least we might attract some summer trade – if the bastards haven't destroyed our reputation for ever.'

'Do the police know who the gang were?'

'No idea. They say it's an extraordinary thing – the trailer was so clean that there was not one single fingerprint anywhere.'

So now there was nothing.

The Highwayman had left her. He had rejected her. He had rejected her without even knowing her. He should have known that their destiny was inevitable. He should have sensed the love and the future as she had done, all these empty months. Now she felt the brutal shove as if she had been pushed away by someone she had known for years. This inexplicable attack stirred up all the fears and now in stark relief, they became one ruthless fact. She was not wanted.

'You should go,' said Miles Falconbridge. 'You'll be late.'

Grace looked at the photograph of her mother on the dresser. Then she got up and left the room.

As the shoot drew to a close, a warmer atmosphere drew the Hatch Hamstone team together. They were united in the collective agreement of those who are looking forward to leaving a country where it is impossible to purchase a decent plate of warm radicchio.

Hair and Makeup had made up.

'Darling I jes *lerve* what you've done with the eyes.'

'*Smoky.*'

'Smoky is *it*.'

Nobody had apologized exactly but the corner where the makeup table stood echoed with the mutual jangle of bangles as Patrick Cox loafers were swapped and an agreement was reached on the correct length for a shantung Capri pant. Makeup told Hair that he had redefined the meaning of the word 'hairpiece' and Hair told Makeup that she and she alone was responsible for the rise of iridescents. ('Darling you've been doing those pearly brow-bones since 1986.') All of this signified that a peace treaty had been signed.

Storm and Tythe had become engaged in order to discuss what they were going to wear to the wedding.

'Alexander McQueen?'

'Too freaky.'

'Calvin?'

'Too straight.'

'Gaultier?'

'Too Eighties. I'm thinking Clements Ribiero – that cute orange moiré taffeta and apricot cashmere tank top. I'm thinking that mango has a lot of potential for chic. And it sure will suit my skin tone.'

'Orange?'

'What's wrong with orange? It's a very uplifting colour. The Dalai Lama wears it.'

'You don't think it's a little alarming, Honey?'

The vice-presidents wandered around benignly telling everybody how talented they were. Hatch himself had faxed from Mexico to say that he loved them all and, by the way, if they had seen the *New York Post*, the rumours weren't true.

Even Styling, fortified by Bach Flower Remedies (consumed neat from the bottle), was in a good mood.

Her agent had rung to say that he had put her daily rate up by $500 and she had managed to sleep with both the vice-presidents. She was wearing a reproduction Vionnet bias-cut dress and a collection of seventeenth-century mourning jewellery coordinated with an expression of self-satisfaction.

The Art Director had been told by a farmer that the bees were flying backwards which was a sure sign that a high wind was due. He cast a moistened forefinger into the air in order to ascertain the direction of currents but, in fact, the last day was bright, dry and warm. He sat in a deck-chair on the beach, ate a chocolate éclair, and surveyed the preparations for the final photograph.

There were beige light-diffusing foundations and good earth eye-shadows. There were precision kohl pencils and nude lip gloss colours. There were booties and shawls and underskirts and miles and miles of gauze. And there were ninety-six hedgehogs.

A woman named Cathy who had driven the van from Wales attempted to control her herd by gently sweeping them with a broom. Problems lay in the fact that the animals were in many different stages of development and, if Cathy was to be believed, each was possessed of an individual personality. Some young ones were snuffling and energetic; some had rolled up into balls; others were running in circles. Several had found a pile of discarded polystyrene coffee cups and, in an attempt to lick the dregs, had stuck their snouts into the plastic cones and, unable to pull back, had become stuck.

'There are supposed to be a hundred,' said Clive, hoping that Carl would not count. 'We paid for a hundred.'

'I know, I'm sorry,' said Cathy, 'I'm afraid Patricia is pregnant, Daniel ate a poisoned slug, Beatrice fell down a drain and Nicholas ran away. It's rather a worry. He's frightfully old and he has a weight problem.'

'He won't go far then,' said Clive, thinking of the fat joggers he saw puffing up and down Venice beach.

'I don't know,' said Cathy doubtfully. 'Last time he went to IKEA. Oh look. There's Donald and Lettice. They're married.'

'For Chrissake,' said Clive, 'How can you tell them apart?'

'Oh it's easy once you know. They are quite intelligent. They respond to their names. Look. Donald, Lettice, over here, Donald, Lettice . . .'

Donald and Lettice did indeed trundle towards Cathy's wellington boot but Clive concluded that this was less to do with their intellect and more to do with the live worm that she was holding in her bare fingers.

'And, ur, how did you get into this field?' he asked with the masochism that is demanded by good manners.

'My dad was a specialist – hedgehogs were his life work. He conducted the definitive field study of their eating habits.'

'Ah.'

'Yes . . . by examining the contents of their stomachs – dead ones of course – he recorded earwigs, caterpillars, snails. That kind of thing.'

Styling interrupted this revolting anecdote by flouncing up, armed with a bouffant fichu, and telling Clive to keep the goddamn porcupines out of her way. If she had wanted to see a mobile cactus she would have dropped a tab and gone to Death Valley.

'They are not porcupines,' said Cathy. 'They are not related.'

'Oh,' sneered Styling. 'Well, whatever they are they are not beautiful.'

Styling surged forward and lowered a white linen 'shepherdess', bonnet on to Grace's head. She performed this operation perfunctorily, for Grace, as always, sat stiff and silent. Now, though, in the absence of hope, she had found hate, in particular hate of a world that was turning her inside out, and whose aesthetic decree was designed to undermine and negate and quash and kill. Waif waif thin thin breasts are in. Hair hair cut it up, cut it off, be like Us.

Styling treated her as she treated all models, as an *objet d'art* to be completed as quickly as possible so that they could all finish the job and go home. The *objet* was a tiny passive part of the elaborate administration that Styling thought of as her talent. She had never spoken to Grace, for Grace could never be of any consequence to her, and Styling only focused her energies on those who could be of use. People like the taller of the vice-presidents, for instance, who owned a chalet in Aspen and who had agreed to finance her range of sportswear. As a fetish, Grace was not expected to opine or motivate or demonstrate.

Mortification washed over her body agonizing and hot. She knew that she could no longer play with this abasement or sit quietly waiting to be defaced. She had allowed herself to be shamed. There was no excuse. She was not even warmed by the money. She had willingly walked towards vacuity.

She snatched the bonnet off. She could no longer be ludicrous.

'I can't,' she said. 'I just can't.'

Styling said nothing but carried the hat towards the Art Director. She could see Grace's point. The bonnet was an eyesore. Hidierama beyond Grotesquissimo, but this was an advertising shoot. There was no room for views.

'*She*,' said Styling, indicating that she meant Grace by pointing a long black fingernail, 'doesn't like *this*!'

She pushed the hat in front of the Art Director's face and shook it.

The Art Director stared at it as if it was the decapitated head of St John the Baptist.

'*That*,' he whispered, 'is Hatch Hamstone's favourite piece in the entire collection. He *loves* it. It has *got* to be photographed.'

'*She* doesn't like it,' Styling repeated.

'It's not her business to like,' said the Art Director.

'I know,' said Styling, 'but who is going to tell *her* that? *Pas moi je pense.*'

The Art Director whispered the details of this tragedy to Clive who communicated the facts to Karl, thinking (mistakenly) that the photographer had built a rapport with Grace and this, combined with his Germanic authority, made him the most qualified mediator.

Karl shrugged. Bored.

'Dey are always like dis,' he said. 'I vill tell her.'

He marched up to Grace, looked down at her, and said, 'If you don't ver dis het you vill not be paid.'

'I don't give a fuck,' said Grace.

Karl was taken aback. He had never seen a person gamble with the sum of $100,000 before. It was a new and disquieting experience. He did not know how to proceed with this unfathomable negotiation. The girl had disarmed him. Money was his only weapon; he had no other except the sheer force of his personality. This, in the past, had been effective. He had spent many years persuading difficult women to obey his orders but they were women who liked money and would have jumped into a septic tank if the daily rate was right.

Hair, Makeup and Styling edged closer. If there was to be a Scene they wished to experience every delicious moment of it. Styling hadn't enjoyed herself so much since the synchronized water-skiers were eaten by a shark in *Jaws 3*. A career was ending before it had begun. Fabulosa.

'You are de best girl I hev ever photographed,' Karl said softly. 'You hev qualities that make you unique. Bitte. Be professional.'

'If you make me wear that hat I will commit suicide,' said Grace.

Karl had no instinct for jokes and could not recognize them. As some people are colour-blind, he was unable to see humour and was forced to follow where others led, joining in long after the laughter had started. He assumed that Grace was joking and he prepared himself for the reactions that teasing demanded. A guffaw began to swell in his stomach and vibrate through his body when he saw, to his horror, that tears were beginning to well in the girl's eyes.

He fell back as if he had been electrocuted and beckoned frantically at Clive.

Clive sprinted forward.

'You must deal with it.'

Clive grabbed Grace's hand, pulled her out of her seat,

ushered her off the set and along the sand in front of the sea. He put his arm around her shoulder, which was cold and bony and very white.

Whispering a hypnotic mix of admonition and compliments he ended with an appeal to her better nature. It was the last day, he said. His job was on the line. Could she find it in her heart to wear the hat for him and thus save an old man the humiliation of an early retirement?

Grace surrendered, but she surrendered so quickly, so utterly passively that her submission disturbed him. Models did not take a stance and then instantly capitulate. There were always telephone calls from agents in Paris and personal managers in Hollywood. There were legal threats from lawyers in New York and faxes from fathers in Chicago. A stance was a stance. Pride was involved.

Her volatility reminded him of LaLa Hurstmonceaux, the famous French beauty, who had slapped Karl in the face while they were shooting a portrait for Italian *Vogue*. Her huge aquamarine and rubellite ring had slashed the photographer's chin causing a scar which was the reason why he had taken to wearing a beard. Actually Karl had not minded the assault – he and LaLa had become (temporarily) engaged a month later, but Clive remembered the scene well. There had been a desperate and dangerous moment out there under the palms of Miami Beach. Grace was like LaLa – she was too odd, too independent, too unimpressed, and she was beginning to smell like a liability.

Clive jogged gracefully back to the set.

'She'll wear the hat – she's just gonna calm down for a minute. She's fine, folks.'

'Gut,' said Karl. 'Dis is de last picture I zink. I haf had enough of these ... these ... *hausfrau!*'

'And I've had enough of aitch-eye-em – *him*.' Makeup whispered to Hair.

'I do not believe the word thank-you has ever passed that man's lips,' Hair agreed. 'He should change his name to Mr No-Manners.'

'He's been horrible to that girl for weeks,' said Makeup, 'I'm not surprised she's having a fit. They should have used Storm then at least she would have been allowed a rest.'

'And I would have gotten to do some hair,' said Hair bitterly.

'And you would have gotten to do some hair,' said Makeup soothingly. 'It's disgraceful how you've been treated.'

The assistants would have glared at their employer but they needed the work and Karl fired people as easily as he breathed.

Styling inspected a pale blue nail varnish and thought about the contents of the perfect capsule wardrobe. The secret, she concluded, was a monochromatic palette and an Hermés shoulder bag.

Grace walked down the beach as the sun began to leave it and, as the light left the day, so her will ebbed away from her. Implacable responses had controlled the automatic motor of everyday life, the walking, the breathing, the sight and hearing that she did not really want. She had only been sustained by the image of the Highwayman, of being saved, and now she felt impelled to surrender to overwhelming disappointment. The future had gone. She was too old. And as she walked into a space where there is no judgement or consideration, she did not think of consequence. She assumed that her disappearance would be of no note to most and a relief to some.

She would move from one existence to another. She did not know what the difference would be and she did not care because she did not care about anything. There was only shallow breath and dull sight and the stealthy planning required to stay out of sight and uninvolved. This was easy. No one ever asked questions. No one ever had.

She was not frightened. She had thought of leaving for some time now, vaguely and without passion. She had often wondered what it would be like and often looked forward to it. She always known that she would go. She assumed it would be before she was twenty-one. She did not want to be twenty-one. She didn't want to be anything. She had never asked for anything. She just wanted to pass on, out of the relentless void, away from the repression of neutrality and torpor. She had wondered for some time if this was it. If it was about indifference, about being untouchable and unexcited, passive and disinterested. Once she had expected more, she had expected to be attracted from withdrawal by adventure, a strange lure, a love. But now she knew that none of this was to be. She knew that that was it. She must go.

There was no more thought. The white dress slid from her shoulders into the shallow froth of the sea's edge, and she walked towards the endless grey, forward and more forward. Calm. Further and further.

'The light will go in under an hour,' said Karl. '*Ver* is she?'

Clive ran back down the beach to where he had left Grace. Seeing the dress sodden at the water's edge he swore and looked out to sea, eyes straining. What was possessing her to swim? He shrieked her name but there was no response and no sign of her head bobbing in the grey waves.

Disfigured corpses crowded his mind's eye. He called the coast guard on his mobile telephone. 'Get here quick,' he yelled, 'I think a woman is drowning.'

The helicopter arrived two minutes later. Lifeguards were winched down into the sea from a ladder as a boat circled the area indicated by Clive.

The Hatch Hamstone fashion crew stood on the sands' edge in shocked silence, as members of the rescue team walked up and down the beach. All eyes strained as the sun went down and warned of the oncoming darkness which would force surrender and bring death.

The vice-presidents shivered and whispered to each other about keeping 'this' out of the press. Then, fingers flying over pocket calculators, they considered the costs that would accrue from legal proceedings.

Hair and Makeup, shocked and silent, did not speak but were both confused. Neither could understand why a young girl 'spotted' by the famous Karl Künterbunt should wish to take her own life. Her future was bright with the forecast of wealth and success. She was destined to experience the warm acclaim that greeted those who were chosen to be beautiful. She would want for nothing and live in luxury and never worry about anything except nails and skin tone. Those who died in fashion were those who could not face the end of a short career, or who had tried but failed, or who had burned out. Ice-cream colours and sleek satin dresses made junkies and whores, this they knew, but Grace had ended before she had begun.

Karl was furious. He had spent twenty years enjoying himself at the top of his profession but the acid presentiment of decline had often embittered the pleasure of power. He had long known that it was only a matter of time before the business bit him. He read his press cuttings and he was aware that he already had a reputation as a sadist and a misogynist. Terrified models had given 'off the record' descriptions of the cruelties implemented in the interests of the dramatic images that were his fortune.

This accident would be blamed on him and he knew that it could ruin him. The world would hang him because someone would have to answer for the mysterious death of a beautiful waif. There would be urban myths and whisperings and they would grow until the telephone stopped ringing and the industry ran to cover itself as he was brought down by an anonymous stranger. He felt like spitting. She was a good model, but there were many. She had not been that special, certainly not special enough to finish him.

Clive was cursed with remorse. He had only been with the child half an hour earlier – his instincts had told him that she was ready to leap into some oddball adolescent tragedy – he knew she was unstable but he had left her alone. He had murdered her.

'It's my fault. I left her. I killed her,' he said to Brent.

Brent tried to remain calm. He patted Clive on the arm. 'No you didn't,' he said. 'This is no one's fault.'

Then a man shouted and signalled and Grace was laid at the water's edge. There was a tangle of rubber tubes as frantic faces bore down shouting instructions. Her chest was punched but still the grey sat resolute on lifeless cheeks, her arms fell, heavy and white; her quiet body lay thin, crumpled and naked.

'Jesus,' said one of the ambulance men as they placed her on a stretcher. 'What has that child done to her face?'

The next day a psychiatrist told Miles Falconbridge that

his daughter was lucky to be alive but that she would remain in danger if she did not receive a long period of counselling.

'Is she mad then?' he asked the doctor. 'I believe she tried to kill herself because she did not want to wear a particular hat.'

The doctor, who was female, did not think that this was unreasonable.

'Your daughter is not mad in the organic sense, Mr Falconbridge, but she is sensitive and intelligent and upset. I believe that she lost her mother when she was very young.'

'Yes,' said Miles.

'Have you ever discussed this with her?'

'Certainly not,' said Miles.

'Well,' said the doctor. 'I would recommend a long period of rest and some expert treatment. I know of a place in Axbridge that has produced some excellent results. Would you like me to refer her?'

A week later Miles Falconbridge drove his daughter to Serenity Hall.

Chapter 15

Tanned men wearing white coats asked Grace how she was and she couldn't answer because she didn't know. Then they asked her how she felt and, again, she couldn't answer because she was full of secrets that she did not wish to tell them. She was alive but nothing had changed except the weather and the furniture. It was sunny now, and there were broken sofas full of people crying and smoking.

The yearning returned. She still wanted him. He was a part of her now, he had become enmeshed with her, she did not even consider letting him go. The Highwayman was her guide. Pacing her mind, he protected her. True, he was sometimes unreliable, an adventurer on the run, but he was still her creation, perfect in height, in appearance, and in character.

She knew that the will could create what was wanted and desire could be manifested by intensity of emotion and perseverance. She spent hours sitting on a bench conjuring him up, staring into the middle distance, miles away, thinking about him. It was odd, then, that when he dismounted from his motor bike on the drive outside Serenity Hall, she could not believe that she was seeing him. It was as if she was observing a paranormal happening – she had been told that such things existed, she knew that they did exist, but their actual manifestation prompted incredulity and panic.

As a conclusion arrived so too did the potential for loss. The blood beat around her head as she moved forward to make absolutely sure. He removed his crash-helmet and she saw the eyes that had loved her for three months. And then, unexpectedly, a minute pinprick of disappointment, for now the longing, as much as a part of her as a limb, was dying. Routed by reality it left a gaping vacancy. The chase was nearly over.

She followed him as he walked towards the herb garden. He was younger than she had imagined, and smaller – only an inch or so taller than herself. Her mind had known only strong features carved with wisdom. He was less graceful and less certain, as became apparent when he failed to see a step and nearly fell into some nettles.

Rupert's mind was on many things. He was girding himself for the Family Visit, an ordeal where he had been forced to give up expecting his mother to apologize for her awfulness because, unfortunately, she had been instructed to let go of the past and forgive herself. Worse, the 'love' word was now interminably on her lips.

She seemed to remember little of the past horrifying years and he envied her her brain death. 'We've got to be honest with each other,' she sometimes said airily, as if this was possible. 'Honest?' he felt like saying. 'If I was honest I'd go down for armed robbery.' Honesty was hardly something to consider in these circumstances. Dishonesty, pure and simple, had propelled her to this place of recuperation – without dishonesty she would still be carrying around the coal scuttle thinking it was her handbag.

She was going to have to be told that there was no more money. The funds had run out. She would have to leave the New Age, return to Fairview Castle and face the bad dreams that were her old memories.

She was talking about opening the hotel again, about bringing some of the people that she had met at Serenity Hall to work with her, and build some kind of collective. Rupert had surveyed the individuals of whom she spoke. They wore Rolex watches. Their shoes were flown in from Milan. They had off-shore bank accounts. They had, in fact, all the things one requires from a business partner. Perhaps they would relieve him of his duties. Perhaps he could shrug off this inexplicable contrition. He resented guilt. She was not his fault.

He rolled a cigarette.

Summer eased over the herb garden causing scents to rise and insects to scurry. Suddenly, without warning, Rupert was enveloped by an overwhelming temptation to weep which, as quickly as it came, was blocked. He had never cried in his life and he did not intend to do so now just because it was allowed and even expected in this so-called safe place. Safety in Rupert's view was only provided by solitude. If there was weeping to be done he would do it in his own time and not to a schedule dictated by acid casualties, European Moon Goddesses and retired super-stars who thought they knew it all.

Nevertheless the sadness was there, ineluctably welling, a

dam about to break, and, when it did, he feared he would drown or choke to death. The tears would never stop, they might kill him. This was what he fought – death by asphyxiation from his own misery.

He looked up and saw a girl child standing in front of him. Bony limbs, white shift, as ephemeral as a ghost. Her beauty held him, he had never seen anything like her, never felt as if he could lose himself in another person. As she walked forward an irrational jealousy consumed him.

She did not say anything because she could not. She had already had all the conversations, said everything there was to say, and she could not, in this terrible exacting moment, fully appreciate that he had not heard them. To her they were already one.

He too was silent, nervous of this intern, but pressurised by the grey eyes, huge alien orbs. The dumb frisson of small talk was not amongst his skills. He did not know what to say.

This silence could have mutated into myriad destinies. Graceful separation hung in the air. Two people were united by death and youth, but two halves could have been divided by a millisecond. The future could have dissolved but an entity invaded the slow present, an entity with newly dyed orange hair, radiant grin, and a mohair jumper in which a peace sign had been embroidered in gold lurex twine.

The voice hailed over the sun-speckled lavender as the bulk sailed into view.

'Darling! You're here! You're early.'

Rupert's new mother ran forward. This was a surprising and unnerving event and one which he had never seen before. Bumps jiggled and joggled.

His new mother embraced her son and the situation with a lack of embarrassment or understanding.

She planted a blemish of crimson lipstick on to his cheek.

'Oh!!' she shrilled, shuddering with happiness, 'You've met Grace! Isn't she lovely?'

Rupert looked again. The small intense face stared up at him and he felt the quiet gentleness that lay within her. Again the physical tug. He smelt the rosemary and, from nowhere, the flood of agony that had so nearly consumed him was replaced with peace. Everything was as it should be.

'Yes,' he said.

OTHER TITLES AVAILABLE

ALL ARROW BOOKS ARE AVAILABLE THROUGH MAIL ORDER OR FROM YOUR LOCAL BOOKSHOP AND NEWSAGENT.

PLEASE SEND CHEQUE, EUROCHEQUE, POSTAL ORDER (STERLING ONLY), ACCESS, VISA, MASTERCARD, DINERS CARD, SWITCH OR AMEX.

EXPIRY DATE .... SIGNATURE ....

PLEASE ALLOW 75 PENCE PER BOOK FOR POST AND PACKING U.K.

OVERSEAS CUSTOMERS PLEASE ALLOW £1.00 PER COPY FOR POST AND PACKING.

ALL ORDERS TO:

ARROW BOOKS, BOOKS BY POST, TBS LIMITED, THE BOOK SERVICE, COLCHESTER ROAD, FRATING GREEN, COLCHESTER, ESSEX CO7 7DW.

TELEPHONE: (01206) 256 000
FAX: (01206) 255 914

NAME ....

ADDRESS ....

....

Please allow 28 days for delivery. Please tick box if you do not wish to receive any additional information ☐

Prices and availability subject to change without notice.